Bad Mothe
Brilliant Lovers

By *the same author*

Absinthe for Elevenses
Cuckoo
After Purple
Born of Woman
The Stillness The Dancing
Sin City
Devils, for a Change
Fifty-Minute Hour
Bird Inside
Michael, Michael
Breaking and Entering
Coupling
Second Skin
Lying
Dreams, Demons and Desire
Tread Softly
Virgin in the Gym and Other Stories
Laughter Class and Other Stories
The Biggest Female in the World and Other Stories
Little Marvel and Other Stories
The Queen's Margarine
Broken Places
'I'm on the Train!' and Other Stories
An Enormous Yes

Bad Mothers
Brilliant Lovers

Wendy Perriam

ROBERT HALE • LONDON

© Wendy Perriam 2015
First published in Great Britain 2015

ISBN 978-0-7090-9386-2

Robert Hale Limited
Clerkenwell House
Clerkenwell Green
London EC1R 0HT

www.halebooks.com

A catalogue record for this book is available from the British Library

2 4 6 8 10 9 7 5 3 1

Typeset in Sabon
Printed in Great Britain by Berforts Information Press Ltd

For Anne Charlton, Goddess of Northumbria!

A mere dedication cannot express my gratitude for
your unstinting and expert help with my previous book

Wendy Perriam's seventeen novels and seven previous short-story collections have been acclaimed for their psychological insight and their power to disturb, divert and shock.

She feels her inspiration as a writer comes from her many conflicting life experiences – strict convent-school discipline and swinging sixties wildness, marriage and divorce, infertility and motherhood, 9-to-5 conformity and periodic Bedlam – have helped shape her as a writer. 'Writing allows for shadow-selves. I'm both the staid conformist matron and the slag; the well-organised author toiling at her desk and the madwoman shrieking in a straitjacket.'

CONTENTS

1.	Mouse	9
2.	Joy	19
3.	Magical Numbers	32
4.	'Can I have it when you go?'	59
5.	'Just yourself?'	68
6.	Presents	79
7.	Lost	87
8.	Boiled Eggs	107
9.	Yew	120
10.	'Ta-ra!'	130
11.	A Cuppa and a Biscuit	150
12.	Marshmallows	161
13.	Venus	180
14.	'Sorry for inconvence'	195
15.	'Unbelievably wonderful!'	208

MOUSE

'If that mouse comes up here on the platform, I'll die – and I mean literally die.'

The young girl shrank back in obvious terror, all but colliding with Jo, who happened to be standing behind her. Following her gaze, Jo peered down at the rails, where a small brown mouse was scuttling harmlessly along.

'Any second, it'll be running up my leg.' The girl turned to face Jo; her expression one of sheer horror and disgust.

'No, honestly, it won't.' Jo felt duty-bound to reassure the poor woman, so acute was her distress. 'It's physically impossible for such a tiny creature to clamber up six feet of concrete.'

'How can you be sure?' The girl kept glancing back at the mouse, as if, at any moment, it would indeed scale the steep incline and pop up at her feet. 'I mean, it must have extraordinary powers to live down there at all, on top of the live rails. You'd think it would get killed when the trains go roaring over it.'

'No, it's small enough to sit safely underneath them.'

The girl shuddered in repugnance. 'I've never seen a mouse on the tube before, otherwise I wouldn't travel by underground – no way! And I'll certainly never set foot on Clapham Common station again. Or do you think there might be mice on every station?'

'No, I shouldn't imagine so.' Jo tried to block out the memory of a large, black, bloated rat she'd spotted just a fortnight ago, actually sitting on the platform at Kilburn station, grooming its whiskers with apparent smug satisfaction.

'Oh my God! There's another!' Panic-stricken, the girl clutched Jo's arm, her voice rising to a wail.

'Why don't you come and sit down?' Jo steered her gently towards a bench, aware that the girl was literally shaking. 'Those mice won't hurt you, I promise. They can't get anywhere near you and, anyway, they're only tiny things, far more frightened of you than you are of them.'

'Impossible!' The girl shook her head so vehemently, her long, curly ponytail bounced and swung on her shoulders. 'Even thinking about mice brings me out in a cold sweat.'

She had indeed turned worryingly pale, so Jo kept hold of her arm, stroking it with what she hoped was a calming rhythmic motion, although anxious about overstepping boundaries. A total stranger might take offence at such uninvited intimacies.

'If only the train would come.' The girl glanced up at the indicator-board, with a beseeching look, as if she could prevail on an inanimate object to be merciful. 'Oh shit! Eleven minutes to wait still.'

'I'm afraid I'm going in the opposite direction – to Morden, and my train's due any minute. Will you be all right on your own?'

'No, I won't, I won't!' The girl made a grab for Jo's coat, holding on with such force Jo was physically prevented from getting up from the bench. 'Don't leave me, I beg you. I feel safer with you here.'

'Don't worry – it's OK. I'll stay until your train comes. I'm in no particular hurry.' In point of fact, she was tired, in pain, and eager to get home, but there was no way she could abandon the girl. At this late hour, stations could be dangerous places and, indeed, two sinister-looking men were standing at the far end of the platform. The mice themselves posed no danger, but the men just might, lured by the girl's attractive figure and crazily short skirt. And the whole atmosphere of this dimly lit, near-deserted, claustrophobic no-man's-land was hardly reassuring.

'Oh, thank you, thank you!' The girl was all but weeping in relief. 'But isn't it an awful cheek – I mean, delaying you like this?'

'It's no bother, honestly. My mother was petrified of mice, so I'm well aware of the problem.'

'And did she ever conquer her fear?'

'I'm afraid not.' It had riled her as a child that her mother should give way to veritable hysterics if the tiniest, most bashful field-mouse dared poke out its nose from some unobtrusive hole. Whereas *she* had adored all animals – big and small, wild and tame; she had even loved worms and beetles, and had once kept a couple of caterpillars, as furry pets, in a tank.

'Well, I have to say I feel for your mum, because I know how hard it is. I've tried everything myself – hypnosis, psychotherapy, CBT, you name it – but I reckon my phobia's so deep-seated, I'll probably never be cured. You see, it first began when I had my tonsils out, aged four ...' The girl's eyes were still fixated on the rails, anxiously watching for the mice; flinching each time they scurried out; relaxing just a fraction of a fraction if they disappeared from view. 'When I was waking up from the anaesthetic – dopey still and definitely not with it – I had this terrifying sensation of a real live mouse trapped right inside my throat. At that age, I wasn't frightened of mice in the slightest, but just the feeling of that slimy body writhing and struggling to get out of my mouth, and its revolting sleek black fur, wet against my tongue, and its long, skinny black tail coiling round my teeth, stayed with me for ever.'

She raised her voice above the noise of a train rattling into the station – Jo's Morden-bound train, which seemed very nearly empty, a mere two passengers alighting and a solitary man getting on.

'The nurses tried to tell me it was only a nasty dream, but it felt far too real and vivid for that. And, afterwards, the fear took hold and I couldn't even read about a mouse in a children's picture-book, or look at one in a toy-shop.'

Jo clasped her hand in sympathy, no longer worried about taking liberties, since the girl appeared to welcome the gesture. And, indeed, the tonsillectomy experience did sound truly hideous, especially for so young a child. 'Was it caused by the pain in your throat, d'you think? After having your tonsils out, your throat tends to feel extremely sore and uncomfortable, so maybe you interpreted that as a living creature scrabbling to get out.'

'Well, partly, I suppose. But I think it's also connected with my brother's clockwork mouse. He had one just the same – a really evil-looking thing, with black, wet-looking fur, and a long pointy snout, and a repulsive skinny tail. He liked to tease me by trying to run it across my bare legs, or tickling my face with its tail. And, once he—' She broke off with a shriek, rocketing up from the bench. 'Oh, Christ! Oh, shit! Another two, would you believe?' Pointing to the rails, with a look of utter revulsion, she then collapsed back on the seat, hiding her face in terror.

Jo peered down at the four little mice, one of which seemed to be frenziedly nibbling at some morsel it was holding in its paws. Sparing the girl the details, she held her arm securely until all four creatures had again skittered off out of sight. 'It's OK now – all clear.'

'It's not "all clear"! They're still down there, aren't they? Look, I must get off this station. Surely those eleven minutes are up by now. Could you check the board for me and see if my train's due? I feel so scared, I daren't look up or down or anywhere.'

Jo checked, only to shake her head in dismay. 'I'm really sorry,' she said, feeling personally responsible that she had no better news, 'but there's some further delay, it seems. There's no north-bound service for another fifteen minutes.'

The girl let out an anguished groan. 'But that's longer than it said before.'

'It's probably a signal-failure. They're very common on the Northern Line, although it's odd they haven't announced it. And the trains going the other way don't appear to be affected.' As if to confirm her words, another south-bound train came rumbling into view, disgorged a couple of passengers and trundled on its way again.

'I can't stand any more of this! I'll have to give up and try to get a taxi – except I live in Belsize Park, which will cost a bloody fortune and I just can't afford that sort of cash. Yet it seems terribly unfair to expect you to stay here, like my nanny. You've just missed your train – and the one before – and I simply can't delay you any longer.'

'Look, it's OK, I assure you. I've nothing to get home for.' True it was way past her usual supper-time, and her arthritic pain was particularly acute, so she'd welcome a double dose of Ibuprofen and some scrambled eggs on toast. But, left alone, the girl might develop a full-blown panic attack if any more mice should dare to venture out. Perhaps a whole colony lived here, enjoying the warmth and darkness, and the safety from cats and foxes. And, presumably, there would be plentiful snacks from people on the platform throwing scraps of food on to the rails. 'Tell me more about your brother,' Jo coaxed, in an effort to distract the girl. 'What's his name?'

'Philip.' She gave a sudden giggle, as unexpected as it was gratifying. 'You won't believe this, but one of my therapists blamed my whole mouse phobia on Phil; said my early bad experiences with an obviously sadistic brother had left me with a basic fear of men, which manifested itself as a fear of mice. Well, that's total and utter crap! Most little boys like teasing their sisters, so Phil was quite normal in that respect, and, anyway, we got on really well. As for men, I've never had any problem with them and I have a really lovely boyfriend at the moment – Toby. Oh, and I'm Michelle, by the way. It's about time I introduced myself.'

'And I'm Jo.' She had been christened Josephine, in honour of her father's devotion to St Joseph and, although always called formal Josephine by the nuns at her convent school, at home, as a child, she had insisted on plain, boyish Jo. 'And what does Toby think about your mouse-fear?'

'Oh, he's very easy-going, so I'm lucky in that way. But I'm afraid it does rule his life – poor man! I mean, we can't live where there might be mice, so it has to be a modern concrete building, preferably the top floor. In fact, this very Friday he's driving down to his parents' cottage in Kent, and there's no way I can go with him, because the place is surrounded by hayfields, so mice go with the territory – literally. And, of course, from now on, I'll never dare risk the tube again, which will restrict us terribly. And we're restricted, too, when it comes to holidays. Caravans and chalets are completely out of the question and, as for a farmhouse, that would be my absolute worst nightmare.'

Jo was suddenly jolted back to her first and only holiday as a child: a fortnight staying on an Irish farm, in 1954. She hadn't given it a thought in decades, yet now every smallest detail was flashing into her mind. Yes, she was on the ferry, steaming out to Rosslare on a thrillingly choppy sea, standing beside her father right on the top deck, pressed against the rail; the wind slapping their faces, tousling their hair, almost trying to rip the clothes from their backs. She relished every sight and sound: the great, powerful ship with its two red funnels and mournful hooter; the flocks of gulls following so close behind, they were like her own personal bodyguard; the huge, white-crested waves giving her a glorious sense of danger, as if, at any moment, they might have to take to the lifeboats and embark on a still more exciting adventure.

In the normal way, there wasn't money for treats or holidays, but her Aunt Agatha had died and left them something called a bequest.

And had left her, as the only niece, a solid-gold St Christopher pendant – worth a mint, according to her father. He wouldn't let her wear it until she was grown-up, because the chain was too long for a child. Besides, it was precious, he explained, and had to be guarded very carefully, so that if, in adult life, she found herself impoverished, she could sell it and raise some ready cash. But she knew, even at the age of nine, she would never consider selling it, because, if you wore a St Christopher medal, it kept you safe on each and every journey, including the Journey of Life, which was vastly more important than any amount of money.

She had learned more about St Christopher at school: he had miraculous powers, having been born a giant who once carried Christ across a swollen river. And, ever afterwards, he protected people from flood, tempest, plague and sudden death and, although none of those seemed a likely peril for a little girl in Kennington, there were other ways he could protect you, so the nuns said. For instance, if you gazed on his image first thing in the morning, you would suffer not the slightest harm all that day or night. So, every morning, as soon as she got up, she would open the luxurious, velvet-lined box, where the pendant was kept until she was old enough to wear it, and look fixedly and prayerfully at the figure of the saint. Soon, the details were imprinted on her mind – his gnarled walking-stick and flowing cloak and the improbably large Christ-child weighing down his shoulders – so just the briefest glance at it imbued her with the certainty that, for the next twenty-hour hours, at least, she would be completely safe from danger.

She leapfrogged back to the present, as Michelle's fingers suddenly dug into her arm. A mouse must have sneaked into view, because the girl was sitting ramrod-tense again, staring down at the rails with a look of the deepest alarm.

'I'll tell you a funny story,' Jo began, determined to distract her once more. 'Well, perhaps not so funny at the time, but you'll empathize, I'm sure.' They were still alone on their seat, although several other people were sitting on the benches further down, presumably also waiting for the north-bound train. 'When I was a little girl of nine, my parents took me on a farm holiday in Caherciveen, in the West of Ireland.' She had loved those exotic Irish words, so hard to spell, but wonderfully weird and wild on the tongue. Caherciveen was overlooked by the Macgillycuddy Reeks, which was the most amazing place-name of them all, and she used to recite it to herself like a magic incantation.

'A farm in such beautiful countryside,' she continued, 'was my idea of heaven, because we were Londoners, born and bred, living in the basement of a dark, cramped house, without so much as a garden, let alone fields and mountains. And our landlord forbade any kind of pet, so it was a huge treat for me to be staying somewhere with sheep and cows and dogs and hens, and even a pony to ride.'

She would never forget that fat, frisky, skewbald mare: the sheer astoundment of its colouring – uneven splotches of chestnut, white and black – and the thrill of riding bareback; the plump, quivery flanks warm against her legs, and the shock of its bouncy, jiggling trot, which all but jounced her off its back, and its eager velvet lips probing her palm when, afterwards, she fed it pieces of apple from the farm's own private orchard.

And her first time feeding the hens had been every bit as magical: the squawk and rush and flurry of feathers, as she tossed the shining gold grain; the flock of greedy birds pushing and shoving each other, with no strict parent restraining them. But best of all the experiences had been watching the milking twice a day: just being so close to big, solid, living animals, and their peculiar, almost embarrassing udders, and the surprise of the milk gushing and frothing into a bucket, instead of being left on the doorstep in boring, workaday bottles.

'Well, when I came back in, after my first enchanting day there, tired and messy and walking on air, my mother said I was to wash and change my clothes, so I'd be nice and neat for supper. I was sharing a room with my parents – to save them money, I suppose – and I was just rooting in a drawer to find a clean jumper, when I heard this shriek of pure unmitigated terror. I whipped round to see my mother clambering frantically on to the bed, her face as white as uncooked dough. And, there, on the floor below her, was the tiniest of fieldmice, equally terrified, I'd guess.'

Michelle gave a dramatic shudder. 'Don't go on! The very thought of such a thing makes my blood run cold.'

'Yes, so it did with my mum. In fact, she insisted, there and then, that we all go straight back home. I just couldn't believe it and burst into tears, but, although my father did his best to change her mind, she was completely deaf to reason. So our one-and-only holiday ended after just one day and we'd wasted all that money, and had to return that very evening, despite the fact we'd already spent two days travelling. There were no motorways in the fifties, you see, and, even if there had been, our third-hand Morris 8 was incapable of any sort of speed. So, the day we left home, we had to set the alarm for five in the morning and drive eight hours to Fishguard, and we arrived so late at Rosslare, we had to stay the night in a b-and-b, before proceeding on to Caherciveen early the next day. That took another six or seven hours, what with avoiding all the potholes in the roads, and having to slow down for sheep or cattle being taken from one pasture to another, or even wild horses leaping out on to the roads!'

As she paused for breath, it was Michelle's turn to sympathize. 'I do feel really sorry for you, Jo. I mean, what a ghastly disappointment for a child! On the other hand, I can imagine exactly how your mother must have felt, and I know I'd be the same. I just hope you could forgive her.'

Jo said nothing, aware that, in point of fact, she had always held something of a grudge. No one could dispute that she'd been a dutiful daughter, cared for both her parents in their increasingly incapacitated old age but, as far as her mother was concerned, a certain coldness and distance had come between them all those years ago, and never quite disappeared. Her mother's continuing phobia had both infuriated and baffled her, as something groundless, irrational and out of all proportion.

'Or I hope at least you could understand,' Michelle added, in a pleading tone, as if she, too, were begging forgiveness and compassion – from her boyfriend, perhaps, or from other friends whose lives she had curtailed.

Jo remained uncomfortably silent. No, she hadn't understood – or not until this very moment, when all at once it dawned on her that, in 1954, her mother would have been much the same age as Michelle, and equally young and vulnerable; basically a decent, gentle person, but in the grip of something way beyond her control. Maybe, she, too, had suffered a trauma similar to Michelle's, but would never have dreamed of mentioning it, of course, in those stoical, buttoned-up days. And, as for therapy, it was unheard of for working-class folk and way beyond her parents' modest means.

'I have to confess, Michelle,' she said, at last, 'I didn't really understand or sympathize. You see, I've always been a fearless type of person, so my mother's terror seemed – well, ludicrous.'

'Oh, please don't say that, Jo! I know people feel the same about me and it only makes me feel worse – guilty and selfish and ridiculous.'

I'm the one who should feel guilty, Jo reflected – guilty for her lack of empathy and understanding. In every other way, her mother had been a kind and caring parent, ashamed of her phobia, yet unable to overcome it; like Michelle in that respect. Yet, she, the obdurate daughter, had failed to show any pity or forbearance, but allowed one childhood incident to impair their whole subsequent relationship; even considered herself superior on account of her natural courage, which was simply a lucky accident, rather than a virtue on her part.

She turned round to glance at Michelle, struck by the unsettling fact that the girl did bear an uncanny resemblance to her mother at that age: the same dark eyes and thick, dark hair contrasting with the fragile, milk-pale skin; the fine-arched brows and delicate oval face. Crazy as it sounded – indeed, all the more crazy for someone who prided herself on her innate rationality – she had the peculiar sensation that this was, indeed, her mother, returned or reincarnated, to teach her a salutary lesson and enable her to make long-overdue amends.

'Hey!' the girl cried, springing up from the bench with a look of mingled triumph and relief. 'My train's approaching, the board says. Oh, thank God! Thank God! And thank you, too, Jo, for being so fantastically kind.'

Quick as the thought, Jo reached up with fumbling fingers and unclasped the gold chain round her neck. 'Have this,' she urged, pressing the pendant into Michelle's hand. 'It's like a sort of talis-man, to give you courage, keep you safe. It's protected me all these years, but I've *had* my life, whereas yours is still in front of you, and I want you to feel safe, as well.'

'What is it?' Michelle asked, examining the image but clearly not recognizing St Christopher.

'Just take it, please. There's no time to explain.' The train was already clattering into the station.

'I couldn't possibly! Gold's worth a bomb, and this feels heavy and solid, and must be really valuable, so why the hell should you give it to a stranger? I'm the one who's in your debt, not the other way round.' Michelle thrust it back at Jo, then, as the doors slid open, darted into the carriage.

Jo, too, jumped on to the train, just for long enough to push the pendant deep into the girl's coat-pocket. 'You're not a stranger, Michelle, and I do actually owe you something.'

'But how could you? I don't understand. I mean, you don't know me from Adam, and—'

The doors were closing, cutting off Michelle's bewildered remonstrations. Jo nipped off the train only just in time and with no chance to reply. No matter. The important thing was that, at last – and shamefully late – she had made some recompense to her misunderstood and unfairly undervalued mother.

And, extraordinarily, she felt lighter altogether, disencumbered from a burden she hadn't realized she was carrying and she knew, in some mysterious, totally inexplicable way, that both she and her mother were finally at peace, and that even Michelle, now with St Christopher as her chaperon, would feel a shade less panicky when next confronted by a mouse.

JOY

JOY....

So jubilant a word, Ken mused, should be rainbow-coloured, glitter-sprinkled, flower-garlanded and audibly Hosanna-ing. Yet, rather than whooshing high into the stratosphere, it was sitting in prim silence on several successive pages of Tesco's glossy Gift Guide. Nonetheless, he had noticed it, if only for its frequency: six sightings in the guide, so far: first, embroidered on a scatter-cushion; then blazoned on a coffee-mug and on a blue enamelled plaque; next, as three separate letters suspended from a silver chain and, one page on, interspersed with the word 'peace' on a roll of festive wrapping paper and, finally, the shout-line on various Christmas decorations.

And, despite the lack of garlands and glitter, those three letters seemed to him the very essence of excess. Joy was a foreign country, as far beyond simple pleasure or contentment as Mount Everest was above Box Hill. A cup of coffee in Starbucks could afford a sense of enjoyment, a new library book even induce well-being, but joy spectacularly outsoared them, comprising, as it did, elements of ecstasy and bliss.

Closing the guide, he decided to make himself a cup of tea, inspired by the polka-dotted Tesco's teapot, with its scarlet lid and spout. Since he had never owned any sort of teapot, he resorted to his usual cheapo teabag dumped in a plain white mug and, while waiting for the kettle to boil, continued to reflect on joy. Had he ever felt it and, if so, why and when? Not for decades, certainly. There was little in his current job in the back office of a recycling centre to cause his pulse to race or his heart to flutter, and, after work, it was straight home, most nights, to his cramped and lonely flat. Even on his pub evenings, joy was hard to come by, what with the inflated price of beer, the ever-increasing decibel-count of what passed for music there, and his colleagues' habit of rarely allowing him a word in edgeways. Fine for them to label him 'the quiet one', when they never gave him a chance.

He took his tea back to the kitchen table, along with a couple of digestives, ruefully aware that, if he sought joy on the biscuit front, he should replace drab, workaday digestives with chocolate-coated, cream-filled confections, sumptuously basking in gold foil. Munching his modest, no-frills biscuit, he tried transforming every bite into heavenly ambrosia – not easy, when the digestive was dry and semi-stale.

However, he did strike gold when, still in search of joy, he began taking stock of his childhood and, suddenly, miraculously, a few long-forgotten memories exploded into life. Yes, he had felt joy, as a six-year-old, at his first sight of the sea – a sea stretching away, away, away, into a far-distant bluey mist, yet which also kept rushing forward in frantic, foamy frills, to thresh around his legs. And, five years later, when he landed his first fish off Brighton Pier, the experience had definitely been joyous. Admittedly, he'd caught only a small pout-whiting, but it was still a source of secret pride; making him almost equal to the gnarled old anglers hunkered down beside him, with their impressive hauls of plaice and dab. Then, two years on, he was fishing again, this time by the River Wey, when he had actually spotted a real live adder swimming right towards him, in a wriggly but determined manner, as if wanting to join him on the bank and whisper something mysteriously snaky into his waiting ear.

But, after that, joy had seemed to vanish. Adolescence brought bashfulness and blushes, acne outbreaks and a new, treacherous voice that kept plunging disconcertingly from baritone to squeak. As for girls, humiliation had been more the general theme than any sort of bliss. Devoutly Catholic Eileen had refused to allow him so much as a kiss; Kirsty had dumped him for a football star, and adorable Susanna had coolly informed him she'd outgrown him, after a mere three months. And, as the years rolled on and somehow he'd reached fifty-five, still with scant success, it was clear that he had 'missed the boat', to use his sister Tessa's phrase. Tessa, in contrast, was happily married with a brood of kids and grandkids, and a husband so faithful and attentive, he resembled a soppy but devoted Labrador.

On impulse, he grabbed his mobile and, after the usual dutiful preliminary enquiries about the health of her numerous tribe, put the crucial question: had she ever experienced joy?

'Joy?' she repeated, sounding a little nonplussed.

'Yes, joy, the real McCoy – it even rhymes, you see! I'm not talking about run-of-the-mill contentment, but something more akin to rapture.'

'Oh, I see. Yes, definitely – when each of my kids was born, especially the first. I can't tell you the elation I felt when the midwife laid Sammy in my arms. I just couldn't stop smiling, Ken, like an Olympian who'd been awarded triple gold. And the whole world seemed a better place, as if all its wars and troubles had ended at that very moment.'

Ken said nothing, unsure how to react. From what he had seen of childbirth on TV, it was a messy, gory, agonizing business – in fact, one of the few things that made him glad to be male.

'And, before that, on my wedding day, I certainly felt joy – I mean, to be marrying my childhood sweetheart, and both of us ecstatically in love. And also being the star of the show in that dress-to-die-for, and with all my friends cheering me on, and Dad in tears of emotion and....'

Ken, for his part, remembered the wedding as something of a trial, drawing unwelcome attention to his own failure in the marriage department. And the celebrations had been so relentlessly protracted, he'd been drooping by the end of the reception and had to steel himself to face the raucous disco-dance, which whooped on till the early hours. But then he was probably just a party-pooper – in which case he didn't deserve joy.

'And I felt joy again this very week, when I took Will and Daisy to the Arndale Shopping Centre, to visit Santa's Grotto. They'd already written their letters to him, which they posted in this big red mailbox, just outside the entrance to his grotto. Then, in we went, and Santa sat them down and asked them if they were good children and always did what Grandma told them – giving me a complicit wink, at that point. And, when they lied through their teeth and said they were little angels, he promised to try to give them exactly what they'd asked for in their letters. And I was over the moon, Ken, just to see their delight. I mean, they were tickled pink by it all: the elves, the sleigh, the reindeer, the bulging sack of presents, the showers of fake snow falling over the grotto....'

Tessa's voice had taken on a lyrical note, causing Ken to wish that he could share her rosy view of defiant Daisy and stubborn Will – not that they were any worse than other small-fry grandchildren. Kids, in general, seemed inevitably to bring chaos, noise, disruption, in their wake.

'But, listen, Ken, talking of Christmas, I do wish you'd change your mind about coming over to our place. I hate to think of you stuck on your own in that poky flat of yours. At least, if you joined us, you'd have a decent meal.'

'I'll be fine – I've told you, Tessa. Christmas is only another day.'

'It's not – it's special, especially with a family around you.'

Yes, that was the trouble. He always felt spare at Tessa and Gordon's – the bashful uncle and great-uncle, who still hadn't learned the knack of bonding with small children, and felt equally ill at ease with their successful, sophisticated parents, all of whom had high-powered jobs, stylish cars and well-honed multi-tasking skills. Forget multi-tasking – it was all he could do to drink his tea whilst completing his trawl through the Gift Guide. And success had been sadly lacking. He had still failed to make any decision about what to buy for Norah, because every time he lighted on something vaguely appropriate, he would worry she might think it odd for him to be giving her a gift at all. Admittedly, he was in her debt, since she had returned his thick, black, woolly gloves, which he'd left behind on the counter last time he was in the newsagent's. She had waited till the shop shut, then come all the way in the dark and cold, so that he wouldn't be without them in the present biting weather.

'Won't you stop for a coffee?' he had dared to say, feeling touched, embarrassed, flustered all at once.

'I'd love to, but it's late and I still have masses to do.'

Although disappointed, he was nonetheless emboldened by her 'I'd love to' – so much so that, once she had left, he stretched out on his bed and pretended she had accepted the coffee. Soon, they had progressed to sherry and a little cosy hand-holding and, eventually, he'd coaxed her to join him on the narrow divan – and, well, after that, it had been fireworks all the way.

'Ken, are you still there?'

'Yes. Sorry, Tessa.'

'Did you hear what I just said?'

'Er, no.'

'I asked if you'd consider coming just for Christmas Day. I know you don't like staying the night and, with such a full house, it's true there won't be much peace and quiet. But at least you'd have a few hours of fun, if you came for lunch and tea.'

'Fun' was almost as challenging as joy. He suspected he'd been born without the 'fun' gene – proof that he *was* a misery. 'But how could I get there, Tessa? All public transport grinds to a halt on Christmas Day.'

'No problem. Gordon can come and fetch you in the car. It would have to be early, mind, so he'd get back before the others arrive.'

'It's a lovely idea, but an awful drag for poor Gordon. And, if he had to drive me back in the evening, he wouldn't even be able to drink. And, anyway, Tess, I've told you, I'll be perfectly OK.' In fact, it would be something of a relief not to be surrounded by so-called festive cheer. The Gift Guide had already set him wondering if he was the only Tesco customer who didn't need Christmas cards or crackers, tinsel, baubles, decorations, holly wreaths, fairy lights, Santa-printed aprons, poinsettia-patterned tablecloths. And, if so, wasn't that a sad reflection on his isolated (selfish) life?

'You've gone all quiet again. What's wrong, Ken?'

'Nothing.' He forced a smile into his voice, to reassure her.

Once he had managed to ring off (declining further invitations for New Year's Eve and Twelfth Night), his mind leapfrogged back to Norah. Motherly, kind and appealingly chubby, she was his ideal type of female. And he had a feeling she'd be a first-rate cook – not the glamorous Nigella Lawson sort, but homely and unthreatening, happily rustling up sultana scones in some cosy little kitchen, her large, maternal breasts half-hidden by a gingham overall. Secretly, he longed to give her something intimate to wear against her soft, pink, yielding skin, but that would seem brazenly presumptuous when they were still strangers, more or less. He didn't even know her surname, or where she lived, or whether she already had a gentleman-friend. Mercifully, she didn't wear a wedding ring, which at least allowed him to imagine taking her to bed without feeling like an adulterer.

He turned back to Tesco's Top Ten Gift Ideas but, as before, nothing seemed quite suitable. Chocolates were unoriginal, books and music a minefield when he had no idea of her tastes, a 'Down-the-Hatch' hip-flask positively insulting, and the set of three body butters was, again, too blatant, although it sparked enticing pictures of her ample body glistening with cocoa butter. As for the scarlet cushion emblazoned with the word LOVE, well, that was a tad premature, considering their current non-relationship. Since early October, when she had first come to work at Martin's, they couldn't have exchanged more than fifty words, in total.

Aware he had made no progress on either the romantic or the present-buying front, he abandoned the Gift Guide and resolved to venture out to a proper store, where there would be a much wider choice. Besides, distraction was always welcome on a Saturday, when time could hang heavy without an immediate family, or a zillion Facebook friends to impress with the latest photos of his white-water-rafting or camel-trekking exploits. If only. Even his recent timid day-trip to Calais, on the ferry, had brought little but successive bouts of humiliating seasickness.

However, despite his gammy leg, he could just about make it to the shops and, in fact, he decided to copy Tessa and head to the Arndale Centre – not her branch, of course (miles too far) but his local one, a short train-ride away. Relieved to have a plan, he set out for the station, his spirits so revived, he actually found himself humming Good King Wenceslas and tapping his stick in time to the catchy tune.

'You can't go wrong with toiletries, sir.'

'Even for someone I hardly know?'

'Absolutely. One of these gift-sets here would be perfect for that very situation – not too personal, yet universally acceptable. How about the Coty L'Aimant?'

'Er, no,' he mumbled, hoping the sales assistant, a terrifying female, with four-inch talons and six-inch heels, wouldn't regard him as 'picky' or 'difficult'. But he seemed to remember from his school-days that L'Aimant had something to do with love, and Norah might regard it as impertinent for him to be galloping towards romance at so reckless and unwarranted a pace.

'Or Dolce and Gabbana are always very popular. This particular set is called "The One" and, as you can see, it's beautifully boxed.'

Norah might be 'The One' in his fantasies, but there was a distressing possibility that she had forgotten his existence, in which case it would be a trifle bold to trumpet her exclusivity in gold letters on a gift-box. 'I need something a little more … neutral.'

The salesgirl must have misheard 'neutral' as 'natural', since she pointed out the Nivea Natural Skin Collection – a fortunate error, actually, because Nivea was a reassuring brand, more associated with shower gels and hand creams than with amorous messages, or suggestively saucy subtexts, and so was, in fact, ideal. Tessa used Nivea sun-block on Daisy's sensitive skin, and he himself had bought their shaving foam last time he was in Boots. 'Yes, that'll be perfect, thank you.'

'Would you like to take advantage, sir, of our free gift-wrapping service?'

He readily agreed, since it would save a trek in search of suitable paper, Sellotape and all the rest of the palaver.

Rejecting the Christmassy-patterned gift-wrap, he opted for a plainish blue, to match Norah's soulful eyes. And, once the beribboned package was safely in his hands, he mumbled his thanks again and, with a sigh of relief, left the stifling shop. However, he was about to head back home, when a large sign caught his eye:

THIS WAY TO SANTA'S GROTTO!

He dithered for a moment. One part of him was curious to see if Tessa's glowing description matched the actuality; another part was worried that, without a child in tow, a grown man would be seen as an intruder. On the other hand, did he really want to sit idle in his flat for the next umpteen hours, trying not to clock-watch? The dilemma was solved by the merry sound of Christmas carols, which seemed to summon him inexorably to the grotto; Hark, the Herald Angels even putting a spring in his, admittedly halting, step.

And, yes, there was almost the exact same scene Tessa had described: the elves, the sturdy sleigh, the brace of feisty reindeer, the showers of innocuous snow – the best kind of snow, neither cold, nor messing up his glasses. (Couldn't specs come complete with windscreen-wipers?) Santa Claus himself was concealed in his inner sanctum, and a long queue of excited children and their parents were waiting their turn to go in. He backed away, nervous of being branded a severe case of arrested development or, worse, a paedophile. But, all at once, he spotted a large red mail-box and stopped dead in his tracks. Will and Daisy had written a letter to Santa and posted it in just such a box and, suddenly he, too, yearned to write one. Forget Teddy bears or dolls or train-sets, forget even the latest video-games – he craved something more elusive, yet of more value than all the toys and games and diversions in the world.

Of course, he would feel decidedly foolish penning such a missive, but who would need to know? So, having found an unobtrusive corner, well away from the crowds, he searched his pockets for a scrap of paper, came up with an old shopping list, scratched out 'bread, baked beans and toilet-cleaner' and scrawled a few lines in the blank space underneath, using his large, flat wallet as support.

Dear Father Christmas.... He preferred the traditional term. Santa Claus was the Dutch name and, frankly, the whole Dutch thing always left him cold. Tulips, windmills, dykes, clogs, were hardly the stuff of passion.

… what I'd really like for Christmas is just plain and simple joy.

No – that was a contradiction. Joy, by its very nature, could never be plain and simple, oozing, as it did, extravagance, exuberance, ostentation, hyperbole. Having deleted the phrase, he added, politely, Thank you in anticipation, K. Gibson.

Still embarrassed by his idiocy, he sidled back to the post-box, then, waiting till a cluster of kids had safely moved away, slipped his folded paper through the slot. A cheery recorded voice crowed 'Thank you!', from deep inside the box and he realized, to his surprise, that he did indeed feel cheery. And, as he pulled on his gloves in readiness for the trek back to the station, Norah's alluring alchemy seemed to have penetrated the grubby black wool, making it thicker, warmer, cosier, even cleaner.

He hovered close to the door, aghast at the scrum of people thronging the small newsagent's – disorganized folk, most likely, remembering only at the eleventh hour that they needed chocolates, gift-wrap, Christmas cards, before everything shut down tomorrow. Norah was there, thank God, but without her usual assistant, and thus coping single-handed with the queue of impatient customers. Nonetheless, she appeared remarkably sanguine – which could hardly be said of him. He had stupidly imagined that, on Christmas Eve, they would have the shop almost to themselves. The last thing he wanted was a bunch of curious strangers watching as he handed over her gift. They might snigger at the sight of him – a guy in his mid-fifties, who hadn't even worn that well – making advances to a woman who, although probably not much younger in terms of actual years, looked sprightlier altogether. And today she had obviously taken trouble to reflect the festive season; her comely curves accentuated by a red-and-green-checked frock, and her not-quite-greying hair adorned with strings of tinsel.

Deliberately, he hadn't dressed up. Norah had never seen him in anything but his shabby cords and drab brown anorak, and, were she to guess he'd tried to transform himself from frump to fashion plate, solely in her honour, he knew he'd feel a fool. Now, however, he regretted the fact that he hadn't at least splashed out on a new shirt, or one of those jokey Christmas jumpers that seemed all the rage at present. He also wished he had timed his visit much nearer to closing-time, when they might have had more privacy. Perhaps he could even have persuaded Norah to let him walk her home.

No, that was a fantasy too far. Probably best for him to go home and forget the whole idea of her gift. Suppose she didn't recognize him? – an agonizing prospect, but not impossible. After all, the last few times he'd popped into the shop, to buy his usual *Daily Mail*, there had been only a vague nod from her; no acknowledgment of him as 'the lost-gloves man', deeply in her debt. Indeed, he had felt a certain sense of pique that his ardent devotion hadn't merited so much as a 'Good morning'.

Disconsolately, he slunk through the door and out into the street, only to turn straight round and re-enter, as a new idea occurred to him. He could ask her advice about chocolates for his mother, and that might spark a longer and more personal chat. His poor old Mum had passed away ten years ago, in fact, but Norah wouldn't know that. And he could always give the chocolates to his sister – as well as Norah's gift-set, which, he now decided, was too ostentatious in these unpropitious circumstances.

As he joined the queue, he thought up a little spiel: his mum preferred milk chocolates to plain and would love something rather special: a luxury brand like Lindt, maybe, or even hand-made chocolates, or a personalized box, imprinted with her name....

No, he was getting carried away, as usual. A small, modest shop like Martin's would probably stock nothing more ambitious than Black Magic or Milk Tray. Anyway, the brand was immaterial – the important thing was to sound spontaneous and casual, then gradually move the conversation from his mother to himself, in the hope of engaging Norah's interest. The present could wait; the first step in his campaign was simply to make her conscious of his presence. Yet his nervousness was mounting as the feckless customers in front of him fumbled for their purses, or dropped their change on the floor, or used credit cards that the machine refused to accept. At this rate, the object of his devotion might begin to lose her cool, or even insist on shutting up shop at the official closing-time and refuse to serve the last few people in the queue. However, as far as her outward demeanour went, she still seemed the soul of patience, cheerfully smiling at some ancient crone, who was trying to pay for her purchases with a slow and shambling succession of one- and two-penny pieces.

And, miraculously, she was still smiling when, at last, he reached the head of the queue.

'Oh, Ken, I'm really glad to see you!' she exclaimed.

His mouth dropped open in astonishment. She had not just recognized him, she had even remembered his name – which he'd told her only in an awkward mumble as she was about to leave his flat, after handing over his gloves.

'You see, I have this tiny thing for you.'

His amazement increased a hundredfold, as, reaching under the counter, she came up with a small, holly-printed, china bowl, adorned with a red bow, and containing, of all things, a rather splendid-looking Christmas pudding.

'It's home-made,' she told him, pushing it into his hands. 'I always make a batch of them for customers and friends, and I wanted you to have one.'

This was the stuff of fantasy and, for a moment, he feared he must be inventing the whole scenario, indulging in his habitual make-believe. But, no, the china bowl was undoubtedly real, as it sat cool and heavy on his palm, and his pleasure and surprise were so rip-roaringly real they had affected his power of speech. 'Th ... thank you,' he stuttered, aware, all at once, that here was his perfect opportunity instantly to reciprocate – and to hell with what people might think. 'And I ... I have a tiny thing for you,' he countered, his king-sized smile all but obstructing the words. Withdrawing the gift-wrapped package from the depths of his old shopping-bag, he passed it across the counter.

'Oh, Ken, how lovely! It looks exciting. But, really, you shouldn't have.'

'It's nothing,' he said, with a deprecating shrug. 'Just, you know, a token, to thank you for returning my gloves.'

He could have continued this exchange for hours, for days, for centuries – maybe dared to use her name: a Norah in return for the two Kens. However, some irate female behind him was muttering 'Get a bloody move on!', even poking him in the back, for heaven's sake.

No matter. As he thanked Norah again and left the shop, nothing could dent his elation. She hadn't given a Christmas pudding to anyone else in the queue, which meant he must be special in some way. And that fact alone was enough to transform the overcast and lowering sky into a glittering vista of resplendent, radiant stars.

He didn't bother with a turkey, of course, let alone 'all the trim-mings', to borrow the phrase from his local's Christmas menu. Norah's pudding was sufficient unto itself as the alpha and omega of this super-special Christmas dinner. He had laid the table with a festive Tesco's paper cloth, and a CD of Christmas carols (free in last week's *Mail*) was playing softly in the background. He had even dressed for the occasion, in his smartest trousers and a crisp white shirt.

He checked the time by the kitchen clock. Dear, kind, thought-ful Norah had enclosed a printed slip at the bottom of the bowl, instructing him to re-heat the pudding for either three minutes in the microwave, or twenty minutes in a pan of boiling water on the hob. He had opted for the hob and, indeed, the eager sound of bubbling was increasing his sense of anticipation.

On the dot of one o'clock, he dished it up, inverting it on to his one-and-only real Royal Doulton plate – a treasure from a charity shop. Norah had made him the pudding with her own sweet, chubby hands, which meant this Christmas would outshine any other in his life, because it proved she felt something for him.

'Look, she makes a whole batch every year,' a cynical voice inside him sneered, 'so you're just one of many recipients – not special in any way, or singled out. Or she may be the bleeding-heart type, who deliberately gives her puddings only to poor, pitiable old souls, like loners, or no-hopers, or doddery, disabled folk. She must have noticed you walk with a limp and—'

'No!' he all but shouted, refusing to spoil this once-in-a-lifetime occasion with negative speculations.

Having tossed all cynical voices into the waste-bin, to moulder with yesterday's potato peelings and this morning's soggy teabags, he seated himself at the table and, with due solemnity, took his first mouthful of the richly fruited pudding. A veritable kaleidoscope of taste-and-texture sensations fought for glorious supremacy in his mouth: the mellifluous moistness of sultanas, the sweet-sharp tang of candied peel, the zing of brandy, the crunch of nuts. And his eyes and ears were likewise engaged, in the jewel-like gleam of glace cherries, and the soft strains of Silent Night. He sat, in a happy trance, listening, as the next carol, God Rest Ye Merry, Gentlemen, cresecendoed through the room. And, when the choir embarked on the refrain: Oh, tidings of comfort and joy, he seized immediately, triumphantly on that last, important word.

Joy! Yes! Here and now, in his small and steamy kitchen, and on Christmas Day, of all days; a day to be endured, most years, rather than enjoyed. And this rare and blessed experience far surpassed enjoyment – it was very nearly bliss – equal, in fact to his six-year-old self's first sighting of the sea, and equal to the proud pout-whiting he'd caught off Brighton Pier, equal to the adder swimming purposefully towards him, across the River Wey; perhaps even better than all three put together, because it was his first taste of joy as an adult.

Of course, despite his euphoric state, he couldn't go as far as to believe in Father Christmas, let alone a maverick one who would have time to answer a grown-up's letter, when millions of children were clamouring for toys. But he *could* believe in romance, and, as he swallowed another spoonful of the luscious, love-filled pudding, he dared to believe in joy, as well – more joy, in the future. Secure in the knowledge that Norah had thought about him, cooked for him, even remembered his name, his confidence was growing like the proverbial beanstalk.

He closed his eyes, better to savour a delectable titbit of dried fig, adhering to his teeth in the same sweetly persistent manner as he hoped Norah would cling to him, one day. Clearly, though, some positive action was required to ensure such an outcome, so, eyes still ecstatically shut, he made a New Year's resolution in advance: he was going back, the very instant the shop re-opened, to invite her out for a romantic, joyous dinner.

MAGICAL NUMBERS

'Oh, shit! I'm terribly sorry.' Lynne gazed in horror at the splotches of red wine already soaking into the man's white shirt – a total stranger, and one who obviously took trouble with his clothes. More wine was trickling down his stylish dove-grey trousers, staining those, as well. 'I can't apologize enough. It was my fault entirely.' Crass idiocy on her part to turn to look over her shoulder while carrying two full glasses back from the bar. She'd been distracted by the barman's hair-do – glaringly peroxided, stiffly gelled and standing up in an exuberant quiff – but that was no excuse. It had made a collision more or less inevitable, and now she and this poor hapless bloke were standing in a small claret-coloured pool.

One of the bar staff was already headed in their direction, with a floor-cloth and a mop, and several customers nearby were watching the scene with interest, further increasing her embarrassment. The man himself, however, seemed remarkably sanguine; no angry out-bursts, no recriminations.

'Don't worry – it's OK,' he said, wiping himself down in a calm, methodical fashion, with a large white handkerchief as pristine as his once-immaculate shirt.

'Let me help,' she offered, rummaging in her bag for some tissues, only to find she'd come out without them.

'No, honestly, I'm fine. It's such a warm evening, my clothes will dry in no time. And tomorrow morning, I'll take them to the clean-ers, so no harm done.'

'Well, at least let me pay the cleaning bill.'

'I wouldn't hear of it!'

'But I must do something,' she insisted, raising her voice above a burst of raucous laughter. Mercifully, the adjoining customers had stopped gawping at her discomfiture and resumed their conversation. 'I feel such a clumsy idiot.'

'It was an accident, that's all. But if you'd like to buy me a drink some time, I certainly shan't object.'

'Of course. What would you like, wine or—?'

'I didn't actually mean now. And aren't you with someone already? You were carrying two glasses.'

'Just a couple of girls from the office. I'm sure they won't mind, if I go and explain.'

The man glanced at his watch. 'I ought to be off any minute, so could we make it later this week? How about Friday?'

'Perfect. Where and when?'

Having arranged to meet at seven in this same pub, he belatedly introduced himself, handing her his business card.

She gave it a quick glance: Andrew Edwards, Data Analyst. 'And I'm Lynne Forster,' she said, scribbling her phone number on a beer-mat, in the absence of a card.

'Great! See you Friday, Lynne.'

The minute he'd gone, she returned to Emma and Nathalie, in the far corner of the lounge bar, and regaled them with the story.

'But you don't know the guy from Adam,' Emma objected. 'Suppose he's a raging pervert or serial murderer.'

'He's hardly likely to murder me in a crowded pub on a busy London street, in full daylight.'

'Oh, come on, Lynne. You know what I mean.'

'I bet he's tall, dark, handsome and filthy rich,' Nathalie put in, 'so Lynne's simply making sure she's in with a chance!'

'If you really want to know, he was about five-feet-eight, with mouse-coloured hair and rather unflattering glasses. To be perfectly frank, he looked a bit of a nerd.'

'So why meet him?' Emma demanded.

'It's the least I can do. I mean, he said he had to leave and, if he's off to some other engagement, it could be jolly awkward for him turning up all wine-bespattered,'

'Talking of wine, we're still waiting for our second drinks,' Nathalie reminded her. 'And, if you disappear completely this time, we'll assume you've collided with someone really hot and he's whisked you back to his Chelsea penthouse for champagne and caviar!'

'I should be so lucky!' Although she wouldn't admit it, least of all to waspish Emma, she did feel a faint ripple of excitement about meeting Andrew again. OK, he might not make the grade in terms of his appearance, but his unruffled demeanour had struck her forcibly, especially in contrast to the aggressive, vituperative men she seemed to have met of late. Besides, if nothing else, it would make a change from drinks with her two work-mates, whom she saw enough of in the office, as it was.

'Fancy a drink this evening?' Emma asked, pausing by her desk.

'Sorry, I'm meeting Andrew.'

'What, again? You must have seen him at least ten times.'

'No, seven.'

'Seven's still a hell of a lot in less than a month. You're obviously besotted!'

'Don't be daft. Of course I'm not.'

'What's the attraction, then?'

'He's … different. Good-mannered and attentive and sort of gentlemanly. I admit that makes him seem a bit old before his time, but—'

'How old is he?'

'Well, older than me, but only eight years or so. He'll be thirty in August.'

'And never been married, you say?'

'No. I suspect he's wedded to his job, and rather obsessional in general – obsessed with numbers, no question. He and I have very different ways of looking at the world. I tend to see things in terms of image – how they strike the eye – whereas he's hung up on algorithms and mathematical formulae and all that kind of stuff.'

'He sounds a total egghead.'

'No, he doesn't even have a degree. And, although I assume he's brilliant with numbers, he also has a side that, frankly, seems irrational. For instance, he pointed out that we met on the fifth of June, at seven o'clock, which gives a sequence of 5/6/7. To me, that's just coincidence and neither here nor there but, as far as he's concerned, it makes our meeting significant, in the sense of "meant to be".'

'That's seriously weird.'

'Maybe it's just connected with his work.' She willed Emma to return to her desk. Fortunately, Graham, their boss, was busy on the phone, but he was doubtless aware, at some level, that the two of them were 'time-wasting' and thus might start his usual spiel about how, with only four staff, it was vital they all pulled their weight. 'I mean, if you're analysing data all the time, perhaps you're conscious of symmetries and suchlike that ordinary people don't see.'

'What I can't understand is how he does that sort of high-powered work without a degree.'

'I'm not sure it *is* high-powered.'

'Well, if he works in the field of Big Data, it's said to be one of the sexiest jobs going, not to mention very highly paid. And since he lives in a snazzy Clerkenwell pad....'

Lynne's attention was still snared on the word 'sexiest'. Although sex with Andrew was good, something vital seemed to be missing – something she couldn't quite define, except he appeared to find it difficult to act with genuine spontaneity. On each of the four occasions, he had followed the exact same, set-in-stone routine: first three minutes' kissing, then three minutes' fondling her body, followed by three minutes' tonguing her breasts, and so on and so on, as if allotted by a stop-watch. Nothing wrong with his technique; she just wondered if, at some point, he might free up a little and dispense with such a methodical pattern, or initiate a different position from his usual man-on-top. It was probably up to her to suggest some variations, yet he was so wedded to his own meticulous method, she feared that might upset him.

Emma was still leaning against her desk, now swigging from a bottle of Perrier. 'Maybe he just calls himself a data analyst,' she said, pursuing the conversation: a terrier with a bone, 'you know, like we call ourselves "publishers", while struggling to turn out a very low-key, indie mag, with a tiny list of subscribers.'

'We're still publishers,' Lynne countered defensively, glancing round with affection at the untidy, cluttered office, with its piles of back issues heaped up on the floor, and the collage on the wall, created from their most striking magazine-covers.

'Except,' she added, 'we *won't* be, if we don't get back to work!'

'Well, I'm only hanging about because I'm waiting for your layouts.'

'Just give me ten more minutes, OK?'

'OK, but don't waste any more time mooning over your so-called data analyst.'

'I *love* you!' Andrew shouted, collapsing down on top of her.

She was too out of breath to speak – as well as too surprised, since he had never mentioned love before. However, most men, in her experience, conflated lust with love, so he was probably just on a sexual high, on account of the fact they'd both come at the exact same gratifying moment, which hadn't happened before. Indeed, up till now, she had found his insistence on remaining in control, even in the sex-act, strangely disconcerting, as if part of him was holding back, dictating the proceedings from some detached, dispassionate cyber-brain.

'That was quite fantastic, darling.'

She noted the 'darling' – another first.

Then, instead of slumping down in his usual semi-doze, he sat up in bed and took both her hands in his, speaking solemnly and slowly. 'Lynne, this may be a bit premature, but I've been thinking very seriously and I want us to get married.'

Dumbstruck, she could only stare.

'We hit it off so well – not just in bed, in every way, and that's incredibly rare. I can't tell you how long I've been looking for a woman with your particular qualities and, now I've found you, I just can't let you go. I want you to share my life, share my flat, share everything.'

Again, she struggled for words. They had known each other barely four weeks and she was ignorant of whole areas of his life, including his family background. In any case, she had ambitions, one of which was to edit a proper, prestigious magazine before the age of thirty. Marriage – and, more so, children – would stymie such a goal. Yet she had to admit it was flattering to receive a marriage proposal, and surely proof she was desirable, which her previous men-friends had frequently led her to doubt. And whatever her suspicions about Andrew's mention of love, this particular matter clearly *wasn't* prompted by lust. He would never take such an important step on a mere impulsive whim and, anyway, hadn't he just told her he had thought seriously about the issue? Besides, she couldn't help being tempted by his offer of sharing everything. His pay was at least quadruple hers and this spacious Clerkenwell flat, with its ultra-stylish furnishings and solid oak-wood flooring, was far superior to her own dingy little bedsit.

She wasn't a gold-digger – the concept was abhorrent – yet, as the child of a single parent, she had always been insecure; moving with her feckless mother from one grotty set of lodgings to another, and invariably short of money for trainers, school-trips, or the latest trendy gadgets all her classmates flashed around. But that was way back in the past, and she mustn't let it influence any decision at this moment. Nor should money come into it. What mattered wasn't Andrew's income or enviable lifestyle, but his reassuring steadiness, generous nature and complete reliability.

'Darling, you're very quiet. I hope this hasn't been a shock for you.'

'Well, yes, a bit, to be honest. I mean, it all seems so...sudden.'

'Lynne, I'm sure you know by now that I never act precipitately. And I'm savvy enough about relationships to realize ours is special, without needing months to prove it. But the last thing I want is to pressure you, so why don't we leave the question open for a couple of weeks, at least. That'll give you time to think it over and maybe discuss it with your mother.'

No, she thought, instinctively. Her mother had never quite forgiven her for leaving home, regarding it as 'abandonment'. And, since she was always supremely critical, Andrew would fail to win her approval, even with all his sterling qualities.

'Let's relax, darling, and not worry about a thing.' He lay back against the pillows, coaxed her down beside him and began gently stroking her hair. And, all at once, she was flooded with an intense – and rare – contentment. She had already decided to turn down his proposal – with the greatest possible tact, of course – but it still made her feel diamond-bright to be cherished and desired.

'So what d'you think?' Lynne reclined back on the trendy, white-leather sofa, next to her fiancé – the word gave her a definite thrill. 'A spring wedding? Maybe Easter week?'

Slowly, he shook his head. 'I'm afraid we don't have much choice of date.'

'What do you mean? Why ever not?'

'Well, it *has* to be this year. In fact, it has to be December the eleventh, at two-fifteen. You see, that particular date and time gives the sequence of numbers: 11/12/13/14/15. And a similar sequence of five won't happen again for another ninety years.'

Could she have heard right? To determine the date of a wedding on such insubstantial grounds seemed totally preposterous. Besides, December was far too soon to get everything arranged in time.

'Numbers have huge importance, Lynne. Many people fail to grasp exactly what they signify, but that doesn't mean—'

'Look here,' she interrupted, caring nothing for numbers, except to fix a more convenient date. 'December the eleventh's only four-and-a-half months off, and it's a hopeless month for weddings, anyway, with all the Christmas hype and everyone desperately busy. And people tend to go away then, so some of my friends will have to miss my Big Day. And the weather's bloody awful and it's the cold-and-flu season, don't forget. But what I really object to is the pressure. My friend Vanessa needed more than a year to plan her wedding, and that's normal, I assure you. You may not realize, Andrew, but there's a huge amount to do – the church to book, as well as a venue for the reception, and my dress and shoes and veil to buy, and loads of decisions about photographers and caterers and florists and what-have-you, and the cake to order, and the wedding cars and invitations, and a budget to be set....'

'Don't worry about the budget, darling. If you want to splash out a bit, that's fine by me. And, as far as the planning is concerned, just give me a list of the things that need to be done, and I'll make sure we get them all ticked off in well under four-and-a-half months. That's my forte, Lynne – organization, efficiency, cutting out unnecessary steps or duplicated efforts, and keeping completely focused on each part of the schedule in turn.'

Unable to contain her agitation, she jumped up from the sofa and began pacing round the room. 'Andrew, you may be super-efficient, but there are some things you just can't do – choose my wedding dress, for instance, or sort out my bridesmaids and *their* dresses. Or draw up a guest-list for me, when you hardly know any of my friends. And you certainly can't take my mother shopping for *her* outfit, or—'

'Agreed,' he said, serene, as always – maddeningly so, in this context, 'but I can do most of the rest. And when it comes to venues for the reception, and photographers and caterers and suchlike, I'll use spreadsheets and a database, and make proper price comparisons and rate every place or service-provider according to a graded system. Then we can see at a glance all the pros and cons of each, and also—'

'OK,' she interrupted. 'It all sounds fantastically efficient, but I still can't understand why a particular sequence of numbers has to overrule everything else.'

'Because numbers must take precedence in certain situations, Lynne, on account of their implications and their power. Take my birthday – the twenty-eighth of June. June is the sixth month, and six and twenty-eight are both perfect numbers.'

'How can any number be perfect?' she retorted. 'Surely a number is a number.'

'No, that's far too simplistic. Perfect numbers are made up the sum of their smaller divisors – for example, six is divisible by one, two and three and, if you add up one, two and three, you get six. And twenty-eight is divisible by one, two, four, seven and four-teen, and the sum of those divisors is also twenty-eight. So, perfect numbers are, by their very nature, extremely rare. The next one after twenty-eight is four hundred and ninety-six.'

Why, she wondered, irritably, were they engaging in such abstruse discussion, when they should be fixing a wedding-date? In any case, his talk of sums and divisors had left her floundering.

'The concept,' he added, with obvious satisfaction, 'is almost unbelievable, yet profoundly seductive.'

Unbelievable, yes, she thought, her high heels tapping out her annoyance on the echoing wood floor, but seductive, not at all. Yet, although she tried to moderate her anger, she produced only a frac-tious splutter.

'Lynne, I hate to see you so upset.' He, too, got up and took her in his arms, to stop her frantic pacing. 'You're probably feeling hassled, even bullied, but I want you to trust me, darling, in knowing that the December date will work out perfectly well.'

'But it's hard to trust you when I'm not on the same wavelength. I mean, all this stuff you find so infinitely fascinating just doesn't strike a chord with me.'

'I grant you it's not easy to explain – or not without going into eso-teric realms, rather like trying to explain religion to a non-believer.'

'So it's just a superstitious thing, you mean?'

'No, absolutely not! It involves crucial concepts, such as harmony and order, correlation, synchronization.... Actually, I learned some of it from my father, who even insisted on naming us children according to a system. I'm Andrew Brian Clifford David Edwards, which gives the sequence of letters: A/B/C/D/E. And my sister's Alice Barbara Catherine Deidre....'

She was torn between laughing in derision, and running a mile. Suppose this obsession with numbers was some sort of genetic disor-der that could be passed on from Andrew and his father to her own kids?

'But,' he said, gently massaging her forehead, to smooth away her frown, 'it would take hours to explore that whole complicated field and, right now, I simply need to persuade you that, if we stick to this once-in-a-lifetime formula of 11/12/13/14/15, our marriage will be blessed.'

She felt herself go limp in his arms, as if her uncertainty and bewil-derment had sapped her physical strength. Yet she was aware of him supporting her in a strangely reassuring way and, although nowhere near convinced about his choice of wedding-date, his own complete conviction was somehow suppressing her doubts. Besides, other, perfectly rational things could also sound peculiar, if not downright crazy – modern physics, for example, or what she could grasp of it from the latest TV series. And, since she was as ignorant about all matters mathematical as she was about quantum physics, who was she to judge such numerical unorthodoxies? If she could ensure a happy marriage by any means, however esoteric, shouldn't she jump at the chance? Her parents had divorced when she was six, and she had never forgotten their blistering rows – each of them using her as a pawn – and then the terrible day her father marched out, leaving her mother bitter and resentful for the remainder of her life. Andrew would never walk out of a marriage, or lose his temper and scream and shout, let alone resort to violence, as both her parents had.

'Let me get you a drink, darling. You still look a bit shell-shocked!'

She allowed herself to be led back to the sofa. Two cushions were placed behind her back; a glass of wine put into her hand. Andrew was nothing if not caring and considerate.

'And I'll rustle up some scrambled eggs, OK?'

'Lovely, thanks.' His scrambled eggs were in the gourmet class, rich with smoked salmon, and perfectly poised between runny and overcooked. Meals apart, he had already done so much for her, simply in being a steadying influence, invariably calm and reasonable. So didn't she owe him something in return – especially on an issue he felt so passionately about?

She hesitated only for a second, before following him into the kitchen. 'I've just made a decision,' she announced, putting her arms around his waist and pressing close. 'We *will* get married at two-fifteen, on December the eleventh.'

'Mum, it suits you, honestly. And it's perfect for a winter wedding.'

Her mother grimaced at herself in the full-length fitting-room mirror. 'I look like a dog's dinner.'

'You actually look extremely elegant. And anyway, you must have tried on fifty outfits by now – I mean, counting the last two Saturdays, as well as today – and there can't be something wrong with all of them. OK, I know you hated the pink creation, *and* the turquoise suit, and that floral thing, and even the gorgeous grey two-piece, but this dress and jacket is definitely the best, I'd say. So why not settle for it, then we can go and have a coffee and rest our feet.'

Her mother shrugged. 'All right, if you insist.'

'I'm not insisting, Mum. It has to be your choice. But we can't spend every Saturday dragging round the shops.' The cramped, claustrophobic fitting-room seemed to be choking on her mother's cheap carnation scent.

'I've said I'll take it, haven't I? – although it's wickedly expensive.'

'Look, I've told you over and over, Andrew's paying.'

'Why should he?' her mother snapped.

'Because he's generous, Mum. And he happens to have the money, which you don't.'

'He's only being generous because he completely overruled you about the date of the wedding. I reckon he's feeling guilty now and just trying to make amends.'

'Oh, Mum, don't start all that again.' Lynne sank into the spindly gilt chair wedged between the mirror and the wall. 'And, anyway,

everything's under control. It's only mid-October, but we've ticked
off almost every item on our list. In fact, I can hardly believe how
smoothly it's gone – thanks to Andrew, of course. He's spared me
a huge amount of hassle. Most brides-to-be do all that stuff themselves, yet he's taken on the bulk of it.'

'If it was my wedding, I'd rather do it myself.'

'Well, it's not your wedding, Mum, OK? And, if you get out of
that dress, I'll go and pay for it.'

'I still think it's way too fancy.'

Lynne restricted herself to an irritated sigh. 'Last week you complained that the grey one was too plain.'

'It *was* – a bit like my old school uniform.'

'Mum,' she said, firmly, 'there's a little café right next to this
department. Once you're ready, just walk a few yards to your right
and you'll come to The Coffee Cup. I'll see you there in ten minutes,
OK?'

'So have you decided on your hen night yet?'

Lynne sugared her coffee and sat spooning the froth from the top.
'Yes – all fixed now. Andrew helped me with that, as well. I kept
dithering, you see, because the normal hen night sorts of things leave
me, frankly, cold. I mean, I've no desire to get trashed in some ridiculously expensive club, and I loathe those sleazy male strippers that
Vanessa had at *her* do. In fact, from what I can gather, they're often
mostly gay and simply pretend to be turned on by a bunch of slaver-
ing girls. And, as for shelling out for some exotic trip abroad, I just
haven't the cash to take all twelve of us. And a chocolate-making
workshop is bound to bring me out in spots, just when I want to look
good for my Big Day.'

'So what has your famous Andrew decided – to pack you all off to
a boot-camp?'

'Don't be stupid, Mum. In any case, he *didn't* decide. He just tried
to focus my mind and asked me all these questions, first to find out
what I didn't want, and then to discover what might appeal. And
when I told him how much I loved ice-skating—'

'Oh, yes,' her mother interrupted. 'If you hadn't broken up with
that dishy Xavier chap, you two could have been the next Torvill and
Dean.'

'Mum, you hated Xavier! You didn't even like his name!'

'Well, what kind of name is Xavier, for heaven's sake? Why couldn't his parents have given him an English name?'

'Because they happened to be Spanish. And, as for us being the next Torvill and Dean, you said any bloke that skated was probably a poof.'

'I never said any such thing.'

She had learned, long ago, that it was too exhausting to argue every point with her mother. And anyway, her thoughts had zeroed in on Xavier: one of her first boyfriends and a Bohemian, artistic type – even a bit of a dropout – but far more spontaneous and devil-may-care than Andrew. No, that was unfair to her fiancé. A devil-may-care dropout would hardly ensure that the mortgage and the bills were paid, and was bound to be a feckless sort of dad, whereas she could rely on Andrew to draw up a fool-proof spreadsheet for the children's every need. He'd know exactly when their vaccinations were due, their eye-tests, dental check-ups, and all the other minutiae of parenthood. And he would research the best schools in the area: entry requirements, curricula, calibre and number of their staff. Besides, *she* could be the artistic one. Opposites attracted, so people always said.

And he was definitely supportive of her work and her ambitions, had even offered to help finance her own online magazine, should she wish to launch one, and agreed they would put off having a family until she had notched up some achievements. She was, in fact, keen to be a mother – a loving and uncritical one, she hoped – but, at twenty-two, she could afford to devote a few years, first, to establishing herself.

'You're miles away,' her mother complained, draining her cappuccino with a slurp. 'You were telling me about Xavier.'

'I wasn't, Mum. I was explaining about my hen night.' She needed all her concentration to avoid losing her temper, or bursting into tears – her customary reaction whenever she met her mother. 'Where were we?'

'Ice-skating,' her mother snapped, apparently every bit as irritable.

'Oh, yes. Well, Andrew asked whether the other girls could skate and, when I told him they could, he spent ages researching all the ice-rinks in or close to London. He eventually suggested we went to the one at Somerset House, because they're putting on a super-special light-show, this year, and you can book various all-in packages, to include canapés and cocktails, or cup-cakes and hot chocolate, as well as entry to the rink, and skatehire and what-have-you. And, would you believe, he went ahead and booked the most expensive package for the lot of us and footed the whole bill.'

Her mother used a moistened finger to mop up the last fragments of her cake. 'So when's it's going to be?'

'Well, I was hoping to have it at least a couple of weeks before the wedding, but Nathalie's not back from Paris till the eighth of December, so we had no choice but to arrange it for the ninth.'

'All I can say is, rather you than me! I can't think of anything worse than tearing round some rackety public rink in the freezing cold.'

'It's lucky you won't be coming, then.' Couldn't her mum say even one nice thing about Andrew's generosity? After all, it wasn't just the hen night he was financing, but almost the entire cost of the wedding. Most mothers-of-the-bride shouldered such costs themselves, often risking hardship in the process, yet *her* mum simply accepted her good fortune as her natural, inalienable right. But then her mother had always found fault and, if her future son-in-law was Jesus Christ Himself, He would be criticized as badly dressed, low-born, eccentric and a leftie. 'Actually, I ought to make a move now. I've masses to do back home.'

'I don't know how you can call it "home", Lynne, when it's Andrew's place, not yours.'

'I've told you twenty times, we share it.'

'Well, I dread to think what your father would say – moving in with a bloke you barely know, *and* before you're married.'

'Look, Dad's not likely to show up again in either of our lives, so we hardly need to fret about it.'

'I wonder if I should try to track him down.' Her mother wiped a smear of buttercream from her mouth and sat musing on the problem. 'I mean, if he knows you're getting married, he might want to walk you down the aisle.'

The very prospect made her blanch. If her father was invited, the whole wedding could be wrecked. There would be shamingly public rows between him and her mum and, if they both got drunk, she could well imagine the consequences: fisticuffs, smashed glasses, the other guests upset and scandalized. She felt a sudden desperate longing to return to Andrew – safe, dependable Andrew, who gave her a sense of security and peace. Kicking back her chair, she sprang abruptly to her feet and grabbed her coat and bag. 'I'm sorry, Mum, but I have to go. I'll ring you later, OK? But, whatever you do, don't breathe a word to Dad about the wedding.'

'I'm sorry, Lynne, but you don't have any choice.'

Mr Vishwa, the orthopaedic surgeon, was a small, stocky man with sallow skin and dark circles under his eyes – exhausted, Lynne assumed, by long hours and interrupted sleep, but that was no excuse for his brusque, officious tone.

'As my colleague's told you already,' he said, impatiently, 'you'll have to postpone your wedding and that's an end to it.'

'I can't,' she repeated, desperate at the prospect. 'It's absolutely essential that—'

'No more argument.' The surgeon ran a weary hand through his lank black hair. 'As I've tried to explain, this is a compound fracture, which means the skin is broken, as well as the bones – and that's more serious. It also means you're at risk of infection, so – let me reiterate – there's no way you can go anywhere tomorrow.'

'But everything's arranged,' she said, blinking back the tears. After months of meticulous planning, how could she shrug off such a large and special wedding as if it were no more than a missed lunch-date or forgotten dental appointment? 'Couldn't I use crutches?' she pleaded, 'or a walking-frame or something?'

'Look here,' he said, with an irritated frown, 'you've broken both the bones in your lower leg, the tibia and the fibula. The tibia is the weight-bearing bone, so if you think you can go gallivanting off the very next day after surgery, you're seriously mistaken. I'm sorry,' he added, glancing at his watch. 'I'm needed in theatre, so I'll leave you with Nurse Bella, OK?' And, with a final curt nod, he strode out of the ward.

The nurse, a much kinder soul, squeezed her hand in sympathy. 'I can understand how awful you must feel, Lynne, having to postpone your Big Day. It really is a terrible shame.'

Lynne clutched her fingers, like a life-raft, glad of any anchor after the last nightmarish ten hours or so of pain, shock and crushing disappointment. 'Are you sure the doctor's right?' she asked, hoping even now for a reprieve.

'Yes, I'm afraid he is. And Mr Vishwa is extremely good, you know, so you're in the best of hands. But, you see, he says you fell very awkwardly and that makes the fracture more difficult to treat.'

'Well, this stupid man crashed into me, full-force – a young teara-way speeding round like a maniac and showing off to his mates. They shouldn't have allowed him on the ice rink at all.'

'He certainly sounds a menace, but try not to brood on it. The anaesthetist has signed you up for a pre-med, which will make you nice and sleepy before you're taken down to theatre. I'm going to fetch that now, Lynne, so I'd like you to do your best to relax.'

Relaxation was impossible, with her mind continually circling back to the whole grim scenario: the head-on collision and her total inability to get up from the ice, the other girls all clustering round in consternation, Vanessa accompanying her in the ambulance, its shrilling sirens an expression of the searing pain. Then the wait in A & E for a member of the orthopaedic team to put in an appearance, while she lay in a curtained-off cubicle, with a harassed male nurse, Raj, popping in and out whenever he could spare the time. She had tried to get hold of Andrew, but he must have switched off his phone and gone to bed, knowing she'd arranged to stay the night with Vanessa and wouldn't be back till late.

It was her mother who had phoned, instead, having been informed as next-of-kin. Then, half an hour later, she had arrived at A & E, by cab, sweeping in like a prima donna and imperiously sending Vanessa home. Hardly any help, in fact, since the latter's sympathetic calmness was now replaced by remonstrations, as her mum wailed about the perils of skating and how she'd warned her daughter all along not to go near an ice-rink.

Raj had finally persuaded her to leave, for the sake of everyone's sanity – although there was still little peace and quiet, due to various disturbances outside the cubicle. Some odious drunk was effing and blinding at one of the staff; a shrill-voiced patient kept complaining about the endless delay, and a quarrel was in full conflagration between a vituperative couple, each blaming the other for their car-crash.

It had been almost a relief to be admitted to this, the orthopaedic ward, where at least the other patients were largely quiet or sedated. And when the staff changed over at 7.30 this morning, Nurse Bella had come on duty and been a gentle, soothing presence ever since.

And here she was, approaching once more – with, presumably, the pre-med. She placed the paper cup of pills on the locker, then drew the curtains round the bed, and passed Lynne a half-glassful of water. 'Seeing as you're nil by mouth, drink just a tiny sip or two to get these down, OK? Oh, and by the way, your fiancé rang again. He sounds a really lovely fellow, so, while you're lying here, why don't you fix your mind on him, rather than on the accident, and think how grand it'll be when you're fully recovered and standing there beside him at the altar, as he slips the ring on your finger....'

And, despite her utter misery and her growing apprehension about the imminent surgery, she made a valiant effort to do exactly that.

'A visitor for you, Lynne.' A different nurse ushered Andrew in – an Andrew half-hidden by a large, cellophane-wrapped bouquet of scarlet roses and white Madonna lilies.

'Oh, they're gorgeous!' Lynne exclaimed, as he laid them beside her on the bed.

He kissed her, tenderly, although the expression on his face was one of deep dismay, as he surveyed the rigid plaster cast encasing her leg from knee to foot; the leg itself propped up on a pillow. 'How are you feeling?' he asked, with obvious concern, glancing next at the drip in her arm, and the cardboard vomit-bowl, placed strategically nearby.

'Not brilliant. A bit woozy from the operation and still in shock, I suspect.' Indeed, she seemed to have lost all track of time and had to rely on clues, such as the black, uncurtained window further down the ward, to deduce it must be evening. 'And, of course,' she added, 'I'm absolutely gutted about having to postpone the wedding,'

He pulled up a chair beside the bed, took her hand in his and gently stroked the fingers. 'Actually, I'm sure we can go ahead – that's what I'm here to discuss, darling. Even if you're on crutches or whatever, we'll find a way, don't worry.'

She stared at him, aghast. 'But, Andrew, the surgeon says it's out of the question. I begged and pleaded – you know that – even said you'd carry me up the aisle, but he was absolutely adamant. I'm not allowed to move, and that's that.'

'He doesn't understand, my sweet.' Andrew's anodyne tone was an irritant on this occasion. 'I hope you explained to him that tomorrow's sequence of numbers won't happen again for another ninety years?'

'He's an extremely busy man, Andrew, so I imagine he has more important things on his mind.'

Her sarcasm was lost on him, since he continued in the same vein. 'And, in another ninety years, we'll both be dead, so this is our one-and-only chance.'

'Well, if you want to kill me sooner than that,' she said, with an unconvincing laugh, 'you're certainly going about it the right way. They've put a rod in my leg and I can't put any weight on it at all. I may be stuck here a whole week, or even longer, so if you imagine I can just jump out of bed tomorrow....'

'Lynne, I couldn't bear the slightest harm to come to you – that goes without saying. But you need to bear in mind that doctors always err on the side of caution, just to cover their backs and avoid the threat of being sued.'

She shook her head in disbelief. Could he really be willing to disobey the surgeon's orders, risk her future health and mobility, for the sake of a sequence of numbers, however unparalleled, mysterious or unique?

He was now holding her hand so tightly, his harsh grip hurt. 'I've cancelled the honeymoon, of course, and the reception. When we spoke on the phone, there simply wasn't time to tell you anything in detail, but you can rest assured that's all taken care of. Fortunately I had good insurance cover on both, so we won't lose out financially. We'll just rearrange them for later, as soon as you're well enough to cope. But, as for the legal ceremony, it's essential we complete that tomorrow – no other day will do. OK, you say you're not allowed to move, but that doesn't rule out a wedding, you know. According to my researches, we *can* get married in hospital.'

'Andrew,' she expostulated, 'not only are you ignoring how bloody awful I feel, but I can't think of anything worse than getting married here! What sort of a wedding would it be, with me lying all trussed up and doped to the gills with painkillers? And, anyway none of my friends would—'

'We'll invite them,' he interrupted, his voice more urgent now.

'For heaven's sake!' she shouted. 'Nathalie and Vanessa have already contacted everyone and told them the whole thing's off. Couldn't you at least have consulted me first, before going ahead with your own private plans?'

'It was impossible to speak to you again. I must have rung a good half-dozen times, but the nurses said you were sleeping or sedated or whatever.'

'Well, that's hardly surprising, when I'd just had major surgery. I'm not free to chat whenever I choose, as if I've come here for a holiday or something. And, in any case, even if I did get permission to get married from my hospital bed, the nurses would hardly welcome a great crowd of people disturbing the other patients on the ward. Can't you see, some of them are extremely old?'

She realized, to her embarrassment, that she was disturbing them already, by yelling so aggressively at Andrew. The wizened old woman opposite was staring, aghast, at the pair of them, and the poor balding lady in the adjoining bed, who'd been crying off and on all night, looked close to tears again. Both of them had broken various limbs and their pain and discomfort was doubtless worse than hers, considering their age – late eighties, if not older, she'd guess. 'Look, I don't want to argue any more.' She made a deliberate effort to lower her voice. 'I'm dead-beat as it is, so I just don't have the energy. I only had the op this morning and it's left me pretty limp. And last night I hardly slept a wink, despite the pills they dished out. What you don't seem to grasp, Andrew, is that this whole thing has been hell on earth – especially my desperate disappointment about the wedding.'

'But, that's exactly why I want to go ahead with it. I'm just as appalled as you are about the prospect of a postponement – and not only because of the special date, but because I *love* you, darling, so I can't wait for us to be officially married. Even if you can't invite your friends, we can still have the legal ceremony here – keep it very brief and low-key, so it doesn't tire you out. And, then, once you're fully mobile, we can have a second ceremony and re-enact our vows, with everybody present. I'm sure the vicar will be more than happy to let us re-book the church, and you can wear your long, white dress and have your four bridesmaids, exactly as you planned.'

'But it won't be the same, whatever you say. And, anyway, you're not even listening, Andrew. I've told you loud and clear, I don't *want* to be married in a hospital ward.'

'There's no other way, Lynne. Tomorrow is our once-in-a-lifetime chance.'

'Yes, so you've told me endlessly – which means that sequence of numbers is more important to you than I am.' How could so cavalier an attitude square with his declaration of love? Clearly, he hadn't the faintest notion how totally exhausted she was, craving only to shut her eyes and rest, not engage in protracted argument.

'Of course it's not more important, but what you don't understand—'

'I'm not sure I even want to understand.' Her voice was rising to an anguished wail.

The nurse came bustling over, having just finished checking the patient opposite. 'What's going on?' she demanded. 'You two are making a hell of a lot of noise.'

'We're fine,' Andrew said, with a reassuring smile, trying to pacify the woman with his customary old-school charm.

'Will you please go,' Lynne begged him. She'd had more than enough of his charm, enough of his treacherously persuasive tactics. How could he ride rough-shod over her wishes, flout the doctors' orders, refuse even to consider her basic physical capacities?

'That really isn't necessary,' he countered, appealing to the nurse directly. 'I think my fiancée would be better with me here, Sister.'

'Well, actually, I'd prefer you to come back tomorrow, simply for the sake of peace and quiet. And, anyway, all visitors have to leave by eight and it's already quarter to. Lynne ought to get some sleep, you know, once I've done her observations.'

'I'd rather stay till eight, if that's no problem. But I can pop outside while you're with Lynne – maybe make myself useful by finding a vase.'

The nurse frowned in patent displeasure. 'You won't find anything big enough for such a huge bouquet. And, in any case, our hospital policy is no flowers in the ward. The water can carry infection.'

'Well, I can bring in a vase myself, and make sure I change the water several times a day.'

'Infection isn't the only risk, so that wouldn't be much help. Some patients are allergic to pollen.'

Lynne clenched her fists in fury. Couldn't he see the nurse was annoyed – not to mention incredibly busy? 'Andrew, I *asked* you to leave. I don't want any visitors at all. I don't even want your bloody flowers!' Seizing the bouquet, she all but flung it at Andrew – which took effort on her part and tired her even more. He failed to catch it and it fell to the floor with a thud, damaging several of the fragile lilies. All the other patients were peering from their beds in mingled shock and dismay. But, if nothing else, it had the desired effect, because the nurse was already ushering Andrew firmly out of the ward.

A second nurse came over to Lynne, who was now sobbing audibly. 'It's only natural you're upset,' she said, soothingly. 'Anybody would be if they had to put off their wedding.'

'It's not the wedding. I'm crying for something much worse – something....' The sentence tailed away. She couldn't actually explain that what upset her most of all was Andrew's skewed priorities: the fact she came a very lame second to some footling sequence of numbers.

'Lord! I've been here all this time, yet I forgot to give you your present.' Andrew reached for his briefcase and withdrew a gift-wrapped package.

As Lynne undid the silver ribbon, she felt the gnaw and throb of pain vibrating through her leg, and the usual discomfort each time she shifted position. Her next painkillers were almost due and it was difficult to concentrate until she'd swallowed them, but she did her best to take an interest in the glossy hardback book she'd just unwrapped. 'The World's Greatest Love Lyrics,' she spelled out from the cover, with its striking illustration of a single crimson rose.

'I don't always have the words, Lynne, to express my love for you, so I wanted these famous poets to do it for me.'

'Thank you,' she said, warily, unable to forget his visit yesterday – what should have been their wedding day. Instead of commiserating with her about their shared sense of disappointment, he'd continued harping on the abandonment of their 'once-in-a-lifetime' date – for him a devastating blow. And that, coupled with his attitude the previous day, had left her shaken and dismayed. Today, however, he seemed completely different and hadn't even mentioned the subject.

Perhaps he felt remorse and was now keen to make amends. He'd certainly been thoughtful in his choice of gift, knowing her love of poetry.

'Shall I read you one or two poems,' he offered, 'to try to take your mind off things? I spent ages leafing through them last night, trying to find the nicest. I even rang a guy at work who used to teach English at Birkbeck, and he advised me to avoid the old chestnuts like Shakespeare's *Sonnets*, and pick out something original.'

A definite improvement, she thought, passing him the book: he'd been thinking of *her*, instead of dates and numbers, and had taken obvious trouble on her behalf.

'But the ones Ed suggested I hadn't even heard of, which made me feel a total ignoramus.'

No way was he an ignoramus, but he had never studied the arts, so she was touched by the fact he was endeavouring to build a bridge between their disparate interests and, again, had expended time and effort on the process.

'After a bit of Googling, I was slightly more clued up, but, even so, that modern stuff doesn't really appeal. I suppose, if verse lacks shape and structure, it offends my mathematical sense, so I'm much happier with traditional poetry that has metre and a rhyme-scheme.' Having pulled his chair closer to the bed, he retrieved the book and checked the index at the back. 'Anyway, I'd like to start with this one, because it's exactly what I'd write about *you*, if I only had the talent.'

He began to read in a deep, solemn voice a poem she knew well and, despite her pain and discomfort, she actually felt herself relax.

She walks in beauty like the night
Of cloudy climes and starry skies;
And all that's best of dark and bright
Meet in her aspect and her eyes....

He broke off to exclaim, 'It's so right for you, Lynne, isn't it – the way your eyes are dark and light at once and seem to change from brown to gold?'

'They're hazel,' she shrugged. 'Not particularly special.'

'They're special to me. And so is your hair – that gorgeous tawny colour, which again combines the best of dark and bright.'

Yes, this was the Andrew she loved; praising her, devoted to her, studying her every feature.

'Anyway, the poem inspired me so much that I had a bash at writing something myself. As I said, I've no gift for it at all, so I couldn't manage any sort of rhyme. In fact, it probably isn't poetry, by any normal definition, but it was intended as a tribute to you.'

'Oh, Andrew, how fantastic! Do read it to me – now, before you finish the Byron.' A personal composition topped even the most accomplished poem in the book.

'Well, it's not exactly Shakespeare,' he demurred, looking uncharacteristically bashful. Nonetheless, he withdrew a sheet of paper from his pocket and cleared his throat in preparation.

'Best read it quietly,' she advised, aware of the usual scrutiny from her fellow patients. They seemed to have no visitors themselves and thus eavesdropped on her and Andrew, perhaps awaiting (yet dreading) another dramatic incident, to top her hurling of the bouquet.

Lowering his voice, he began to recite:

'Lynne is fossilized rainbow,
Lynne is throwing a double six,
Lynne is the cherry on a knickerbocker glory,
Lynne is a double-yolked egg.'

'It's amazing!' she interjected. 'How on earth did you come up with those wonderful images?'

'Heaven knows! Just thinking about you, I suppose, and how much you mean to me. There are thirty lines, in all, and I felt I could have gone on for ever.'

How incredible that the numerical genius should have become a poet overnight. She could forgive him everything. 'Well, I want to hear it all.'

'Just a sec.' He removed his jacket, draping it on the back of the chair. 'It's always frightfully hot in here, especially compared with outside. You may not have noticed, but there were even a few flakes of snow this morning, which inspired one of the lines in my poem. Here it is,' he said, returning to his script: 'Lynne is the diamond sparkle in a snowflake.'

'That's lovely,' she enthused. Almost enough to restore her severely damaged sparkle.

'Shall I go on?'

'Yes, please!'

Lynne is the filling in a walnut whip,
Lynne is the purr in a leopard....

As he continued, she was struck by the genuine word-power in the lines, despite his insistence on his lack of talent. Their surprising originality revealed a whole new side to him and, indeed, she almost resented the nurse who'd brought the painkillers, since it forced him to break off. However, she swallowed the pills in two quick gulps, so he could resume his reading straight away – right to the end, this time.

'Honestly, it's the nicest present I've ever had. In fact, I'm going to frame it and put it on our wall, then, if Mum starts having a go at me, I'll just tell her I'm not all bad!'

'I suspect your mother's only ... difficult because she wants love herself and feels deprived and lonely.'

'You're right. And you're certainly much more patient with her than I am.' Her mum had marched in yesterday, fulminating about the aborted wedding – the waste of effort, time and cash – which had resulted in a full-blown row, whereas Andrew treated her mother with diplomatic restraint, never rising to the bait and shouting back. But then wasn't he always patient, always forbearing and tolerant, except in his obsession with numbers and dates? And was that really so heinous, in light of his general decency and kindness?

'But that's quite enough from me! I just hope I haven't tired you out. How are you feeling now?'

'Not too bad. I think it helps that I've accepted the inevitable, rather than wallowing in self-pity. And my friends have been fantastic. They've all sent lovely texts and emails, and most are planning to visit. And even my boss was surprisingly sympathetic, so Nathalie said. When she explained the situation, he just consulted with the others, and they eventually agreed they'd manage somehow – cover for me, if possible, and, if not, call in a temp.'

'Well, that's a weight off your mind. I know you feared he'd blow his top.'

'Perhaps he's only just realized I'm indispensable!' She gave a deprecating laugh – the first time she'd laughed since the accident. 'Anyway, once we've arranged another date for the wedding, everyone, Graham included, has promised faithfully to be there.'

'Actually, I do have another date in mind.'

She tensed, noting the change in his voice. 'I don't want to fix it *now*, Andrew – it's far too soon. I have to know how well I'm doing before we make an alternative plan.'

'Don't worry, darling, this isn't till April – April the first, in fact. Yes, it may be April Fools' Day, but it's also a magical sequence again, or will be if we schedule the wedding for two o'clock. That gives 1/4, for the first of April, another 1/4, for the year 2014, and a third 1/4, for 14.00 hours.'

'But,' she said, doing a quick calculation, 'that's only three-and-a-half months away.'

'Well, surely you'll be better by then.'

'There's no guarantee. The surgeon said it can sometimes take longer and, in any case, you can never rule out setbacks or complications. And I'll need physio, of course, and all that sort of stuff. Besides, it's not just a matter of recovery-time. The last thing I want is to rush the wedding. I must be totally fit for it, so there's not the slightest risk of having to cancel again.'

Andrew reached for her hand. 'But it would mean so much to me, darling. I still don't think you realize quite how hard it's been, having to abandon that sequence of 11/12/13/14/15, but at least this new one will help to compensate.'

Angrily, she pushed his hand away, unable to endure more pestering and pressure. Here he was, back to his obsession, and just when their relationship appeared to have taken a turn for the better. Admittedly, she was impressed by his poetic flair but, were he to plough through every poem ever written, in an attempt to share her interests, that would be mere flimsy gauze laid across an iron-and-steel intransigence. This wedding should be a symbol of their union, their mutual love and commitment, not a matter of so-called magical numbers. Perhaps she had been kidding herself all along, excusing his monomania on the grounds of efficiency and order.

'It's absolutely crucial, darling, that we don't choose a date at random. In fact, I doubt that I could go through with the ceremony, unless it was happening on a day that had numerical significance. I'd feel the marriage had got off to a bad start and might actually be doomed to fail.'

Could he be mentally disturbed, she wondered suddenly? Indeed, it struck her only now how few friends he seemed to have. Most of those on their guest-list were *her* associates, and even his best man was little more than an acquaintance, so maybe people avoided him as a fanatic and a numbers-freak. But avoiding a husband wouldn't be quite so easy and such fanaticism might constrain many facets of their life together. Suppose he insisted on choosing their children's names in the same peculiar way his father had, or even try to time their conceptions and births to fit some rigid formula? If a baby was born prematurely, or well past its due-date, would that affect his love for it?

'Another alternative,' he said, trying to take her hand again, despite her obvious resistance, 'would be three-fifteen in the afternoon, on the fifteenth of May, 2015, which provides the sequence: 15/15/15/5/15. But, numerically speaking, it's far less satisfying, on account of that lurking "five". Maybe,' he continued, his entire attention still fixated on sequences, 'three-twenty on the first of May would work better, giving us 15/20/15/20/15. But, of course, both those dates are a hell of long way off, so I wouldn't really want....'

She had actually stopped listening, her mind now veering to a different problem – one more fundamental, since it inhibited their sex-life. Far from diminishing, his need to be in control seemed even greater, invariably holding him in check, as if he were driving a car with the brakes on. Xavier, in contrast, had been unbridled and free-spirited, and his refreshing spontaneity had released in her a depth of passion she never felt with her fiancé. So why was she engaged to him at all? And how could she have failed to see that sexual compatibility was 'absolutely crucial', to borrow his own phrase? The fact he had used that phrase about the wedding-date, rather than their intimate married life, meant their priorities were utterly at variance.

'Time for your observations, Lynne.' Nurse Bella had breezed up to the bed, with her usual cheery smile.

'Shall I wait outside?' Andrew asked the nurse.

Yes, Lynne begged him, silently, longing to be left in peace, free from any more discussion. Her head was aching, as it was, simply from the shock of these sudden demoralizing insights.

'No need,' the nurse replied. 'And, I'm glad to tell you, Andrew, that Lynne's doing wonderfully well. Because she's young and strong and basically very fit, she'll heal much faster than older patients tend to do.'

Once the nurse had filled in the chart and bustled off, Andrew returned to the attack, now sounding almost triumphant.

'You see, she says you'll recover really fast, which means the April date should be fine.'

Lynne shook her head, wearily. All anger had leached away. There was only deep fatigue, coupled with shame and disbelief at her own obtuseness. April Fools' Day. She had been a fool all along, blind and deaf to the obvious.

'And it'll be spring by then,' he persisted, 'which is perfect for a wedding.'

She didn't answer. Early April could be bitter-cold – as cold and bitter as she felt towards him now.

'And if you do have any setbacks, darling, there'll be no real need to worry, because I intend to take on all the rearrangements, just as I did with our original plan. So, even if you're still limping a bit or whatever....'

She let him ramble on, making no further objection. He would always want his own way when it came to dates and numbers – that was now beyond dispute – and, since dates and numbers were paramount and could easily extend to a host of different areas, she herself would have little leeway or autonomy. Closing her eyes, she slumped back on the bed, letting his arguments wash over her, until he finally realized she had no intention of complying. In the ensuing silence, she heard the old lady's pathetic whimpers, and then the tramp of feet as a doctor strode into the ward and on to the bed in the corner.

'Well, if you refuse to consider April,' Andrew said, at last, 'we'll just have to go for May the following year. At least, by that time, you'll most definitely be better, even if – God forbid – you suffer every complication in the book.'

'No,' she said, opening her eyes, with an effort.

'D'you mean no, you won't be better, or no to the May date?'

'No to the May date. In fact, no to all magical sequences. No to the wedding itself. There isn't going to *be* a wedding, Andrew.'

And that, she thought, with a surge of overpowering lightness and relief, was the most magical thing of all, because – serendipitously and in the nick of time – she had managed to escape an onerous life sentence.

'CAN I HAVE IT WHEN YOU GO?'

For Sylvia, my wide-thighed, hot-mouthed, luscious-lipped, silken-skinned seductress....

Unable to repress a smile, she took in every detail of the inscription: the extravagantly sensuous adjectives, the bold italic script looping across the flyleaf of the book, the dashing signature penned with such panache it ended in an exuberant spray of ink-blots. The sixty years since the affair seemed to contract like an accordion, as she felt Roberto's mouth again, its sheer seeking, probing, daring, insolent greed.

Leafing slowly through the pages, she remembered how, after they'd made love, he would insist on reading to her, as if, once her body was sated, he must give equal stimulation to her mind. Sometimes, he would read these very lyrics, reciting them aloud in the original Ancient Greek and adopting a lulling, rhythmic voice, very different from his usual staccato tone. Even after all this time, she could still recall how strangely soothing, yet intriguingly exotic, the unfamiliar tongue had sounded, and the way she had tried to catch each syllable as it lilted through the room; each a fragile butterfly that must be captured and preserved.

And here they were still – those iridescent butterfly wings fluttering in her head, centuries after the poet's death, and a good fifty after Roberto's tragic drowning, in a shipwreck off Zanzibar.

Reluctantly, she closed the book and transferred it to the 'keep' pile, which, she noted anxiously, was already considerably bigger than the pile to give away. She simply hadn't realized how onerous it would be to reduce her possessions to the bare minimum necessitated by her almost-certain house-move. Her clothes had proved less of a problem. Who needed half a dozen winter coats, least of all at Beaufort Lodge, which, on her two recent visits, had seemed stiflingly hot and airless? And most of her shoes were now too tight or too frivolous, so it had caused only a minor pang to ditch the strappy scarlet sandals and perilously high heels, the splendiferous silver evening-pumps and knee-length calfskin boots. Indeed, they'd been due for the dump an age ago but, somehow, she had clung to them, if only as reminders of her glitzy youth.

But, of course, books were more important altogether and trying to weed them out was like uprooting the most exquisite blooms from a well-loved, long-tended flowerbed, leaving it bare and barren. Already, each gaping hole in the shelves rebuked her for having eradicated some vital part of her life-story. Before she'd started the cull, the trajectory had been unbroken, charting her evolution from nursery rhymes and fairy-tales, to Arthur Ransomes and Enid Blytons, then on to college text-books and bound sets of Dickens and Hardy, followed by the Stendhal, Flaubert and Baudelaire she'd amassed when living in Paris, then her Daphne de Maurier phase, after she bought a place in Cornwall, and on and on, in the same haphazard way, through all the subsequent decades. And the men in her life – lovers and both husbands – had contributed their own clutch of books; Roberto's Aeschylus, James's T.S. Eliot, Mark's Freud and Jung, Adam's Lawrence Durrell. But wherever she lived or with whom, the books had always gone with her and, once she was lucky enough to own a large, capacious house, she had assumed she would end her days with them.

Or she had until last month, when the prospect of Beaufort Lodge first reared its unwelcome head. Each of its tiny rooms boasted one patently inadequate bookshelf, which meant all her dictionaries would have to be relinquished, for a start. Just the two volumes of the so-called Oxford Shorter would take up half that shelf on their own. She was just debating whether she could keep them in the wardrobe, when the phone shrilled through her thoughts.

'Yes, hello? Sylvia Lipton speaking.'

'How are you, Mrs Lipton? It's Heather Murphy here, from Beaufort Lodge. I'm ringing about your provisional reservation. I'm sure you'll understand we can't hold your room indefinitely, so I was wondering if you'd made a final decision. Of course, if you'd like to visit again, you're more than welcome – any time at all. And if you have any further queries, I or the general manager will be more than happy to help. I also want to remind you about our annual Christmas bazaar, which we're holding at the Lodge this coming Saturday. It'll be a perfect chance for you to get to know the other staff and say hello again to those residents you met when you spent that lovely day with us. So we do hope you can join us.'

This coming Saturday she had booked to attend a lecture at the British Library on 'Boccaccio and His World' – definitely preferable to tombolas, bric-à-brac stalls and overpriced mince pies, not to mention the fake festivity bound to wreath the occasion like faded, tarnished tinsel. The trouble with geriatric homes was their ludicrous pretence that old age should be celebrated, rather than deplored. Every brochure she had studied so far went overboard on smiles: radiantly smiling staff conducting sing-alongs, or cutting ninety-ninth birthday cakes; ecstatically smiling inmates sipping sherry with Matron, or creating works of genius in the Crafts Room. Yet, on her actual visits, genius, sherry and smiles had all been noticeable by their absence. And, indeed, who but a fool would keep grinning fatuously when faced with the realities of pain, loss, grief, dependence and disability?

Heather was now elaborating on the enormous relief some residents felt when released from the 'burden' of owning their own house, with all the attendant chores and responsibilities. Far worse, Sylvia thought, to own nothing but a toothbrush and a nightie, and have no source of stimulation beyond carpet-bowls and Scrabble. 'Look,' she said, cutting through the treacly tide of words, 'could you give me just a couple more days to make up my mind?'

'No problem at all, Mrs Lipton. But remember, all of us here at Beaufort Lodge are hoping to give you a really warm welcome in the not too distant future.'

The warm welcome she didn't doubt, but could it compensate for losing her individuality and becoming just a revenue-stream, a set of ailments, a room-number? Left to herself, the answer would be an emphatic 'no', but with Colin to consider – her only child, born late, after two miscarriages, and thus infinitely precious – things were more complicated. Although she had tried her best not to lament, or resent, his move to Australia, in October – a move vital for his career-prospects – it meant he was increasingly concerned about her health and strength now that he no longer lived close by. And, on his recent trip back home with Kate and the girls, he had sat her down in the drawing-room and explained his apprehension about her trying to cope on her own, with him 10,000 miles away – no more popping in to lend a hand, or keep a watchful eye on her – then he'd taken her on an inspection tour of several local care homes.

So, by the end of the visit, with Kate apparently sharing his anxieties, she had felt honour-bound to put the house on the market and start the dismal process of downsizing. Yet, every time she saw the traitorous 'For Sale' board, flaunting in the front garden, or attempted to clear out another cluttered cupboard, her resolve would waver and she would find herself prevaricating again. Which was actually quite pointless in light of the fact that Colin had already booked his next flight over – a mere six weeks away now – to assist her with the move, and to authorize the estate agent to take over the whole business of the house sale. So, in loyalty to her son and daughter-in-law, she ought to be tackling some of the outstanding tasks, rather than drifting around indulging in futile memories.

Determinedly, she went upstairs, to make a start on weeding out her large collection of letters. She kept the cache hidden in the linen-chest beneath a stack of Egyptian-cotton sheets, which Beaufort Lodge would never countenance, Egyptian cotton being difficult to launder, unlike their flimsy nylon. She was glad Colin wasn't present to witness her wheezy struggle as she hauled out the heavy box, managing, eventually, to deposit it on the bed.

Long ago, she had sorted the contents into separate bundles, tying each with a different coloured ribbon. On top were the holiday postcards; a veritable kaleidoscope from friends, now mostly dead, or mouldering in homes like Beaufort Lodge. Having read a random two dozen – describing grape-harvests in Burgundy, or sunsets in Miami, or fog and floods in Venice – she decided to ditch the lot, as proof of her new resolve. Next, she unfastened the sheaf of Colin's letters, each one of them preserved, from prep school through to public school, then his gap-year in Peru, followed by four years at Cambridge, his spell at Stanford, his various foreign postings and, in addition, a host of letters from his exotic foreign holidays. He had always been a dutiful son; kept in touch, given her no cause for worry as to his health or whereabouts, and the only reason the letters ceased was because of his move to her own small Surrey town, once his daughters were born, partly so she could be a hands-on grandma.

It had been a wrench to lose that vital role, all the more so because Becky and Robin seemed to have changed disturbingly since they'd been living in Melbourne, and even spoke with a pronounced Australian twang. She also felt increasingly cut off from them now that she no longer knew the details of their house and school and friends. Instead of being a crucial, day-to-day presence in their lives, she was now reduced to a voice on the phone; a return-address stamped on her airmail envelopes.

She dragged her attention back to the tide of correspondence. Postcards she could consign to the waste-bin, but not the written record of her beloved son's life and career. She had actually offered him the treasure trove to keep as his personal archive, but tidy, efficient Kate had intervened, saying she didn't believe in hoarding reams of sentimental stuff and preferred to keep her house uncluttered.

Still indecisive, she slumped down on the bed, struck by the sheer variety of envelopes and paper: pages torn from school exercise-books, cream-laid vellum, flimsy blue airmail sheets, headed company notepaper, luxurious hotel stationery, even scribbles on the backs of foreign menus. And the stamps would gladden any philatelist's heart – stamps adorned with birds, flowers, castles, bridges, crowned heads, multi-coloured flags. Couldn't someone, somewhere, give those stamps a home? Her love-letters posed still more of a problem, since they were far too confidential to be read by anyone – even the refuse collectors – and might well shock her steady, sober son.

But, as she untied the scarlet ribbon, the writing on the envelopes set off a tide of memories: Christopher's frantic scrawl as tempestuous as his life; Mark's elaborate script, with its fancy, flowery flourishes, contrasting with his controlled, pedantic temperament; Adam's neat, crabbed, constipated hand affording no hint of his wildly generous love-making. But, as always, it was Roberto who drew her back, enthralled her, so the first letter she opened had to be one of his – the now yellowed paper tattered at the edges.

Since our first night together, I am in thrall to you for ever, beautiful, mysterious, enchanting Sylvia....

His prose had always been passionately purple. Others might deride it, but his ardent words never failed to ignite her and, even now, she could feel the familiar stirring in her body, the tumult in her mind.

Impulsively, she rammed her fist against the box-lid, wincing at the pain in her hand, but suddenly furious with Beaufort Lodge for all the things it banned. Pets were unhygienic, electric blankets dangerous, personal items of furniture too bulky for the rooms – all that she could accept, but why should they outlaw passion, sex, romance? 'We aim to meet all your needs,' the brochure stated, piously, 'health, dietary, spiritual and social.' But what about the pressing need for touch – the contact of bare skin against bare skin – and for union, communion, devotion, adulation, strings of singing adjectives? Could she really be the only octogenarian who still desired such things, still craved to be ravished and enraptured, refused to settle tamely for crossword puzzles, Chinese chequers, crochet?

Yes, apparently – at least judging by the tedious Tuesday she had spent at Beaufort Lodge, lunching with companions who talked of nothing but their ailments and the recent heinous fee-increase, then decamping to the lounge with them, to watch hours of daytime television, and hearing not one intelligent comment about politics, poetry or art. A few lugubrious residents had discussed their grim childhoods in the War, and the pains and perils of bringing up their own children, but had touched on nothing arresting or inspiring. Of course, she would hardly expect them to confide in her, a stranger, about ungovernable passions or intimate relationships, but, by the end of that dreary day, she knew she didn't belong there and couldn't imagine tamely settling for so vegetative a life, merely sitting, sleeping, staring.

When the phone rang again – the smart-phone Colin had given her, a definite advance on her no-bells-and-whistles landline – she grabbed it eagerly, remembering he'd arranged to ring at 10.30, her time. It never failed to upset her that Melbourne was eleven hours ahead, which seemed to underline the fact that, while he and Kate and the girls belonged in a rosy future, she'd been left mouldering in the past; their two universes now cut adrift, divorced.

'How are you, Mum?'

'I'm fine, darling.'

'And how's the clearing out going?'

'Not too badly.'

'I hope that nice Mrs Brindle is giving you a hand?'

Sylvia declined to answer. 'That nice Mrs Brindle' – the overbearing bossy-boots who lived two doors down – seemed determined to cart off the entire contents of the house to the Oxfam shop, or the municipal rubbish-dump, on the pretext of neighbourly good will. Wasn't her harvest poor enough already, for God's sake: two husbands and two babies dead, half-a-dozen lovers reduced to dust, and her all-important life's work ending in failure? But, since she had never burdened Colin with any hint of loss or regret, she changed the subject to the innocuous one of the weather.

'Oh, it's been really glorious here, Mum. We've been out in the garden all day, soaking up the sunshine. And, even though it's dark now, it's still wonderfully warm.'

She glanced through the window at the sleety rain and murky grey sky – another reminder of the gulf now stretching between them: her son relishing a balmy summer, while she shivered in the cold.

'Sorry, Mum, I missed that last bit. Becky's yelling at me! OK, Becky, I heard you first time. Yes, you can have a word with Grandma. Mum, I'm just passing the phone to Becky, all right? Back in a tick.'

'How are you, Grandma?' the child asked, politely.

Kate had always taught the girls manners: to say please and thank you and not speak with their mouths full, to acknowledge all birthday and Christmas presents, and to enquire with some show of concern about their grandmother's health.

'I'm fit as a fiddle, sweetheart.' Her increasingly troublesome bronchitis was of no interest to a twelve-year-old, and even Colin hadn't the slightest inkling of her recently diagnosed heart-murmur.

'Hey, Grandma,' Becky continued, once the dutiful enquiry was discharged, 'you know that cuckoo-clock – the one on the dining-room mantelpiece – can I have it when you go?'

The phrase jolted, as if Becky had snapped a rubber-band against her face. What did she mean by 'When you go': when she moved to Beaufort Lodge, or when she departed this life? Could Becky secretly be hoping for her imminent demise, so that she could lay immediate claim to the clock? In fact, both girls had put in bids for several of her possessions – the dressing-table set inlaid with mother-of-pearl, the pink leather vanity-case, the jewellery-box and many of its

65

contents. She'd been inclined to give them everything they wanted while they were actually staying with her, so that they could take the objects back with them on the plane. But Colin had pointed out that they'd already exceeded their baggage allowance, and told them, firmly, 'No, girls, wait till Grandma goes.'

At the time, the words hadn't struck her with any sinister import, but now their ramifications hit home with troubling force. The catch-phrase, You Can't Take it With You When You Go, seemed to be echoing in her head, with its unavoidable reference to death: why fret too much about material possessions, when one would be inevitably parted from them? And, yes, when it came to clocks or jewellery or dressing-table sets, she could, indeed, jettison such things, but not her *life*, for God's sake! She wasn't ready to go anywhere, either to meet her Maker, in whom she'd never actually believed, or to move to Beaufort Lodge. Why should she have to fit the mould expected of the elderly: passive and resigned, soulless and incurious, all her emotions extinguished or tamped down? Colin, Kate and the girls all had unconfined and vibrant lives. On their recent visit they'd enthused about the fabulous climate, the variety of sports, their luxurious house just a stone's throw from the sea, and Colin seemed delighted by the challenge and opportunities offered by his new job. So couldn't she, too, have a life – an independent, idiosyncratic life, in which she made her own decisions, with no one interfering or dictating her daily timetable? And, if that was unfair to Colin, or even unforgivably selfish, then she'd just have to bear the burden of the guilt. Guilt had always been the price she'd paid for living unconventionally, going her own way.

Suddenly, she realized that Becky was still waiting for an answer. 'Yes, of course you can have the clock, darling. I'll give it to Daddy when he comes over again in January, along with anything else you or Robin want.'

She wouldn't ask him to cancel his flight – that would only cause serious ructions, impossible to resolve long-distance – nor would she entrust so important a decision to a letter or an email. No, she must wait till he was with her in person, then she would sit him down in the drawing-room, as he had done with her, and explain how strongly she felt about being written off, or carted off, or exiled, or uprooted, or dispatched in either of its senses.

When he reclaimed the phone from Becky, she was no longer simply faking her good cheer, but experiencing a sense of genuine liberation, which he noticed instantly.

'Mum, it's good to hear you sounding so upbeat.'

'Yes, things are going well,' she said, with suppressed but palpable glee.

Having chatted for a little longer, he finally rang off, and she did a tiny, triumphant hop-skip around the room, as if physically rejuvenated. Then, sitting on the bed, she began reading Roberto's letters – all passionate twenty-three of them.

Heavenly creature, I want to lie against your gorgeous body for ever, worship every inch of your skin, drink great draughts of you. You are becoming a drug of addiction. Without you, I am lost....

As the extravagant phrases pirouetted in her head, she could actually feel herself becoming young and beautiful again; desired, adored and cherished. So long as she kept these letters, she could remain a 'heavenly creature', stay girlish and untarnished, live in eternal springtime, instead of limping and shambling into winter.

I feel every different colour in the love spectrum, from thrusting purple to the most tender probing pink. Glorious Sylvia, no other woman could exert so great a hold on me. From this day on, I vow to be your champion and slay any dragon that ever dares to threaten you....

The only dragon that threatened was officious Heather Murphy and, suddenly – indeed, daringly – she seized the phone again and dialled Beaufort Lodge, with a not-quite-steady hand.

'Miss Murphy? It's Sylvia Lipton speaking. I'm ringing to let you know that I have now made up my mind – yes, just in the last half-hour. I've decided not to join you, after all, so would you please cancel my reservation? ... Well, actually, it's difficult to explain. Let's simply say a new, exciting alternative has unexpectedly presented itself....'

Miss Murphy, ever-persistent, was making one final bid to elaborate the advantages of residential care, but Sylvia was already spiralling up on the thermal of the future, its new challenges and vistas, soaring as high and free as a falcon towards a whole new lease of life.

'JUST YOURSELF?'

'Just yourself?' the manageress asked, as Ellen stepped in to the crowded King's Road café.

No, she bit back. I've brought along a whole football team. Can't you see?

Did the woman have to make her feel so unwanted and superfluous? But, of course, a singleton hogging a table-for-two was clearly uneconomic. The manageress didn't even bother to smile; simply led her to a dark corner at the back and, having slammed down the menu, strode off to greet some newcomers – a couple, naturally.

Ellen unbuttoned her coat, glancing round at the brightly lit and stiflingly hot establishment. No one else seemed to have had the temerity to enter it on their own. All around her were groups or couples – normal people with friends and partners and futures. It had been a mistake to come here at all, but it had felt equally wrong, on her fortieth birthday, to leave work and go home alone. Admittedly, her work-mates had made a bit of a fuss of her in the office; bought a proper iced cake and some Cava, but Derek, with typical boss-man stance, had soon put a stop to the merriment.

After a brief look at the menu (or its cheaper dishes, anyway), she decided on the lasagne – not that any waitress seemed interested in taking her order. Perhaps singles were ignored here, as in the wider world. The whole of society was geared around coupledom: double rooms in hotels; meals-for-two in Tesco's; half-bottles of wine increasingly rare and always over-priced. She couldn't afford wine anyway, although at least she'd had a tipple at lunchtime. True, Cava was hardly sophisticated, but her work-mates' kindness had touched her. There had even been a glitter-sprinkled card, signed by all the gang: Rosie, Jenny, Linda, Beth and Anne. Derek made a point of employing only women and liked to strut about like a cock with his brood of hens. Apparently, most people met their future partner at work, which might explain her current lack of a mate. She had tried Internet dating, of course – didn't everyone, these days? But the no-hopers she had met so far had failed to match their 'Profiles' in age, appearance or success, and seemed to have few skills except deceit. The 'company director' had turned out to work in a call-centre, and the 'advertising executive' was little more than a glorified salesman.

The waitress was just bustling up to the table next to hers. Ellen signalled to her, waving the menu for emphasis.

'Won't be a sec,' the girl said, then disappeared for a good ten minutes. The only other waitress was patently overworked; rushing about in near-panic, with too many customers to serve.

On a sudden impulse, Ellen stood up and made for the door. There was now a small cluster of people waiting to be seated, so she'd actually be doing them a favour by vacating her table-for-two. Not that anyone seemed to notice she had gone. However, as she walked out into a deluge of sleety, stinging rain, she regretted her action as typically self-defeating. Better to be sitting foodless in a cosy fug than battling, head-down, against the elements. Spotting a soggy, crippled umbrella abandoned inside-out on the pavement, she paused to open her own sturdy, storm-proof brolly; wished she could storm-proof her life; make it impervious to gales and squalls.

Fortunately, the downpour began to peter out as she strode, in the dark, murky night, towards the bright warmth of the tube. Stopping at the lights, she was joined by a swarthy-looking man, with long, straggly hair and a shapeless old grey coat. While they waited for the pedestrian light, he suddenly stooped down to pick up something from the gutter and, nudging her excitedly, held it out on his palm for her to see. Jolted, she stared at the wide gold wedding-ring, which he was now examining more closely, presumably to check the hallmark.

'Real gold!' he exclaimed, as he crossed the road beside her, then continued to walk alongside, down the street. 'Me Russian,' he confided. 'In London six weeks.'

Beginner's luck, she thought, wryly, to light on such a treasure, when he'd only just arrived in England, whereas she'd never found so much as a fifty-pence coin, during all her years of living here. However, she gave him a courteous smile and, thus encouraged, he grabbed her arm and pulled her to a stop, insisting that she watch while he tried the ring on all his fingers in turn.

'Too small,' he wailed, screwing up his face in disappointment, as each finger proved too fat to fit the ring. 'For lady,' he said, returning her smile and thrusting the ring towards her. 'You have. Bring you good luck.'

She dodged away, imagining some frantic wife not daring to tell her husband that she had lost her wedding-ring. 'You need to take it to the police,' she told him. There might well be a reward, so he could still be in luck.

He shook his head so violently, raindrops cascaded onto his coat. 'No! No police. Papers not in order. You take. Ring for lady. Real gold. Bring you luck.' He jammed it on to her wedding-finger, where it fitted so surprisingly well, she was reminded of Cinderella's slipper in the fairy-tale.

She stood a moment looking at her hand; her life upgraded in an instant; no longer a lonely singleton, loveless and adrift, but with an adoring partner awaiting her at home. And, with Valentine's Day just forty-eight hours off, she would have the longed-for flowers, the beribboned box of chocolates, the intimate dinner in a romantic riverside restaurant. Yes, she could feel her husband's hand just slipping beneath the table to gently stroke her thigh and....

The man's hoarse voice interrupted the fantasy. 'Me no job. Me hungry. You give me money and you have ring.'

'No,' she reproved, slamming the door on the romantic riverside restaurant. 'That would be stealing, so, if you refuse to take it to the police, then I will.' No question of claiming the reward for herself, which constituted another form of theft – or so her law-abiding mother was pointing out, from some realm beyond the grave. 'He found the ring, so any recompense is his.'

Turning her back on her mother's sepulchral presence, she repeated her advice about the police but, unceremoniously, the bloke snatched the ring from her finger. 'No police,' he insisted. 'Police send me back to Kursk. Papers not in order.'

She wrestled with her conscience. Her devoutly Christian parents had trained her since early childhood to be scrupulously honest. Yet this ring was clearly valuable and thus could offer her the chance of fulfilling a long-held dream. She knew absolutely nothing about gold, but Derek had happened to say, just last month, that it always increased in value at times of economic crisis and was currently fetching extremely inflated prices. So, if she sold the ring, she would have the cash to sign up with Connect, as Rosie at work had done. Rosie, equally disgusted by the frauds and cheats she, too, had encountered online, had decided to use professionals, instead. Connect relied on trained psychologists to find each client a perfect, lifelong mate, with the end result that Rosie's whole existence was transformed: she was now Mrs Simon Murray, revelling in married life and already three months' pregnant.

Ellen winced as the bloke nudged her in the ribs. He was nothing if not persistent and was holding out the ring once more, clearly determined to overcome her scruples. Yet those scruples were so deeply entrenched, it did seem truly heinous to resort to stealing to ensure her own future happiness. 'Look,' she told him, wearily, 'if you're scared of the police, take it to Lost Property, instead.'

He stared at her in bafflement; his vocabulary obviously not extending to such concepts.

'Me hungry,' he repeated, his tone entreating, almost desperate. 'Me not eat three days. You give me money and you have ring.'

Ellen realized they were blocking the pavement, and that several irritated people were having to squeeze past, already harassed by the large, inconvenient puddles. Wasn't it equally immoral, she tried to persuade herself, to allow a man to starve? For all she knew, he could be homeless as well as hungry, obliged to sleep on a sheet of cardboard in some freezing alleyway, and rely on the non-existent kindness of peevish Londoners like these. And, anyway, did she have to stick so closely to her parents' high-minded precepts? They'd been dead for twenty years, for heaven's sake, and, even when alive, had never been concerned with her feelings or well-being, only with her moral rectitude.

'OK,' she said, suddenly decisive and, snapping open her bag, she extracted a ten-pound-note from her purse.

Ungraciously, he grabbed it from her and thrust it in his pocket, only to hold out his hand for more. 'Thirty,' he demanded.

Ellen struggled between annoyance at his discourtesy and a grudging admiration for his sheer sense of entitlement. If only *she* possessed such confidence, she might be a manageress by now, or even work for a big corporation, with her own expense-account and company car. In point of fact, she was often forced to economize and, anyway, since last July, when she'd been robbed in broad daylight by an aggressive young hoodlum who'd threatened her at knifepoint, she deliberately avoided carrying large amounts of cash. However, she did find another tenner, which she handed over, reluctantly.

'More!' the Russian repeated, whilst pocketing the second note. Her sympathy was dwindling fast, yet having done a quick calculation, thirty pounds still seemed a reasonable outlay if she managed to sell the ring for, say, a cool five hundred. After only a moment's hesitation, she scrabbled in her purse again for a last, crumpled fiver and three pound-coins. He could see perfectly well that he had cleaned her out completely, but she brandished the now empty purse, to prevent any further argument.

He did have the grace to smile his thanks, before shambling off in the opposite direction; turning round to holler out a final 'Bring you luck!' Although her rational side refused to entertain the concept of luck, she couldn't help but thrill again to the sight of her 'married' hand; the gold-emblazoned wedding-finger proving to the world that she was wanted, coupled and deeply loved. Despite the cold, she was loath to put back her glove, wanting everyone to see the ring; view her as a beloved wife, successful and secure.

On the journey home, she had to contend with rush-hour crowds and signal failure on the District Line, yet her new status seemed to put a gloss on everything, as if she'd been gift-wrapped, mind and body, in glittery gold foil. She imagined her fellow commuters regarding her with new respect; some of the females downright envious. And, to her considerable surprise, she had succeeded in banishing her parents' ghostly voices, so that she barely felt a twinge of guilt. Indeed, as she ascended from the tube and strode towards her apartment block, even the puddles looked enchanting, gleaming in the light of the street-lamps, as if they contained shards of brilliant stars.

'Hi, Ellen, stop! It's me!'

Swinging round at the sound of the voice, she saw Susanna just entering the block, a pace or two behind her. The woman lived one floor above and was the nearest she had to a friend there. People kept themselves to themselves in Granville Court.

'How you doing, Ellen? I haven't seen you in an age.'

'I'm fine,' she said, believing it, for once, and, suddenly expansive, invited Susanna in for a coffee.

'Actually, I'd planned to go to the launderette. My laundry-basket's overflowing! But who cares about a few more dirty clothes? So, yeah, you're on!'

Ellen fumbled for her key. Susanna was enviably easy-going, in contrast to her own rigid lists and schedules, which included various after-work routines, normally set in stone. However, just for once, she would break with normal practice and make an effort to relax.

'Wow!' Susanna exclaimed, as Ellen let her in. 'Your place looks like a show-flat. Mine's a complete and utter tip! But how on earth do you keep it so tidy and uncluttered?'

With a little daily discipline, Ellen refrained from saying, although demonstrating her point by hanging up both their coats and putting her bag away in it's rightful place. Clutter was dangerous as well as unnecessary. If you allowed it to take hold, life could spiral out of control. 'Make yourself at home,' she said – superfluously, she realized, since Susanna had already done so and was now sprawling on the sofa. 'How do you like your coffee?'

'Sweet and strong, please. Three sugars.'

Jolted by Suasnna's sangfroid as the woman kicked off her shoes, to reveal large holes in the toes of her tights, Ellen went to fill the percolator. As she stood measuring out the coffee, she wondered whether to mention her birthday or not, but finally decided against it, for fear of seeming a failure. Any truly popular person would be celebrating with a whole group of well-wishers.

It was not until she had handed Susanna her cup that the woman noticed the ring. Ellen took her time in explaining how she'd obtained it; first needing to reassure herself that, since she and Susanna had no friends in common, the woman was safe as a confidante.

'Oh, Ellen, you've been had! That whole ring thing is a scam. I'm amazed you didn't twig. It's been all over the papers.'

Ellen swallowed. The word 'scam' had lodged in the throat like a piece of gristle.

'Wh … what do you mean?' she stammered.

'Well, apparently, loads of beggars and scroungers are trying it on. They get hold of a cheap ring, spray it with gold paint, or varnish, or whatever, so it looks like the genuine article, deliberately slip it from their pocket on to the pavement, then pretend they found it by chance. And they always trot out the same story about it being too small for their finger, so that they can flog it for cash to some unsuspecting person. But I can't believe you fell for it! I mean, there was a piece in the *Daily Mail*, just last week, warning people off.'

'I don't read the *Mail*,' Ellen countered, uneasily aware that perhaps this was a punishment; her parents proving the error of her ways, even from the Other World.

'It's been in the *Standard*, too – you know, saying how widespread it is and advising people to be vigilant. It's mainly women who are gulled, they said, because us females are more likely to fall for a sob-story – and, of course, more interested in rings!' Susanna gave a guffaw, which made her fat face wobble. Little wonder, Ellen thought, surveying her shapeless bulk, that she, too, was single, at forty-eight. But perhaps she was one of those radical feminists who regarded men as the enemy and marriage as legalized rape. A ridiculous opinion. Didn't most fairy-tales end with a wedding and 'happy ever after'?

'The *Mail* piece said a lot of these fraudsters work the same pitch night after night, often in the rush-hour and usually somewhere posh – all of which fits your own experience. I mean, the King's Road must be full of wealthy bods to dupe.'

Bristling at the word 'dupe', Ellen sought to justify herself. 'But he showed me the hallmark, Susanna.' Hardly had she spoken, when she realized that wasn't true. Certainly, he'd made a pretence of examining the hallmark, but she'd be too stupid to check on its authenticity herself.

'If there's a hallmark, I'll eat my hat,' Susanna crowed, with another infuriating laugh. 'Here, let me see.'

Ellen eased the ring from her finger. Already, it felt lighter and less precious, as she passed it to her friend. No, Susanna wasn't a friend. Just as the ring wasn't valuable – only a painted sham. Could you trust anyone or anything?

Susanna held it up to the light and peered at it closely. 'I'm sorry, Ellen, but you've been well and truly conned. This is no more gold than I'm Napoleon! I just hope you didn't give him too much cash.'

'No,' she lied. 'Only a couple of quid.'

'It's probably worth a few pence, in fact, but never mind – no harm done.'

Harm *had* been done, Ellen reflected, miserably, and it wasn't just a matter of deceit. Her twenty-four-carat-dream of future happiness was now revealed as base alloy.

She sprang up in sudden fury. 'I'm going back,' she announced, 'to have it out with him. How dare he cheat members of the public!'

'Don't be daft! He won't be there now and, anyway—'

'You just said they worked the same pitch,' Ellen interrupted, '*and* in the rush-hour. And since it's only five past seven, there'll still be plenty of people around – more dupes for him to fleece.'

'Ellen, it's cold and dark, and if he *has* pissed off home, you're just wasting time and effort for the sake of two measly quid.'

'It's not the money,' she fumed. 'It's the principle.' Hope was as precious as gold and, unusually for her, she had allowed herself to hope. After all, Connect's scientific expertise in matchmaking, the in-depth interviews they insisted on conducting before registering any client, and their wide-ranging compatibility-checks, there'd been an excellent chance that she would, at last, have met a decent, honest, efficient, tidy man. Of course, any personally tailored introductions agency was bound to charge over the odds and, although her salary covered not just the basics, but even extras like inexpensive holidays and occasional visits to a nail-bar, it certainly wouldn't stretch to paying Connect's high fees. Which is why the ring had seemed a gift from the gods – a gift now proved a sham.

'Ellen, do calm down! Let's finish our coffee and have a good old natter.'

'I'm sorry,' Ellen countered, 'but I'm determined to find that swindler, even if it takes all night.' No way could she stay here 'nattering', while the bogus Russian laughed all the way to the bank. He was probably not Russian at all, but a Pole or Lithuanian – someone with every right to be in the country and no reason to fear the police.

Susanna gave a shrug; drained her coffee in a couple of noisy gulps; grabbed her shoes and strolled barefoot to the door.

'Don't forget your coat,' Ellen said, fetching hers at the same time, although giving the woman time to disappear, before emerging into the corridor herself. It was inexcusably rude to have banished a harmless neighbour so abruptly, but she was just too het up to engage in vacuous chat.

In less than half an hour, she was back at the exact same spot where the man had first waylaid her. Frustratingly, there was no sign of him, although the King's Road was still crowded, as always. Well, she would simply wait, despite the sullen weather. At least the rain hadn't started again and she was so hot with indignation, even the cold no longer seemed to register.

She took up her position in a doorway, so as not to block access to the crossing, but which afforded her a view in four directions, so that, if the bloke did show up, she could accost him instantly. All she could see at present were people – mainly couples – linking arms as they sauntered down the street, or striding into restaurants with the in-built confidence that came with being a twosome. Another person completed you; gave you worth and validation, but, in light of her age, any such completion for her was now extremely unlikely. Forty was a watershed – not just the worrying issue of one's biological clock, but the fact that men were evolutionally programmed to seek younger, fertile partners. Which made it all the more galling that she had lost her chance of signing up with Connect. According to their brochure, they specialized in older clients: discerning professional people with experience of life, so, with the agency's skilled help, she might have met a surgeon or an Oxbridge academic.

Again, she stared down at the ring – furious with it now, yet somehow reluctant to remove it from her finger. Suppose Susanna was wrong? The woman was hardly an authority on anything, considering her slovenly habits and dead-end job. And, even if she was correct about the whole business of the scam, and the Russian had deliberately slipped the ring from his pocket, then pretended to see it glinting in the gutter, this particular ring could still be valuable. Perhaps it had belonged to his grandmother or even great-grandmother, and was worth money on account of its age and provenance alone.

All at once, she froze. The bloke had suddenly appeared, on the opposite side of the road – the same grey coat; the same greasy, unkempt hair. Her mind was in a turmoil as she watched him walk towards the traffic lights, anger and resentment battling with a last desperate spark of hope. Despite her bitterness, one part of her yearned to believe in him. He hadn't looked like a crook. His eyes had an honest expression and he'd sounded genuinely hungry, and truly frightened of the police. If only she could question him about the ring's antiquity or origins, but his English was far too basic to understand such subtleties.

Still torn between longing and suspicion, she saw him sidle up to a small, slender girl waiting at the lights, then, exactly as he had done with her, stoop down to pick up something from the ground. Her former indignation reignited like a firework, as she realized that the poor young girl would imagine – as she had done herself – that the ring was just a lucky find, discovered by pure chance. Susanna was right. It *was* a con, and he *did* work the same profitable pitch; probably duping scores of women, as he repeated the ruse again and again. No doubt he had hundreds of rings; mass-produced for him, most likely, by a whole gang of imposters, all with a stake in the swindle. Yes, she could see him in his true colours now, as he laid the ring on his palm and held it out for the girl to see, just as he had done before.

Enraged, she darted across the street, weaving her perilous way between the oncoming traffic, yet willing to risk an accident in her haste to warn the girl. The poor creature looked barely out of her teens and seemed so trustingly vulnerable, she would have no idea she was the victim of a scam.

'Don't give him money!' she cried, seeing the girl already opening her bag. 'That ring's completely worthless. It's just tin, or brass, or something. He's simply taking you for a ride.'

The girl rounded on her in annoyance. 'I don't know who the hell you are, but piss off, OK, and mind your own bloody business!'

'I'm only trying to spare you,' Ellen retorted, still determined to warn the girl, despite such base ingratitude. 'He conned me, too, an hour ago. There's a whole load of them trying it on. Don't fall for it! We have to take a stand.'

The girl's only response was a vicious shove that left Ellen not just winded but with no choice save to back off. Shakily, she edged away and went to lean against a shop-front, watching the girl hand over at least three banknotes, although she couldn't tell their value in the dark. Maybe she, too, was in the grip of a dream – a dream that could only be fulfilled by selling a precious ring. Perhaps she, too, craved a partner, even at her young age. After all, women were evolutionally programmed, just as much as men – in their case to find a mate and reproduce.

As Ellen thought of her own mate, now never to materialize; of her own might-have-been children, now so cruelly aborted, she stepped towards the gutter, about to wrench the ring from her finger and hurl it down the drain. Why kid herself any longer? She was alone and on her own, with no happy ending, no perfect, hand-picked spouse.

But then, all at once, she heard, in her head, the sneering manageress's greeting: 'Just yourself?' How *dare* she be so dismissively patronizing? How dare anyone belittle her, simply because it was, indeed, 'just herself' against the world? She would keep the ring and wear it; glory in it, even; resurrect the thrill she'd felt when she'd first slipped it on her finger. The important thing was not its actual value but the fact it made her feel so different – transformed and validated – and was thus precious in itself.

Moving a little closer to the lamp-post, she admired its gleam and sparkle on her hand. In the world's eyes – and in hers – this was genuine gold. And even her parents were strangely, mercifully silent, perhaps glad, for once in their lives, that the daughter they had never wanted now actually felt loved.

PRESENTS

If Roddy were a train, Debs thought, he would fling himself about with the same headstrong fits and starts as this lurching, jerking tube. At the next disconcerting judder, she all but lost her balance and fell against the knees of those lucky enough to be sitting, reminded again of her obstreperous younger brother. Born in an unseemly rush when her father's frantically speeding car failed to whisk her mum to the labour ward in time, he'd developed into a hyperactive boy, constitutionally incapable of cruising along at a smooth and steady pace. However, not even madcap Roddy could dislodge her from cloud nine, where she'd been blissfully perched since viewing the Archway flat for the third and final time. On the previous occasions, the snooty estate agent had treated her like a child – and no wonder, with her parents in tow – so she had insisted on going alone today to signal her independence.

'Sorry,' she mumbled, as an extra violent jolt sent her reeling into the woman standing next to her – a woman not unlike her mother, being overweight and shabby. Not that she was in any mood to criticize her parents, since it was they who were providing the deposit on the flat. And her father had even offered to help her with the decorating, while her mum had been touring the shops in search of curtain-material, and was already talking pelmets and tie-backs. Curtains were just so uncool, but it was decent, nonetheless.

That was the trouble with her parents. They were decent but over-protective, generous but smothering. If she ventured too far from their boring suburban semi, they imagined she'd be instantly raped or mugged, and kept issuing dire warnings about the dangers of North London! As for Roddy, he was probably jealous of her leaving home, since, at thirteen-and-a-half, he could hardly follow suit. He was bound to miss her, though, if only because he'd no longer be able to nick her Clearasil, or 'borrow' her magnifying mirror, and then drive her insane by leaving them in his room.

The train rattled into Camden Town, where a crowd of people jostled their way out. Gratefully, she plumped into a free seat; booted Roddy from her mind and began deliberating on paint colours. The shade-cards were pure poetry: Frosted Grape, Sunday Sonata, Oriental Coral. She would definitely go wild, if only as a reaction to her parents' tame Magnolia. Maybe Roasted Red for the sitting-room; Thunderous Sky for the bedroom, and something really zany for the cupboard-sized kitchen and—

A sudden racket at Euston interrupted her thoughts, as a gang of black lads pushed into the carriage; all shouting, swearing, and determined to make their presence felt. Now *she* was the one with someone pressing into her knees, since the tallest of the blokes loomed hot and huge above her; his muscly arms sheened with sweat and rippling with tattoos. They were all so physical, for God's sake; big, burly types, with shaven heads, and wearing aggressively ragged jeans. As she peered through the cluster of bodies, she saw that one of the guys was carrying a puppy – a poor wretch of a thing, yelping piteously. The man was clutching it too tightly, ignoring the fact it was a living, breathing creature – too young to have left its mother, by the looks of it – and not a piece of baggage that could be jammed against his chest.

All thoughts of the flat vanished, as she imagined its possible fate. They might drown it, just for a laugh, or fix a firework to its rump and stand jeering and applauding as it careered around in panic, unable to throw off the exploding, sparking coat-tail. She knew nothing about dogs, so she couldn't tell what breed it was and, anyway, it was half-concealed by the cruelly clamping arm. But suppose it was a pit-bull? Just a month ago, she'd seen a TV pro-gramme where pit-bulls were pumped with steroids to bulk them out and make them more belligerent. And the owners filed their teeth into sharp, unnatural points, to intimidate the public, and used the dogs almost as gang-members, to secure better terms on drug-deals.

She longed to grab the pup and take it home, but that was out of the question, with her mother's allergy to animal fur. The only family pets were goldfish, but a goldfish was so soulless. It couldn't sleep on your bed at night, or snuggle close when you were feeling a bit hopeless and needed a wet nose on your face or a consoling paw in your hand. Perhaps she could keep the dog in her flat, though. Admittedly she'd be at work all day, but she could take it out in the evenings in the two small parks nearby. In fact, wasn't that the perfect way to make friends? People always said dogs broke the ice and prompted conversations. She might even meet a guy and, since there'd been no one around since the disastrous bust-up with Jake, she was pining for some love interest – maybe an older man, this time, a snazzy dresser, with cash and class. Jake wore a gross red anorak, and still liked One Direction – pathetic for a guy of nineteen.

She closed her eyes to set the scene more clearly, the crowded carriage fading into a secluded little park. And, yes, a posh-looking golden retriever had come rushing up to *her* dog, and she and its distinctly fanciable owner were bonding every bit as firmly as the two sniffing, circling dogs. Love at first sight didn't have to be corny.

Come off it, Debs! Get real....

Roddy's voice shattered the romance. Her brother was so *basic*; failing invariably to grasp that dreams could be reality. She wouldn't have the flat, for instance, if it hadn't started as a dream. And Roddy it was who had first shortened her name to 'Debs', which, much to her annoyance, soon became 'official'. If she met the golden-retriever-man, she would use her full name right from the start. 'Deborah' had class.

At Charing Cross, there was a further disturbance, as the rowdy group began shoving out of the carriage – all except the one with the dog. As the closing doors cut off their yells and curses, she fixed her attention on the pup once more. It was clearly terrified and still squealing in a sickening way. Her natural instinct was to report the bloke to the RSPCA, but how could she, when she didn't know his name? Maybe better to be less hostile and simply offer to buy the dog at a price he couldn't refuse. OK, she didn't have that sort of cash, but her dad might shell out – again. She was his favourite, after all. His 'little girl', he still called her – and would probably continue calling her, even when she was an ancient thirty-something.

Shit! The train had reached Waterloo where she was meant to change for the mainline. If she didn't get back to Tolworth soon, her parents would start imagining that she'd been raped at knifepoint by some psychotic maniac. But how could she shrug off responsibility and abandon that helpless creature to its fate? No one else seemed bothered. The majority were elbowing their way out – irritable commuters dashing for their trains – while the others slumped heedless in their seats, distracted by their headphones, or riffling through the *Standard*. Not that *she* was any better, when all she had done so far was fume in silence. She needed a plan of action – maybe approach the guy and get into conversation, then ask him outright about the dog, to see what he intended. But the thought of going over to him, with a dozen people watching, and having to raise her voice above the rumble of the train, held her rigid in her seat. Wouldn't it seem more natural to wait till he got out, then dart up to him in the street; make it appear a chance encounter, not a calculated stalking?

As the train rattled on its way, past Kennington, the Oval, Stockwell, Clapham North, she deliberately kept her eyes down, to avoid the bloke's attention, so that, when she finally confronted him, he wouldn't twig she'd been tailing him since he first got on at Euston.

At Tooting Bec, he made a lunge for the doors, hoisting the puppy over his shoulder, like a small, saggy refuse-sack. Grimacing in fury, she followed him out of the carriage, keeping him in view as he hurtled up the escalator. Once in the street, he maintained the same frenetic speed and she had to run to keep up; weaving in and out of infuriating people dawdling along at a snail's pace or blocking the pavement with their great, clumsy, show-off buggies. And, because it was scorcher of an evening, clusters of drinkers were standing outside the pubs, all blithely assuming that other people had nothing else to do but tip lager down their throats.

Although out of breath and sweaty and still blundering along in her not-meant-for-running shoes, she tried to work on her action plan. She couldn't involve the police – it wasn't a crime to carry a dog – but, if she tackled the brute on her own, he might turn violent and pull a knife on her. Yet her mind was seething with horrendous images of the dog-abuse she had seen online: owners starving their pets until they were living skeletons, or keeping them tied up all day on tight, neck-strangling chains. Some monstrous individuals even tortured dogs deliberately: beat them, stabbed them, left them to die. One sadist had cut the ears off his bull terrier, to make it look more macho, and an unspeakable Hitler-clone had actually put his pup into a washing-machine running at full speed, then dumped its sodden corpse in the municipal rubbish-tip. If *this* puppy suffered such horrors, she would be to blame in part, just for standing by and doing nothing.

The guy continued striding down the street, until, all at once, he lurched to a halt and paused a moment outside a seedy café. Concealing herself a pace or two away, she watched, appalled, as the pup struggled to escape. He simply gripped it tighter, ignored its agonizing cries, then sauntered in to the café; the dog of no more importance than the canvas bag slung across his shoulder.

Cautiously, she edged a little nearer and peered in through the café window; saw him slouch over to a table for four and plonk himself down on a chair. Was he about to meet some new gang-members – sell the dog to them, perhaps, to treat in that brutal fashion? Noiseless as a shadow, she slunk in through the open door and took a seat in the corner where she could escape the fellow's notice yet watch his every movement.

He ordered a coffee – she did the same, keeping her voice as low as possible. She must screw up her reserves of courage and approach him now, before any more of the gang showed up. He could hardly knife her in front of the staff: two hulking waiters who looked reassuringly streetwise. Nonetheless, her heart was thumping in her chest as she rose to her feet, determined to measure up to her father's lofty standards, his unshakeable belief that a single individual with a conscience and integrity could actually make a difference in the world. It only took one voice, he said; one brave person who dared to take a stand.

But as she stepped purposefully towards him, there was a sudden jangle of bracelets and a waft of sickly scent, and a big, curvaceous black lady erupted into the café, a gangly black youth following close behind. As the pair lumbered towards the table, the bloke jumped up to greet them and there were hugs and kisses all round – the poor puppy squashed still further as it was momentarily engulfed in the woman's mountainous boobs.

However, to Debs's sheer surprise, the guy used his free arm to fumble in his canvas bag and drew out a fuzzy pink blanket, patterned with cutesy paw-prints, and, having wrapped it round the dog, then transferred the creature from his arms to the woman's.

'Happy birthday, Mum!' he said. 'Meet Lucky.'

The woman's smile was so wide it split her face, and her eyes crinkled up with pleasure as, tenderly, she cradled the dog and rocked it like a baby, gently cooing and clucking. The boy seemed just as fond; stroking the puppy's floppy ears; even planting a kiss on its head. Its cries stopped, miraculously, as it snuggled closer to the woman's pillowy chest, daring to relax, at last. Debs's own surge of relief was mixed with shame about how wrong she'd been. He wasn't cruel at all – probably just embarrassed to be carrying a scrap of a puppy in front of his macho mates, and clearly not accustomed to handling new-born creatures.

She sat back in her chair; glad there was no one else in the café, so that she could tune in to the family, feeling almost part of their cosy little circle. The guy ordered tea and cake for his mum, and Coke and ice-cream for the boy – his younger brother, presumably, since they looked noticeably alike.

'Anything else for you, miss?' The waiter had returned to remove her empty cup.

'Yeah, I'll have another coffee.' Somehow, she couldn't tear herself away and, in any case, she needed a second caffeine shot. All her gruesome imaginings – which now seemed horribly unfair – had left her as limp as a lettuce-leaf.

She kept her eyes on the mother, who obviously doted on her sons, reaching out affectionately to pat the elder one's hand, or ruffle the younger's hair. Yet, never for a moment did she ignore the little dog; one arm circling it securely, as it nuzzled against her chest. And, when the tea arrived, she poured milk into her saucer and held the puppy up, so it could lap the milk from a comfortable position. Once the milk was finished, the boy smeared his fingers with ice-cream and held them out to the dog to lick. And, judging by its response, ice-cream was a number-one hit. The small pink tongue flicked back and forth so fast, it seemed to have a life of its own, quite separate from the dog itself.

As the mother dabbed a fleck of ice-cream off her turquoise satin blouse, Debs was suddenly conscious of her *own* mother. By now, she would be worrying Big Time; imagining her daughter lying battered and bloody in some North London alleyway, or already in the mortuary, laid out on a slab. Guiltily, she dialled her parents' number, only now aware of just how late it was.

'Oh, Debs, thank heavens you've rung! Dad was getting frantic.'

'It's OK, Mum. I'm still in one piece!'

'Thank God for that! And no problems with the flat?'

Debs fiddled with her hair. The pause seemed ridiculously long.

'Debs, are you still there?'

'Yeah.' She glanced across at the family, united and secure; exchanging jokes and banter. 'Well, actually, there *is* a problem.'

'What do you mean? What's happened? Oh, I know the kitchen's tiny, but you said that didn't matter, because—'

'It's not the kitchen, Mum. It's....' What the hell was she saying? The flat had seemed near-perfect, on all three viewings.

'Well, what?'

She couldn't explain. It would sound pathetic, utterly uncool. But only now had it struck her that you could miss a mother – terribly. No one to care whether you were OK, or in a heap. No one to cook you proper porridge in the morning, or have your supper waiting when you came back, knackered after work. No one to make you a hot-water-bottle, if your period pain was bad, or sew new eyes on your old, balding teddy bear.

'Sweetheart, have you lost your tongue? I asked you, twice, what's gone wrong with the flat?'

'Nothing's gone wrong. And it's not exactly the flat, Mum. It's the, er, whole idea – you know, me leaving home and everything.' You could even miss a brother, she realized, with a jolt. OK, Roddy drove her spare by leaving the top off her Clearasil, or playing his drum-set when she was trying to have a lie-in at weekends. On the other hand, a flat could be deathly quiet. Isolated. Lonely. Maybe even dangerous, if her parents happened to be right about the perils of North London.

'You mean you've changed your mind, love?' She couldn't fail to hear the relief in her mother's voice.

'Yes. No. I'm not exactly sure.' No one to call you 'love', or 'sweetheart', or their 'favourite little girl'.

'Well, you'd better decide as soon as possible, because Dad plans to give the sewing-machine a right old going-over tomorrow. But, if you think you won't be wanting the curtains, I'll tell him not to bother.'

'I *will* be wanting them, Mum.' Perhaps they would do for her Tolworth bedroom. There was nothing really wrong with pelmets, not in Tolworth, anyway. And making curtains for someone was like giving them a present: a gift of time and effort – as was slogging up to London to decorate a daughter's flat. Presents meant a lot; meant someone cared and bothered. 'Let's discuss it when I get back, OK?'

'But when will *that* be, darling? You're much later than you said, you know, and we were getting really worried.'

'I'm on my way!' Without waiting for her second coffee, she flung a fiver on the table and strode towards the door; smiling openly, unabashedly, at that loving, caring – completely essential – family.

LOST

'Oh, no!' cried Primrose, as the tube doors hissed shut behind her, at the very moment she realized she'd left her handbag in the carriage. She stood, horrified, incredulous, watching the train rumble out of the station, taking with it the keys to her flat, her travel-pass, her credit card and all her money, and several treasured possessions. She experienced their loss like a physical assault on her body – stomach churning, heart beating frighteningly fast – curdled with a sense of mortifying guilt. How could she have been so careless and so stupid?

Easily, it seemed. Exhausted by the long and tedious film, she had nodded off on the journey back from the cinema and only jerked awake in the nick of time, as the train pulled into her station. She had made a grab for her walking-stick and for the old canvas bag that held her travel-cushion, but, in her flurry to get out, must have somehow missed her handbag, which was now winging its way to the end of the line. Should she catch the next train in pursuit, ask the staff here for advice, or...?

Indecisive in her present state of shock, she tottered over to a bench and sat unmoving, feeling frighteningly denuded. In the absence of keys, cash and travel-pass, she was grounded and inoperative, not to mention shut out of her home. Worse, she seemed to hear Violet reproaching her from some realm beyond the grave, since it was Violet who had given her the bag – a luxurious one, real crocodile-skin, silk-lined – along with the matching leather purse and a tortoiseshell powder-compact, now both lost, as well. Her own bag had been shabby, cheap and shinily synthetic, but Vi had always been generous, paying for shared treats, or passing on barely worn clothes, and, during her last illness, had pushed the almost-new, designer bag

87

into her hands and asked her to keep it in her memory.

Primrose and Violet: two small, shy blooms, reared in adjoining flowerbeds, growing up together and remaining close ever since. The loss of Vi herself had been painful enough, without losing an object of such great sentimental value and one that still retained faint traces of her friend's floral eau-de-cologne. Indeed, she felt so prostrated, she simply didn't have the energy to go chasing off to Walthamstow in the fragile hope of finding the bag. So expensive an object would doubtless have been nabbed the minute she had shambled off the train, still half-asleep and dazed.

Two or three people had now joined her on the bench and others were flowing on to the station, but to them she was invisible, of course; just a sad old crone, easily ignored. Leaning on her stick, she eased up from the seat and limped towards the exit, mounting the escalator with her usual caution. A broken leg, on top of everything else, would hardly improve the situation.

Only when she reached ground level did she realize that, without her travel-pass, she couldn't even get out of the station. However, having explained her dilemma to a swarthy, turbaned fellow, standing by the automatic gates, he kindly let her through. In fact, he seemed so affable, she found herself pouring out the whole story, her voice rising in panic as she realized the full implications of her loss.

'Try not to worry, my love. There's just a chance your bag might have been handed in.'

'Already?' she asked, seizing on the smallest grain of hope. 'I assumed it would have been stolen.'

'Not necessarily. Some people are good-hearted and do the decent thing. Tell you what – let me ring the next three stations down the line and make a few enquiries.'

He led the way to a small, glass-fronted booth and, having disappeared inside, began talking on the phone. His obvious kindness and concern were like a soothing salve laid on a raw, smarting burn. Since Arthur's death, kindnesses were rare. And he had called her 'my love', which also touched her deeply. She had been no one's love for years.

As he continued his phone-calls, she watched his face for any signs of hope, wondering what nationality he was. Indian? Pakistani? Bangladeshi? Throughout her rural childhood, she had never seen a black or Asian face and, after her marriage and the sixty years in Sidcup with Arthur, things hadn't been markedly different. And, although here in Seven Sisters – where she'd moved to be close to Violet, who lived in neighbouring but more salubrious Highbury – she was surrounded by Africans, Jamaicans, Kurds, Turks and a whole host of other ethnicities, it had proved hard to get to know such a person – or, indeed, anyone in the area. Why should younger folk be interested in an outworn ninety-three-year-old? When Vi was still alive, they'd had each other, of course – two fellow nonagenarians united against the world – but her dearest, longest-standing friend had died six months ago, and the pain of her passing still throbbed like an open sore.

'No luck yet,' the man reported, 'but don't lose hope, my dear. It often takes a while for things to be handed in. You need to contact the Lost Property Office and they'll do a proper search. Do you have email?' he asked, passing her their brochure.

She shook her head, feeling her usual shame at owning neither a computer nor a mobile, both of which seemed more crucial in the modern world than owning a heart or head. But the long years of Arthur's illness, followed by his dementia, had closed her own life down. Acting as his carer had proved a fulltime job, and, when she was finally forced to move him into residential care and sell their house to meet the ever-mounting costs, she was busier than ever, dealing with estate agents, showing prospective buyers round their neat little Sidcup semi, trying to find herself a new place, as well as fit in twice-daily visits to her increasingly incapacitated husband. And, after his sad and sparsely attended funeral, she had simply lost energy and heart. The once-enticing sounding IT courses for the over-sixty-fives had now lost all appeal. How could computers be of interest when her childhood sweetheart and life's companion had died incontinent, fighting for every laboured breath and failing even to recognize his wife of sixty-seven years, as she sat clutching his scrawny hand, her tears falling on his age-blotched skin?

'I'm afraid I don't even have a computer,' she admitted. 'I know it seems awful in this day and age.'

'Not at all. My wife's the same. She refuses even to touch our laptop and just leaves all the online stuff to me.'

'Well, she's lucky to have you,' Primrose observed, noticing his lustrously black, long-lashed eyes. Arthur had been resolutely English in his looks: fairish hair, pale blue eyes and over-sensitive skin that flared up in the sun.

'*She* doesn't think so!' The man gave a big, booming laugh. 'But back to your lost bag. Don't worry about email, because you can call in at the Lost Property Office in person. All the details are here in this leaflet.'

'But how can I go anywhere without a travel-pass, and with no credit card or cash to buy a ticket?'

The man looked baffled for a moment, before passing her another brochure. 'You'll need to report their loss, as well. Here's the number to ring for lost or stolen Freedom Passes, and they take calls on Sundays, up to eight o'clock, so you can do that right away. You can also phone the Lost Property Office, if you can't get there in person, without shelling out for a ticket, but they won't be open till Monday morning, eight-thirty. As for your credit card, that's more important than all the rest, because if you don't cancel it immediately, someone else may use it and start running up huge bills on your account.'

She shuddered at the very thought, having always been scrupulously careful not to overspend.

'There's bound to be a customer helpline, and those are usually open twenty-four hours a day, three-hundred-and-sixty-five days a year. So I strongly advise you to phone them the minute you get home.'

'I can't ring anyone,' she said, feeling more and more distressed. 'My only phone's a landline, you see, and without my keys, I'm locked out of my flat. I do keep a spare set with my neighbour, but she might be out and, anyway, she's always rather fierce.' Faced with the prospect of wandering the streets all night, not to mention being landed in debt because some stranger was using her card, it was all she could do not to break down in tears.

'Do you have your neighbour's number? I can give her a ring, if you like, to check she's in.'

'Yes, *please*,' she breathed. This man was a veritable saint, doing everything in his power to help her out.

'We're not allowed to make calls indiscriminately but, since this is an emergency, there shouldn't be a problem. So, if you come with me to the office, I can get an outside line there.'

Fortunately, it wasn't far – just a few yards from the booth – although, once inside, she felt awkward about disturbing the three members of uniformed staff, all sitting at computer screens and clearly hard at work. But, like the majority of people, they gave her little more attention than if she were a discarded chocolate-wrapper tossed into the waste-bin.

'So what's your neighbour's number?'

She fought panic for a moment, fearing she'd forgotten it. It was written on a piece of paper, stowed safely in a zipped compartment of her purse – useless in the present circumstances. She had once attempted to learn it off by heart, in case of just this sort of mishap, so, shutting her eyes, she summoned up her full powers of concentration. And, falteringly and slowly, the digits began to creep back into her mind: the seven and the three fours at the end, followed, more swiftly, by the prefix. Thank God her memory was still more or less intact, whatever else was failing. Having jotted down the number – along with her neighbour's name, Mrs Cronin – she passed them both to the man, watching in an agony of apprehension as he dialled out on the office phone.

'Good afternoon. It's Mohammed Ahmed here, from London Transport....'

How exotic his name sounded! She tried to imagine being married to a Mr Mohammed Ahmed, instead of to a Mr Arthur Simpson.

'Ah, Mrs Cronin, you're in....'

She could have hugged the woman in sheer relief, just because she was *there*, yet she also felt a surge of dread at the thought of her irascible neighbour's wrath. 'Did she sound cross?' she asked, once the obliging Mr Ahmed had rung off.

'Well, not exactly a laugh a minute!' The man gave her a complicit grin, which she did her best to return. In truth, though, she felt infinitely fatigued, not just from the stress, but from the prospect of all the calls required to regain her vital access to trains, buses, shops and even films. She relied increasingly on the cinema, these days, as a way of passing the empty hours, with free heating thrown in, as a bonus, and special discount rates at some of the chains; even free tea for pensioners.

Aware that two other passengers were waiting to speak to Mr Ahmed, she apologized for taking up his time and thanked him profusely for his kindness.

'No problem, my love. It's all part of the service.'

As she left the station, she stored that final 'my love' in the savings-bank of her mind, to provide some credit and comfort during the lonely evening ahead, then exited the station and turned into the High Road, surprised to see it was dark. The clocks had gone back a fortnight ago – a fact she kept forgetting, until each oppressively endless evening reminded her again. The High Road was as busy and noisy as usual, with buses roaring past, and a sense of being dwarfed and deafened in such a major thoroughfare. Everything in Sidcup had been on a smaller scale: quieter, safer, less anonymous and overwhelming.

It also never failed to strike her how hugely Sundays had changed. In her young days, everything was closed and you stayed peacefully at home – cooking the roast, of course, but never breaching God's designated Day of Rest by hanging out the washing or cleaning the front step, let alone indulging in any whoopee. Indeed, people rarely ate out on any day of the week, except for special celebrations. Whereas folk flocked to restaurants nowadays at all hours of the day and night – pizza chains, McDonald's, Starbucks, Café Nero. They even breakfasted in cafés (which did seem a step too far), shelling out a fortune for tiny bowls of porridge her mother used to make for ha'pence. And here, in the High Road, were people eating, drinking, shopping, travelling, regardless of the Sabbath.

She turned right into Broad Lane, taking the path across Page Green Common – or what was left of it. Vi had told her once that, a century or more ago, it had been considerably larger, with a pond and seats and a proper fence enclosing it, instead of just a small open space. Still, nice to have a patch of green at all, and some tall, attractive trees.

Despite her deep anxiety about her lost bag and credit card, she stopped, as usual, by Arthur's tree, sending up a silent prayer that her husband was now totally at peace and had regained his former health and mental clarity. He had always had a passion for trees – knew all the different species and even their botanical names – and, although they had never had a garden, their weekend walks in the various Sidcup parks had kept him contented enough, with occasional longer forays to Elmstead Woods or Beckenham Place Park.

So, immediately after her house-move, she had hunted for a tree that might appeal to him – something as strong and sturdy and singular as *he* was – so she could adopt it, so to speak, as they'd once planned to adopt the children they had never, sadly, managed to conceive.

'Miss you, Arthur darling,' she whispered, looking up into the tangled network of branches. 'Your leaves are beginning to fall, my sweet, so be sure you don't get cold.'

Autumn was always a challenge – season of loss and decay: loss of warmth, of light, of leaves, of growth. Simply being old brought losses enough, without nature shrivelling and dwindling on such a melancholy scale. Still, at least Guy Fawkes Day was over. The noise of the fireworks seemed to shake the very foundations of her flat, and she felt awkward being pestered for a 'penny for the guy' when it was a struggle to give generously to every child who asked. She jumped as a lone firework suddenly whooshed into a shower of sparks high above the houses. One or two had been going off sporadically, during the last few days, always startling her with their mini-explosions. And, when she peered down at the grass, she could see some of their burnt-out carcasses, lying sodden and blackened right here by Arthur's tree.

She shambled on, passing the little primary school, then turning left into Hanover Road, glancing at every person who went by, in the hope of some acknowledgement. In Sidcup, there'd been a constant stream of 'Good mornings' or 'Good afternoons', friendly smiles, doffed hats. Now, no one wore hats and everyone seemed in such a tearing hurry, there wasn't time to stop and chat. Also, she felt cut off from all the black and foreign faces. However much she might want to get to know them, they inhabited a different world that seemed to bar her entry. Once, she had stopped outside the local Apostolic Church, peering through the open door and astonished by the sight that met her eyes: people in colourful robes and exotic headgear singing and dancing on a stage, to the rhythmic, jazzy sound of a live band, and the entire congregation shimmying and jigging in the pews. She had felt a secret longing to join in, if only as an antidote to the severely silent Methodist services she had attended as a child, yet there hadn't been a single white face among that exuberant throng, so she had simply slunk away, feeling intimidated, excluded.

She must be grateful for her blessings, though. Despite the tragic loss of Violet's final precious gift, she still had her health and sanity, food in the fridge and a solid roof above her head. In fact, she was glad to reach the flat, notwithstanding the vicious rant from Mrs Cronin, who came storming to the door, saying she had no intention of being at her neighbour's beck and call every time she lost her keys. Since it had never actually happened before, the harsh words stung like hail, but safe, at last, at home, she immediately hunted out the folder that held her official documents and dialled the Barclaycard helpline.

'Hi, there,' said a recorded voice. 'Welcome to Barclaycard! To help me find your account, please say or tap in your credit-card number.'

Having failed to realize she would need it, she was obliged to ring off and rummage in the folder again for one of her monthly statements.

'Hi, there,' the voice repeated once she had redialled – a strange form of greeting to her ears. Wouldn't 'Good afternoon' be more respectful?

With some difficulty, she tapped in the card-number. Her fingers were increasingly stiff, these days.

'I'm sorry, but that card doesn't sound like one of ours,' the anonymous voice observed.

Had she misread a digit, perhaps? Her sight was failing, like so much else. Reaching for her stronger glasses, she tried a second time, relieved to hear the cheery 'Thanks!'

'Now please say your date of birth – for example, the twenty-fifth of March, 1980, would be 25, 03, 80.'

'18, 06, 20,' she obediently responded, hardly believing she could have lived so long. In 1920, the British Empire still covered a quarter of the world, and horses and carts still delivered milk, bread, beer and coal, and there was no radio or television and only silent movies.

'OK. And now what is the full postal code for your card's billing address?'

As she was about to speak, the line suddenly went dead and, suppressing a groan of frustration, she was forced to go through the whole rigmarole again, until she was back to supplying her post-code.

'I'm sorry, I didn't hear that. Could you please repeat it?'

This second call, it appeared, was fated to continue in the same stop-start manner as the first. However, she was finally put through to 'one of the team' – an Indian-sounding gentleman with an exceptionally strong accent, which, combined with her hearing loss, made it difficult to understand. In fact, by the time she had explained the situation and the man had asked her to spell out her name and post-code (again) and several other details, she was exhausted by the effort of listening to hard-to-grasp instructions, and having to strain her faulty ears to hear anything at all. But, at last, and to her huge relief, he confirmed that he had blocked her card and promised to send a replacement.

To celebrate, she actually poured herself a thimbleful of sherry – another gift from Violet – and sat down with it, in the small, cluttered room. It had taken a while to adjust to the lack of space in what was basically a bedsit. However, without sons or daughters to visit her, or grandchildren to stay (the adoption plan had foundered when Arthur suddenly changed his mind and insisted on trying even longer for their own child), she didn't actually need more rooms, so this 'studio flat', as they called it, was, in fact, perfectly adequate.

She had planned on making the other phone-call after a brief sit-down, but, whether lulled by the sherry, or aware that her energies had reached their lowest ebb, she decided to postpone it till the morning – when she could also ring Lost Property. This sad and stressful Sunday had been quite long enough, so, tuning in to the Antiques Roadshow, she made a conscious effort to relax. Just for an hour, she intended to indulge in the glorious fantasy of owning some jewel or lamp or painting that turned out to be worth a fortune. Then she could move back to Sidcup and buy a house with a garden, full of exotic trees for Arthur.

'Welcome to the Freedom-Pass helpline!'

Her spirits sank at the sound of another recorded voice. How long ago it seemed since real flesh-and-blood people had answered the phone. But on this occasion, at least, she wasn't expected to press a whole succession of numbers in a long-winded attempt to speak to anyone at all.

'Yes, may I help you?'

An Indian voice again and every bit as difficult to decipher as the Barclaycard man last night. Eventually, though, she managed to grasp that, to obtain a substitute pass, she must pay a ten-pound replacement-fee and, in the absence of a credit card or cheque, a postal order would be acceptable.

The mere mention of a postal order changed her mood entirely, bringing an instant surge of euphoria. She had totally forgotten her post-office account, as well as the joyous fact that its pin-number and card were kept not in her lost purse, but right here in the flat, along with her other official documents. Which meant she could actually draw out some money straight away, and also purchase the all-important postal order.

The foreign man was just telling her the address and, as she copied it down, she tried to keep pace with his rapid-fire speech, although continually having to interrupt and ask him to spell out words she'd failed to catch. Laurencekirk, she wrote, wondering where it was – north, south, east or west? There were so many places she had never visited, and probably never would now. Arthur had preferred to stay on home territory, even when he was fit and well.

'Once we receive your fee and a covering letter,' the heavily accented voice continued, 'with your name, address and date of birth, the replacement Freedom Pass should be with you within four or five working days.'

Her relief redoubled at the thought that, by early next week, she should be able to travel again. The Freedom Pass was well named. Without it, the prohibitive cost of bus and tube and train fares would trap her as a prisoner in her flat. In fact, she decided to set out for the post office right away, before ringing the Lost Property Office. She didn't need a bus or tube – it was only a short walk away – but what she did need was the security of no longer being penniless.

Forty minutes later, after a long wait in the queue, she was infinitely consoled to be handed three crisp ten-pound notes – not that thirty pounds would go far, especially as she had to relinquish a third of it, to pay for the postal order. And then she'd need food, if only a tin of beans. Nonetheless, once she had popped back home to write the covering letter and send it off with the fee, she was strongly tempted to splurge a little of the cash on buying a ticket to Baker Street, so she could visit the Lost Property Office in person. Surely that would be safer than resorting to the phone again, with the risk of being cut off or misunderstood? What finally swayed her, however, was the dismal prospect of spending the rest of the day indoors, with neither distraction nor company. At least, if she ventured out again, she would have an aim and purpose, with the added bonus of seeing some fellow human beings.

Yet she was shocked by the price of the ticket. It was so long since she'd paid for her travel, she could hardly countenance the huge increase in fares. It would be worth it, though, if the precious handbag was restored, along with its treasured contents, so she simply had to trust in what Mr Mohammed Ahmed had called people's basic decency.

Timidly, she entered the Lost Property Office and joined the queue of people waiting: two young girls, with ultra-short skirts and ultra-long hair, a swarthy-looking man in a navy pinstriped suit, and an elderly couple standing (enviably) hand in hand. Always hungry for conversation, she tried to engage the latter in a little harmless chit-chat, but they turned out to be foreigners and failed to understand.

So it was something of a relief when she was eventually summoned to the Enquiry Desk, to be greeted by a man who spoke loudly, clearly and with no trace of a baffling accent. Having supplied him with all the details of yesterday's journey and a description of the bag, he raised her hopes, at least momentarily, by explaining that he was going to check if the item had already been handed in, and would she please take a seat. Subsiding on to one of the uncomfortable plastic chairs, she glanced at the person beside her, again hoping to exchange a friendly word or two. But the woman was on her mobile, as were the two girls now waiting opposite. How wonderful, she mused, to have so many friends one could chat to them all day.

When requested to return to the desk, she was informed that nothing had been handed in that fitted her description. 'But don't worry,' the man said, brightly. 'Items usually take up to seven days to arrive. And you don't need to do anything more – just leave the rest to us. We'll be searching the whole network and will contact you immediately should your bag be found. And, if nothing turns up within twenty-one days, then you'll also be notified, but, after that, there's nothing else we can do, I'm afraid. Right,' he said with a final look at the computer-screen, 'all signed and sealed. No worries!'

No worries, she thought – if only! She was seldom free of anxiety and right now it had increased at the mention of twenty-one days – an eternity to be left hanging around, torn between hope and despair, and unable to take her usual bus and tube trips, at least until next week. She did, in fact, consider staying right here for a while, if only to relish the warmth and the chance of a chat, should she meet a friendly soul not cemented to a mobile. But, seeing that all the chairs were occupied and realizing she would only be an obstruction, she had no option but to leave.

However, once outside, she managed to pass some time studying the items displayed in the window – tracing her own life-history in the various abandoned objects, each labelled with its description and the date and place it was found. A rusty old iron, from 1934, jolted her back to her mother, ironing sheets and towels, bloomers and liberty-bodices – heating the iron the old way, on a stove, and toiling patiently for hours with no thought of alien concepts like 'women's liberation'.

She, too, had been a dab hand at ironing, even at fourteen, and could knit and sew and darn and polish brass – all unnecessary skills now, along with letter-writing and cooking from scratch; gone the way of pounds and ounces, shillings and pence. She was a dinosaur in the modern world, lacking all the new skills; baffled by self-service checkouts, online banking, Wi-Fi, Facebook, Google and all those other mysterious things, constantly mentioned on the News.

With a sigh, she peered at a clutch of books from the forties and a stash of LPs from the sixties, a reminder of much-loved novels and songs from those far-off, much-missed days. And the 1951 top hat was identical to the one Vi's husband had worn at their wedding. But who, she wondered, would be likely to leave a top-hat on a bus, or – even more peculiar – an iron? Forgotten phones and cameras were far more understandable and, examining the large assortment here, she saw, that as each decade wore on, they became smaller but more complex.

She, too, had grown smaller, shrinking an inch or two in height and losing her once voluptuous breasts; even her lips contracting, so that she now had a pinched-looking mouth. In fact, she was repulsed by her reflection in the glass. Even with her failing sight, she could make out the great dark pouches under her eyes, and her hair reduced to a baby-fine fuzz, so scant in parts it revealed pink, shiny patches of her scalp.

But no point hanging around any longer, depressing herself and getting cold in the process. Once back home, she would treat herself to a nice, hot mug of soup, and have it as late as possible, so it could serve as lunch-and-tea in one. Until she knew the fate of Violet's bag, economy had to be her watchword.

The twenty-one days that had passed with no word from the Lost Property Office weighed so heavy on her spirits, she seemed to be carrying a great sackful of stones. Obviously, the official search had proved fruitless, and, any time now, she would receive a notification confirming that dismal fact. Admittedly, she now had her replacement credit card and travel-pass – and a cheap plastic purse from a charity shop – but nothing could compensate for losing her final keepsake from Violet. And the fact she had been so careless in the first place seemed to underline her general state of decrepitude. Suppose she developed dementia, like poor Arthur? Who would know or care?

She wandered disconsolately along West Green Road, avoiding the big Tesco's, as usual. There were just as many bargains here, without the glare and confusion of a large, anonymous supermarket. Today, however, she felt more and more out-of-place as she passed Afro Hair and Beauty, Halal Meat, Caribbean Spice. These exotic stores made *her* into the foreigner; not the people inside them, shopping for yams, matooke and plantains, or the women having their hair braided, plaited, straightened.

As she mooched on past Oriental Foods and Eden Store Gospel Music, she couldn't help recalling the friendly little local shop in Sidcup, owned by Mr and Mrs Thoroughly English Brown. No way was she racist – indeed, she longed to have a black or Asian friend – but the harsh truth was she didn't belong here, simply by virtue of the fact that she didn't know the culture.

She stopped to look in a shop selling bags, wondering who had stolen Violet's and whether they had filled it with their own possessions, or were using the tortoiseshell powder-compact, the crocodile-skin purse and Vi's stylish pink umbrella that folded down into a handy compact size. Did the thief feel guilt or remorse, or were those outmoded concepts like chastity and temperance?

Having finally bought a loaf, two apples and a tin of mushy peas, she headed home, battling against the spiteful wind. Crossing the road via the Seven Sisters subway, she imagined having seven sisters herself, instead of being an only child. Then, she might well have had nieces and nephews – indeed, great-nieces and -nephews by now. She even found herself christening her make-believe sisters: Poppy, Daisy, Jasmine, Iris, Rose and Marigold. Or, instead of giving them all flower-names, perhaps she could call them after months: April, May, June…. No, there weren't enough suitable months. You could hardly christen a daughter December, January or February, when those were such gruelling months, with perilously icy pavements, coughs and colds and chilblains, and – worst of all – lonely Christmas Days.

There had been signs of Christmas since late October and, in this first week of December, one couldn't escape reminders of the so-called Festive Season: turkeys and satsumas in the shops, twinkling lights strung along the High Road, an illuminated reindeer outside the Town Hall. The Big Day invariably required a plan, to make it more endurable: a nice boiled egg for breakfast, a walk to Page Green Common, to commune with Arthur's tree, then back for the Queen's Speech and a couple of mince pies and – hopefully – something uplifting on television to get her through the evening.

Once home, she checked the post and having discarded the usual flurry of leaflets from kebab houses and Chinese takeaways, she picked up the large white card from the Lost Property Office – easily identifiable from the drawings of golf-clubs, cameras, umbrellas, bags and other lost objects. Turning it over, she steeled herself to read the official notification that her bag was irretrievably lost. Instead, she lighted on something completely unexpected: Dear Mrs Simpson, We may have found the property you lost….

Delighted, yet still fearing disappointment – 'may have' was far from certainty – she rushed to phone them, as requested. They had to verify that the bag was hers before they could return it, or so it said on the card.

But, yes, it *was* hers, the man confirmed and, even more miraculous, all its contents appeared to be intact: the purse, with its cards and money, the umbrella and the powder compact, even the bag of jelly babies, which she sometimes bought to comfort herself, when mourning her lack of real babies.

She set out again in high spirits, bound for Baker Street, this time, her mood entirely transformed. But, as she entered the Lost Property Office, she couldn't help but wonder if the whole thing was a dream, because there, standing in the centre of the room, was a radiantly pretty young girl, dressed in a long flowing dress, with a wreath of flowers on her head, and, beside her, a handsome man in a suit, with an orchid in his buttonhole. The pair looked weirdly incongruous in the unatmospheric surroundings of grey vinyl floor and white polystyrene ceiling-tiles and, for some unknown reason, they were actually posing for photographs – surely most peculiar, in a Lost Property Office, of all places.

Pinching herself to ensure she was awake, she stole over to one of the plastic chairs, hoping the woman beside her could shed some light on the proceedings.

'Oh, it's quite a saga!' the woman exclaimed, obviously keen to share the drama. 'Those two are just about to be married.'

'What, *here*?' Primrose asked, in astonishment, although keeping her voice low, so as not to disturb the couple. Had the Lost Property Office become an unusual new venue for weddings, like Lords' Cricket Ground or the Lexi Cinema?

'Oh, no,' the woman laughed. 'They're on their way to the Register Office. The bridegroom just told us the whole story. What happened was he bought his fiancée a wedding ring from some really pricy jeweller's – cost a bomb, he said, because he wanted to do her proud and not stint on anything. But – would you believe? – a fortnight ago, he went and left it on a train!' The woman edged closer and began speaking in a conspiratorial whisper, so that Primrose had to strain to hear. 'I reckon he'd had one too many. He said he was out on some stag-night thing, with half-a-dozen mates and, on their way home, he was showing them the ring and they were all passing it round and larking about. Anyway, when they got off the train, he assumed one of them had hold of it and only realized later it must have got dropped in the carriage. Between you and me, I guess they were all so plastered they didn't know their ankles from their arses – if you'll forgive my language!'

The woman paused for breath a moment, before continuing in the same excitable fashion. 'Anyway, the next morning he rolls in here to report the lost ring but, as the days go by and no one hands it in, or gives him any news, he gets more and more pissed off at the thought of having to make do with some old cheapo ring, because no way can he afford to buy another proper gold one.'

Primrose glanced at her own ring, remembering how Arthur had saved up for months and months, sacrificing his usual pints in the pub, cutting down on tobacco and filling his pipe with shreds of bark, instead; even selling his treasured stamp collection, to raise some extra cash – and all to give her a ring so dazzlingly extravagant it would reflect the depth of his love. Perhaps this young man had done the same. Certainly, he was gazing at his bride with the same devotion and adoration Arthur had shown to her during more than six blessed decades.

'But, wait till you hear this!' the woman crowed, nudging Primrose in the ribs, to regain her full attention for the remainder of the story. 'They phoned him – literally, half an hour ago, to say someone had handed in the ring at that very moment. So he rushes straight here with his bride – I mean, actually *en route* to their wedding, because they're now a bit pushed for time – and, once the ring is safely in his pocket, he's like a dog with two tails and starts pouring out the story to all us people waiting in the queue. And we all say congratulations and take pictures on our phones and stuff. Then the manager hears the kerfuffle and *he* comes out and wants a proper photograph – I suppose for the records or something. That was just a minute ago. See the guy with the camera, in the blue trousers and white shirt?'

Primrose nodded, enchanted by the tale, which brought back such cherished memories. Her own wedding day had been so supremely happy, even the war couldn't spoil it – not the bombing, or the rationing, or the fact her wedding dress was made from a pair of dingy, once-white lace curtains. The only thing that mattered was that she was marrying the most wonderful man in the world. In fact, as soon as she had finished here, she planned to go to Arthur's tree to tell him the whole saga. And she shouldn't be kept too long, because the bridal couple were just this minute leaving, headed for the Register Office, to a chorus of 'Good luck!' and 'Congratulations' from the onlookers. A cluster of people went trooping out along with them; folk who'd obviously been hanging around only to witness any further developments – fortunate for her, because there was no one left in the queue now, save the woman who'd been talking to her, who offered to let her go ahead.

'Thanks so much,' Primrose smiled. 'And thank you for telling me the story. It's certainly a drama!'

'Well, this place must see all human life. *And* death,' the woman added, with a grin. 'There's this bloke I know at work who went and left his dad's ashes on a number twenty-four bus. You'd think he'd be more careful, especially as they were in a proper fancy urn, not just a plastic bag or something.'

'And did he get them back?' asked Primrose, feeling less guilty now about her own carelessness. Arthur's ashes were in pride of place on the mantelpiece. Why scatter them, when she could keep him safe at home?

'Yes thank God! There was a plaque on them, engraved with the old boy's name, and I suppose that must have helped.'

Primrose felt very nearly happy, what with this long, engaging chat and the free diversion of the bridal couple, not to mention her precious bag about to be returned. And, once she had finally paid the fee for the restoration of her property – a mere four pounds for a bag worth hundreds – she left the Lost Property Office with a definite spring in her step.

On the tube back, she kept the tightest hold of her booty, first stowing the house-keys deep inside her pocket, so they'd be instantly at hand and she wouldn't have to fumble in the recesses of her bag. She'd had a new set cut, of course, but she preferred these original ones, because the heart-shaped key-ring (now tarnished, sadly) had been a gift from Arthur. She sat, marvelling at the fact that someone had actually resisted the temptation of stealing such a valuable bag, proving that people *were* decent, as Mr Mohammed Ahmed said. She had seen him on duty at the station, several times during the last three weeks, and he had not only recognized her but seemed happy to converse. She now knew the name of his wife (Omera) and his two sons (Faisal and Bashir), and had even seen their photos on his mobile. Omera looked a lovely young lady – beautiful and gentle, with a bashful smile and huge black eyes.

However, when she came through the gates on this occasion, he failed to notice her – although hardly any wonder, since he was dealing with a group of aggressive lads, all shouting and shaking their fists. So she left the station and made straight for Page Green Common, shocked to see Arthur's tree now completely bare. On her previous visit, only forty-eight hours ago, it still had a thin cladding of leaves, but today its naked branches were silhouetted against the leaden sky, and dead brown leaves were heaped in fragile drifts beneath the trunk.

'Arthur, my sweet,' she whispered and, once he'd registered her presence, she told him about the bridal couple and how their mutual devotion had reminded her of her own wedding, despite its very different setting in a peaceful little country church. Listening intently, she seemed to hear his reply in a sudden crackling and rustling from the moving carpet of brittle leaves, as they were bullied by the wind. He was telling her that not even his death could negate their marriage or their solid and unshakeable bond and, in light of that consoling fact, the loss of mere possessions scarcely mattered. So, even if Violet's bag had failed to turn up, she would still be rich and blessed, because she and Arthur had each other.

She stood stock-still as a sudden thought occurred to her: did she even *need* possessions, now that she'd reached so advanced an age? After all, they could be as much a source of grief and worry as of pride and pleasure. Perhaps Arthur was trying to tell her that it was time to yield to nature, as these wise old trees were doing; to accept being bare and denuded, in the hope of a re-greening in the spring. She had long ago lost her belief in any conventional sort of heaven, with angels playing harps and God in a long white robe, but, as the years wore on, she had begun to sense the existence of some mysterious realm where leaves were always green, the air invariably warm and mild, and where she could live with her husband for ever, in love and tenderness. And maybe Violet would be there, as well – her dearest friend restored, a greater blessing by far than the return of a mere bag.

Suddenly decisive, she told Arthur she'd be back, before turning on her heel and retracing her steps to the tube, walking urgently, determinedly, despite her clumsy stick and the persistent nagging of the wind. Fortunately, there were no longer any customers distracting Mr Ahmed, who was standing by the automatic gates, with no one else in earshot.

'This is for you,' she said, passing him Violet's bag. 'To thank you for your kindness. I'd like you to give it to your wife.'

His face expressed both astonishment and worry, as if he feared she might have taken leave of her senses. 'No, I couldn't possibly take it, Mrs Simpson. That's a very expensive handbag, by the looks of it.'

'Yes, top quality – I can vouch for that. But I have no more need for it, you see, whereas Mrs Ahmed might find it useful and it should certainly last her a good long time.'

'But you *lost* your bag. I mean, that's how we first got talking. And you've been telling me about it ever since – how distressed you were that it hadn't been found and that you were giving up all hope. So, did someone return it, after all, or is this a different bag?'

It was impossible to explain and, anyway, she didn't want a whole rigmarole of refusals and protestations. 'I'm afraid I can't stop, Mr Ahmed. My husband's waiting for me.'

'Your husband? But I thought you said—'

'Things have changed,' she said.

Nonetheless, he continued to demur, insisting he couldn't take, and would never dream of expecting, any sort of gift for simply doing his duty.

Finally, she was forced to push the bag almost rudely into his hands, shaking her head with such vehemence when he attempted to return it, he looked a little startled. But they could stand arguing for ever, so she had to take a firm line. 'I'm sorry, Mr Ahmed,' she said, in her most resolute tone, 'but I really do have to go.'

And, with that, she turned her back and left the station and, although she *was* a little worried about having seemed brusque or even overbearing, she knew his wife would be delighted and might even understand.

Once out in the street, she headed again for Arthur's tree, feeling strangely lighter without a handbag or possessions.

'Sweetheart,' she whispered, her voice lost in the roar of the traffic, the hiss of the buses' automatic doors, as they opened and shut, disgorging passengers. Yet the noise and the crowds barely registered. She was aware only of her husband's love, cloaking her, awaiting her, enduring for eternity.

'I'm on my way,' she murmured and, despite the dingy High Road and the sleety rain that had just begun to fall, she felt totally suffused with the peace and joy and beauty of her Wedding Day.

BOILED EGGS

'Hey, guess what I read about Prince Charles in the *Mail* today?'
'Haven't a clue.' Neil pulled out into the fast lane, to overtake the erratic elderly driver in front. 'What about him?'

'Well, they said he likes boiled eggs for breakfast, but, instead of having a couple cooked hard or soft, or whatever, he insists on having a whole range of them prepared – one boiled for exactly three minutes, one for three-and-a-half, one for four, one for four and-a-half, *et cetera, et cetera,* just so he can take his pick, according to his whim at the time. I *ask* you! What a spoilt prat!'

'Not necessarily.' Neil checked in the mirror on the elderly driver, in his equally ancient Rover. The traffic ahead was slowing, prompting the old fellow to come up dangerously close. 'Perhaps he's just a perfectionist, or taking a close interest in the eggs from his various farms – seeing how they taste at different degrees of hardness and softness. After all, he *is* passionate about food, not just growing it organically, but making sure every process in the supply-chain is up to the mark.'

Lara gave a non-committal grunt. In her opinion, Charles was a wimp, a bore and a hypocrite, but Neil was clearly more tolerant. In fact, she'd been struck by his basic decency when they'd first met at Carole's party and he'd helped her mop up her spilt drink; even sponged her jacket in the sink to prevent the wine leaving a permanent stain. Of course, the fact he was so much older probably accounted for such thoughtfulness but, already, after just two weeks, she was beginning to get a taste for going out with a guy in his forties. Neil had a proper job as a civil engineer in a big construction firm, and a decent car, and his own two-bedroomed flat, which made her student friends seem rather gauche and shallow in comparison; all, like her, stuck in rented flat-shares in grotty parts of London, and with no transport beyond second-hand bikes.

'I wouldn't mind having minions cook me eggs and wait on me hand and foot,' she said, with a grin, thinking of her messy flatmates who couldn't even be bothered to wash up. 'Mind you, it probably means His Royal Highness would starve if the servants all walked out. I doubt he can boil an egg without a huge amount of help!'

'Maybe not, but he's hardly a slouch when it comes to other things. I mean, he campaigns for the environment, and cares intensely about climate change, and heads a whole raft of charities. In fact, I knew this young guy once, who came from nothing and was going nowhere, but his entire life was changed by a grant from the Prince's Trust. It made all the difference that someone was actually there for him – to give him hope and encouragement and make him feel he wasn't crap.'

So Neil was also an idealist, she mused, feeling slightly guilty that her own energies were focused on herself – her ambition to achieve fame as an actor, rather than leave drama school and spend her life waitressing in Starbucks. To be honest, she didn't give a toss about the environment. She also now regretted her remark about HRH being unable to boil an egg, which seemed a tad hypocritical, when her own culinary skills were nil. Indeed, she couldn't help worrying that, during this weekend away, Neil might be expecting her to cook, or at least to have packed some provisions for supper in the cottage tonight, or tomorrow morning's breakfast. She was so used to eating in the student canteen, or phoning out for takeaways, food-shopping rarely figured in her life, and she'd actually been more concerned with packing the right clothes for a romantic idyll in Devon than with sparing a thought for milk or bread or teabags.

'Shall we stop at the next services and have a bite to eat?' Neil suggested, as if tuning in to her fears.

'Yeah. Great idea!' Thank God she was let off the hook as far as rustling up some Gordon Ramsay creation was concerned, although her worry about cooking was vastly overshadowed by her worry about sex. She barely knew this guy. Admittedly, they'd kissed – and he was a pretty fantastic kisser – but they hadn't taken it any further, so he was blithely unaware of her inadequacies.

She stole another glance at him: his hair so thick it was like a horse's mane and much darker than her mousy crop. And his long, lean legs, emphasized by tight blue jeans, seemed a reproach to her own plumpish, fleshy thighs. Did she measure up in any way, she wondered? Her face and figure were passable, but she didn't have the sort of looks that could inspire the heights of passion or devotion.

'The only problem is,' Neil said, picking up on his previous remark, 'there isn't another service-station till Exeter. The last one was only three miles back.'

'Doesn't matter. I'm enjoying the drive.' In truth, she felt much more at ease in the car than actually arriving and being faced with the reality of going to bed with someone more or less a stranger. It would be horribly embarrassing, at such an early stage, to try to discuss her sexual fears and failings, and, with every mile they travelled, it became increasingly clear that she should have got to know him better before agreeing to this weekend. On the other hand, it had sounded so idyllic, staying in his parents' cliff-top cottage (with his parents safely out of the way, in Provence), and she'd felt an urge to be spontaneous, for once, and just say an impulsive 'yes', instead of being ruled by her usual swarm of insecurities. And, anyway, she yearned for more experience, if only to deepen and inspire her acting, which needed to be fuelled by a full, adventurous life. A weekend with an older man in a sixteenth-century cottage, once inhabited by a notorious pirate, and with wild waves crashing on the strand beneath, would definitely be a change from her normal run-of-the-mill weekends, mugging up on play-scripts or chilling out in the pub.

'Well, we're lucky as regards the traffic. It's surprisingly light, especially for a Friday.' Neil accelerated again, finally throwing off the battered black Rover, which up till now, had been tailing them with obstinate persistence. 'Even with a stop for supper, we should be there before dark. And remember, we're coming up to the longest day, so it'll be light till ten or so. Hey, why don't we celebrate – have a picnic on the beach or something, the night of the summer solstice.'

'Oh, yes – light bonfires and dance naked through the waves!' She longed to be more daring; throw off all her fears and break away from the influence of her mother, who had probably caused them anyway. Her mum lived a confined and conventional existence, stuck in a poky bungalow, and barely able to cope since her husband walked out, five years into the marriage. After his desertion, their life had changed entirely, not just because money was short but because her mother had become cowering and diminished; her only remaining thrill collecting triple points at Tesco's. And she was forever sounding off about the treachery of men; how they couldn't be trusted and never stayed around, so, as the child of such a marriage, she'd vowed, long ago, that, if there was the slightest chance of her partner doing a bunk, she would get in first and be the one who did the leaving.

'Darling, you're turning me on already.' Neil placed his hand on her thigh and began stroking it, suggestively. 'The thought of your body glistening-wet in the moonlight, and your mermaid hair streaming down your back, and your nipples stiffening in the breeze, and….'

Hell, she thought, her apprehension growing with his fantasies. He was bound to be used to the kind of females who gasped and moaned like porn-stars and had breasts so huge they'd need scaffolding to hold them up, rather than a bra, so it would be a definite disappointment to bed a nervous, uptight student, with almost no experience. He might even decide to break off their relationship and return to his wonder-women, whom she imagined having orgasms with such frequency and ease they would qualify for the *Guinness Book of Records*. Appalled by such a humiliating prospect, she shut her eyes and tried to blank out everything except the drone of the engine and the steady, lulling rhythm of the road, broken only by a sudden whoosh, when some speed-fiend hurtled past.

'Please, God,' she prayed – although uncomfortably aware that He probably didn't exist – 'let us *never* arrive. Neil desires me now – which is fabulous – but I want to keep it that way, not have him disillusioned.'

'Oh, Neil! Oh, Christ! It's wonderful.' She collapsed against him, out of breath, heart pounding, body sheened with sweat. His own heart was beating so wildly against her chest, his arms clasped so tight around her, she had lost all sense of where she ended and he began. He didn't speak – no need. If a guy had to ask 'Was it good for *you*?', then patently it hadn't been. But Neil had used his own experience and skill to sweep her far beyond her normal timid boundaries and, for the first time in her life, she'd come *with* a man, at the exact same moment.

She lay luxuriating, her face against his neck, their legs entwined, savouring the sense of union, completion. She loved this man, because, by some magical alchemy, he had refashioned her muted, meagre self into a exuberant, full-blooded woman. And, suddenly, the lines she'd spoken on stage last month, playing the lead in the student production of *Romeo and Juliet*, became authentic and alive, as if only now did she fully comprehend them.

My bounty is as endless as the sea,
My love as deep; the more I give to thee,
The more I have, for both are infinite.

Words like 'infinite' and 'endless' were totally correct. Indeed, all the erotic poetry she'd ever read was imbued with new depth and truth through Neil's miraculous powers. Even the reference to the sea was apt, because it was prowling underneath their window, the insistent waves softly breaking, breaking, breaking on the shore: the soundtrack to their lovemaking.

'Sleepy?' he asked.

'No, excited still. I'm on such a high, I can't come down!'

In response, he clamped his mouth against hers, as if her very words had ignited him again. Could he really recover so quickly, repeat that amazing performance? It must be way past midnight by now – except there *was* no time in this new realm; no norms, no rules, no limitations, nothing to stop them making love all night, the whole weekend, all week, all month, for ever.

'Neil, are you awake?' she whispered, gently disentangling her body from his slumped and solid form.

His only reply was to turn over on his stomach, to shield his eyes from the eager morning light nudging through the window. She had deliberately left the curtains open, so she could watch the skittish moon flirt in and out of the clouds, and observe the different shades in the sky, as it slowly lightened from black to charcoal to bruise-grey to silvery-pink. Too hyped up to sleep much, she had simply lain exulting in this whole transformative experience, staying in the most romantic place on earth, with the most sensational man she had ever met.

Yet, far from feeling tired, she was so energized, she wanted to slither down the cliff-face and race along the beach, or take off like a seagull and soar across to France. It would be unfair to wake poor Neil, though, since his job was so demanding, he was forced to rely on weekends to catch up on his sleep. When, at getting on for 3 a.m., he'd finally collapsed, exhausted, he'd said he hoped she wouldn't mind, but he just had to have a lie-in this morning and had no intention of stirring before eleven.

However, it was impossible for *her* to lie still any longer, let alone return to sleep. So, with the utmost caution, she eased herself out of bed, gathered up her clothes, which he'd peeled off last night in a thrillingly sensuous manner, and took them into the bathroom. There, she quickly washed and dressed, then crept downstairs and left a hastily scribbled note on the table, explaining she had gone out for a walk. And, not stopping for a drink, or for her jacket, she bounded out of the front door, closing it so carefully it made not the slightest sound. But, as soon as she was out of earshot, she skittered along the winding road that led down from the cliff-top, relishing the fresh morning smells of sea and grass and gorse. The place seemed deserted, apart from the gulls wheeling overhead, so it was easy to pretend that she'd just bought this whole wide stretch of cliff and now owned it as her private possession, sacred to her and Neil. She would ban all other visitors, and even his parents would have to give up all claim to their cottage and stay indefinitely in Provence.

Once she reached level ground, she ran still faster; the sun warm against her face now, the wind tousling her hair into crazy disarray. She had no idea where she was headed; she just needed to be on the move, like everything else around her. Tall, feathery grasses were rippling in the wind; clouds scudding across the sky; ungainly cormorants skimming the waves; the waves themselves frothing and flailing on the sand.

Careering on, she was almost disappointed to see houses, pavements, lamp-posts – boring, townie things that had no place near a wild, untrammelled ocean. She was about to turn round and go back, when she spotted a small general store, its windows plastered with special offers for sausages and coffee, fish fingers, Fairy Liquid. She skidded to a halt, an idea taking root in her head. The idea needed money, and she'd dashed out without her bag or purse, but she always kept a spare tenner in the back pocket of her jeans, which would come in very handy right at present.

Elated, she sailed into the shop, smiling at the thought of laying on a little surprise for her incredible new man.

She surveyed the table with definite satisfaction. The blue-and-white-checked tablecloth set off the vase of flowers, also mostly blue. She'd found them growing wild on the cliff-top and picked a few of the tiny, fragile blooms. Back in the cottage, she'd unearthed some poppy patterned crockery from the bottom kitchen-cupboard; laid out plates and mugs and egg-cups, and a large ceramic bowl that now held an array of fresh fruit. Of course, she'd had to think very carefully before deciding what to buy, as a tenner would hardly stretch to a feast, but Neil's parents already had the basics in their larder – tea, coffee, marmalade, cereal, milk and sugar – so she'd been free to use her money for the best organic eggs, a fresh, crusty loaf and slab of butter, and a good selection of grapes, nectarines and plums.

Everything was ready now, except the eggs themselves. But, since the whole point of this breakfast was that each should be boiled for a different length of time – one for exactly three minutes, one for three-and-a-half, one for four, and so on – she decided she'd better wake Neil before she actually cooked them. If he took a while getting up, it would ruin her plan of making him a genuine 'Prince Charles' breakfast.

First checking it was gone eleven, she ran upstairs and tapped on the bedroom door, about to announce herself as His Royal Highness's personal valet, summoning him to his favourite royal repast.

No answer. He was probably so deeply asleep it would take more than a knock to rouse him, so she breezed into the room, only to stop dead. The bed was empty, the duvet flung back. He must be in the bathroom – although strange she hadn't heard him, since it was directly over the kitchen and the pipes made a gurgling noise.

But he wasn't there, nor in the second bedroom, so she catapulted downstairs again to check the lounge – no one – then zoomed out of the back door and surveyed the small cliff-top garden and the expanse of land beyond. Not a sign of him.

Only when she walked round to the front of the cottage did she notice that the car had gone, which was definitely peculiar, since he'd told her last night that he'd done quite enough driving for one short weekend and had no intention of getting in the car again until it was time for them to leave on Sunday. There was no *need* to drive, he'd said, with the shop so close and the village less than half a mile away, boasting a variety of pubs, all serving excellent food. In fact, they'd both agreed that a relaxed weekend – strolling, lazing, making love – would be infinitely preferable to getting stuck in traffic on polluted, tourist-clogged roads. So where the hell had he gone? And why had he got up earlier than he said, when he'd been adamant about sleeping late?

'Neil!' she called. 'Where *are* you?'

The sound echoed back, as if mocking her, so she darted back inside to grab her phone. But, when she dialled his number, she found his mobile was switched off. Why, for heaven's sake? And couldn't he have left a note, explaining where he'd gone? He must have seen *her* note, so surely he would reciprocate – unless, of course, he was deliberately trying to avoid her.

She rang again – still nothing. And, suddenly, her mother's voice was chiming in her head. 'You can't trust older men. They're bound to let you down.' Her father had been much older than her mum, which, she claimed, had made him selfish, unpredictable and arrogant. So was Neil repeating the pattern, proving her mother right?

No, that was plain ridiculous. Why should he have left her when things had gone so well? Except perhaps they hadn't – in *his* view. She'd been so full of her own preening little triumph, she had hardly spared a thought for how it might have seemed to him. All along, she'd feared he'd find her tepid, even boring, but it could have been the opposite: he regarded her as greedy and voracious, focused on her selfish pleasure, taking rather than giving. Or perhaps she'd been too demanding, urging him on and on, regardless of the fact he had put in five hours' driving, after a long, pressured day on-site, whereas *her* only pressures had been whether to paint her nails purple or puce-pink, or wear her hair loose or in a bandeau.

And she'd been greedy, too, in the motorway café, ordering loads of food and gobbling it too fast, with no concern for what *he* was eating, no offer of titbits from her overloaded plate. So maybe, in the cold clear light of morning, he'd concluded he was better off without her. There was also the matter of his high ideals – those very issues they'd been discussing over supper. She had made no real attempt to disguise her lack of interest in river pollution or sustainable farming, so he was bound to judge her harshly, as someone wrapped up in herself, with no zeal for improving the world.

Phone in hand, she again ventured outside and started prowling round and round the cottage, from front to back, from front to back, keeping a careful watch for him; ears straining to hear his car or voice – a futile exercise, because there was no sound of anything except the restless sea. She also kept a constant check on the time. He'd been gone so long, he couldn't merely have driven to the village and, if for some unknown reason, he'd popped to the shop by car, she would have met him on her way back, a good three-quarters of an hour ago. However, she couldn't clock-watch all morning, or stay out here indefinitely walking in endless circles and fruitlessly phoning every few minutes. So she forced herself to return to the house and try to get a grip, simply trusting he'd be back.

But, once in the lounge, she was unable to relax, or read, or even sit still, so she resumed her nervous pacing; this time up and down the room, although still trying to reassure herself that, in another few moments, he would sail in through the door, with some simple explanation for his sudden disappearance. Yet unsettling, frightening memories began stirring in her mind, of that nightmare Saturday when her father had walked out in the same sudden, inexplicable manner. Despite being only four at the time, she could still recall her mother's grief and shock, and the black, choking cloud it cast upon the house; her mum no longer able to cook or clean, only to sob and storm.

Another thing that struck her with a chill was her growing realization that she knew scarily little about Neil's character or background. He was actually just a pick-up, someone she'd happened to meet at a party. Even Carole, the party hostess, had seemed vague about his identity. 'I don't know who you mean, Lara. I suspect he was just a gate-crasher. But what the hell? The more the merrier!'

They'd laughed about it at the time, but now a surge of apprehension began prickling down her spine. He might be a total neurotic who derived his kicks from ensnaring women, only to leave them in the lurch. Granted, he'd been decent enough at the party, mopping up the wine-stain, but that could have been a ploy, a deliberate ruse to gain her trust. Just as all the spiel about climate-change and human rights might be a clever smokescreen to present himself in a favourable light. One read about men like that; men who could charm and flatter before wrenching women's lives apart – her own father, for example, at least according to her mum. Or Neil might be a downright sadist, a woman-hater, with an innate desire to punish the entire female sex. Perhaps he too, had been burdened with an unbalanced, bitter mother, who had perverted his thinking from an early, impressionable age.

Her guilt was giving way to anger. How dare he treat her like that, or pose as a friend of Carole, when he was an imposter, an intruder? Her mother was right – you couldn't trust any man. In fact, when she thought back to her first boyfriend, Ben, he, too, had dumped her, refusing to discuss their relationship in person, but cravenly resorting to a brief, insulting text. Neil was probably equally unwilling to face the hassle of long-winded explanations, or the risk of tears and arguments, so preferred simply to push off. How mortifying – indeed maddening – that, having always resolved to be the first to leave, fate had forced her to break that vow, not just once but twice. Anyway, how could she leave in this present situation: 200-odd miles from London, with no means of transport and no station within reach? She was trapped here, in effect, unless she phoned for a taxi to the station, which would more or less clean her out.

As she passed the sofa in her frantic circling, she slammed her fists against its smugly solid, green-plush back, taking out her fury on a dull, inanimate object, because she couldn't lash out at Neil.

But, just at that moment, she heard a noise – a car coming up the cliff-road and, as she dashed to the window, she saw Neil's sleek grey Citroën carefully nosing its way along the narrow, winding track. Her relief was overwhelming, yet it couldn't suppress the churning seethe of all her former emotions: anger, resentment, repugnance, indignation. Her first instinct was to hide, unable to face him in such an agitated state. But he had come into the cottage now and was calling out excitedly, ignoring the fact that he had thrown her into a turmoil of panic, grief and rage.

'Lara!' he called, again. 'I'm in the kitchen. Come and see what I've got!'

She forced herself to move, although her body was so tense, every step required effort.

'Look!' he crowed, holding up a string of fish – revolting-looking, dead things, with bloodied gills, glazed eyes.

'Three fat mackerel! That's quite a catch! I went out specially so I could surprise you with a fresh fish breakfast. They're delicious fried in butter.'

Her smile felt false and forced. She should be overjoyed that his absence had been purely for her sake – a desire to please and surprise her, with absolutely no intention to abandon or betray her.

'I used my father's rod. He taught me to fish when I was a kid of only ten. There's this dirty great rock a mile or so away, jutting out into the sea. The water's really deep there and the fish come in from the Atlantic and swarm past Berry Head. I've even seen a whale-shark in that spot, and porpoises by the dozen.'

His excitement was patent, but she felt only dejection. Admittedly, she wasn't keen on fish – and angling seemed cruel anyway – but what really hurt was that he had spoiled her own surprise. How could 'Prince Charles' eggs compare with fresh-caught mackerel; the humble village shop with a deep and dangerous ocean?

'What's wrong?' he asked, picking up on her mood, at last.

'Oh, nothing …' she said, forcing another smile. 'I was just a bit worried about where you'd gone. I kept ringing you and texting and—'

'I'm sorry, darling. I had to turn off my phone because there were other anglers on the rock and they hate any sort of noise. It disturbs their concentration, you see.'

'Well, couldn't you have left a note, at least?'

'I'm sorry,' he repeated. 'I suppose I was so excited about cooking you a special breakfast, I just went tearing off without a thought.'

Instead of reproaches, she should be hugging him and thanking him. He loved her, was concerned about her, had sacrificed his lie-in to lay on a surprise. Yet there was an aching sort of hollow in her heart – a hollow where her father should have been. And the triumphantly laid table and meticulously timed eggs now seemed stupid, childish, a waste of time and money. In any case, she had lost her appetite.

'Well, all this talk of breakfast is making me feel peckish and, anyway, it's getting late, so I'd better gut these fish.' He took them over to the sink and she watched in horror as he picked up each in turn, sliced off its head with a brutal-looking knife, slit open its slimy belly and yanked out long, repugnant strings of bloody entrails.

'Do you prefer hard roe or soft, Lara? I have two hard here and one soft.'

'If you really want to know, I've never eaten roe in my life. I'm not even sure what it is.' If he thought her ignorant, who cared?

'It's the eggs of the fish – you know, like caviar.'

No, she didn't know. Fish fingers had been more common in her life than any posh or pricy foods.

'It comes in all sorts of colours. This one's pinkish-red but, in other species, the roe can be black, white, yellow or bluey-grey.'

With a disgusting sort of plop, he transferred the squelchy, glutinous mass into a plastic pot. She averted her eyes in revulsion. The roes would stink out the kitchen, pollute her 'Prince Charles' eggs – although the eggs were clearly superfluous. He would have probably spurned them, in any case, if she had gone through the whole rigmarole of cooking them for different lengths of time. In fact, it was beginning to strike her how little she and Neil had in common – no shared taste in food, no concern for similar interests. He might agonize over sustainable farming but, when it came to cruelty – cruelty to fish *and* women – he couldn't give a damn. As he began washing the fish under the kitchen tap, the water ran blood-red, and that somehow seemed significant.

'If you want to be more specific,' he said, breaking off for a moment to explain, 'soft roe is the sperm of a male fish, and hard roe is the spawn of a female. What happens is that the females lay their eggs in the river or the sea, then the males ejaculate on top, and their sperm fertilizes the eggs, right there in the water.'

Frankly, it felt insulting that he could talk so dispassionately about sperm and ejaculation, and about males and females mating, with no reference to their sex last night, nor any sign that he desired her still. It hadn't escaped her notice that, since he'd come in, he'd made no attempt whatever to kiss or touch or caress her, so, exactly as she'd feared, he'd obviously lost all sexual interest and it would only be a matter to time before he dropped her altogether. Yet, *she* was the one who had vowed to be the first to leave in any doomed entanglement, so she was honour-bound to go – go *now*, this minute, not allow him to soft-soap her with lying, weasel-words, or poison her with a breakfast of fried male sperm. OK, she couldn't afford a taxi, but if she died of exhaustion walking untold miles to the station, even that was preferable to ending up like her mother, being unceremoniously dumped.

Turning briskly on her heel, she stalked out of the kitchen and out through the still open front door. And began to run full-pelt, not along the road, as earlier, but down the rocky, tussocky cliff-face – dangerously, precipitately, not caring if she tripped and broke her neck. Everything was already broken, and she was weeping for that brokenness, and for her own rigidity and folly and sickening self-destructiveness, weeping, above all, for her unknown, uncaring father, her lost, aborted childhood.

YEW

'You ought to celebrate, Sarah, not beat yourself up about it. If you want my honest opinion, you're well rid of him, in any case.'

No, she didn't want Pat's opinion; nor was it 'honest', since Pat had taken a strong, irrational dislike to Daniel, the very instant the two had met. She held her peace, however, and took out her annoyance on her espresso, savagely stirring in an overdose of sugar, until spurts of hot black liquid overflowed the cup.

'You're right, Pat,' Avril chipped in. 'When an ex gets remarried, the best thing to do is show you don't give a monkey's. When Simon tied the knot again, I took myself on a day-trip to Paris, got sozzled on champagne and revelled in my freedom.'

'Yes, one of the girls at work did much the same,' Pat remarked, between mouthfuls of her cheesecake, 'except *she* went all the way to California on the day of her ex's wedding, hired an open-top sports car and drove along Highway 120, singing at the top of her voice. She refused to feel sorry for herself, or envy the new wife.'

Meaning *I* do both, Sarah didn't say, taking a gulp of her scalding coffee. At least the pain of a burned mouth helped control her irritation. Didn't these so-called friends realize she still loved Daniel, body, heart and soul, and thus detested his new bride-to-be? The very thought of their wedding made her sick with grief and jealousy, and the fact of Clare and Chloe being bridesmaids only complicated things still more. She wouldn't dream of spoiling her daughters' excitement, prompted largely by their flamboyant bridesmaids' dresses and the thrill of their first flight. The only grain of comfort in the whole galling affair was that, thanks to Amanda, she didn't have to accompany them to Italy. Amanda, ten years older than Daniel, was completely different in temperament from her exuberant, extravagant, mercurial, moody brother – a boon on this occasion, since the calm and capable woman had offered to chaperone the girls and act as stand-in mother.

'Seriously, love,' Avril said, putting a hand on Sarah's arm, 'the last thing you should do is mope around at home. I'm free that particular Saturday, so why don't you and I book ourselves in for a Pamper Day at the spa – have the whole works: massage, facial, manicure...?'

'It's sweet of you, Avril, but I'd actually prefer just to spend the day in the garden, clearing up the fallen leaves and having a good old bonfire. That'll be as therapeutic as anything.'

'Sounds thrilling!' Pat said, sardonically. 'But look, if you change your mind, or don't fancy Avril's spa-day, give *me* a ring, OK? I can't promise Highway 120, but I'll certainly lay on some sort of diversion to keep your mind off Daniel.'

'Thanks, both of you. I appreciate it.' It was a physical and mental impossibility to keep her mind off Daniel. He had been her life, her lodestar and – so she'd thought until fifteen months ago – her future. It was different for Pat and Avril; both long-divorced and childless and seeming positively to relish being free to do exactly what they chose and embark on wild affairs. As a newly single parent, her life was more constrained, nor could she even contemplate sleeping with any man but Daniel.

'Well, I'd better make a move,' she said, extracting a note from her purse, to pay for her two coffees. 'The girls are with their grandma and she hates me to be late.' Granny Taylor, although not, in fact, particularly fierce, was as good an excuse as any. She could hardly admit her urge to escape this crowded, claustrophobic café and especially the din from the adjoining table, where a group of women kept breaking into peals of raucous laughter. Since the divorce, laughing seemed unwarranted – indeed, very nearly blasphemous.

Pat and Avril were clearly in no hurry to leave and, once they had waved her off, she glanced back over her shoulder to see them already deep in conversation – discussing her, maybe: how ridiculously fixated she was on her shit of an ex-husband and totally blind to his deficiencies. Not true. It was simply that his deficiencies were out-weighed by his good points: his vivacity and ebullience, his thirst for knowledge of every kind, and sheer enthusiasm for life – infectious qualities, which, from the age of eighteen, when he'd first erupted into her life, had kept her buoyant and inspired, if sometimes reeling. Without him, she was flat champagne, tepid coffee, stale cake, soggy toast.

Clare and Chloe had, at last, stopped calling out for drinks of water, or yet more bedtime stories, or a continuation of their discussion over supper as to whether witches and wizards actually existed. After a final pause outside their bedroom door, she trailed downstairs and poured herself a glass of wine. The sofa still felt achingly empty without Daniel's bulk and solidity pressing against her side – a big man, in every sense. The sofa bore his traces: a cigarette-burn on one chintzy arm; a star-shaped beer-stain on the seat and, along the back, a faint grease-mark from his mane of irrepressible black hair. Stains and holes and grease marks had become as precious in her mind as his cache of love-letters and the romantic inscription on her wedding ring – a ring she refused to remove, whatever her present status as discarded, superseded wife. She even missed his habit of purloining most of the duvet, leaving her chilly and uncovered, or of wolfing the whole huge chunk of cheese she had bought to last a week. They were simply part of his endearing greed; the way he regarded life as a tuckbox or a treasure-chest to be raided and plundered at need. Tragically, that treasure chest now included Gabriella: impossibly young, exotically blonde and, from the moment she had first encountered Daniel, set relentlessly on being the next Mrs Langham, whatever the impediments in her path.

She banged her glass down on the coffee-table, imagining she was punching Gabriella's gorgeous face. Yet, as the mother of two daughters, she had to retain her dignity; not warp their young minds by exposing them to ugly scenes. It was imperative to prise her thoughts from the nuptials, as they approached nearer every day. Not easy, when the wedding photographs seemed already to have been taken and were now displayed in full colour in her mind: the radiant bride clamped mouth-to-mouth with the besotted groom; the spiteful Sienese sun daring to shine all day, and the two enchanting bridesmaids becoming increasingly sparky and kittenish at all the extra attention from their new Italian relations....

'Enough!' she said, out loud, striding to the window and staring out at the murky darkness of the garden. No, she couldn't spend the wedding day placidly incinerating dead brown autumn leaves, whilst longing to fling her rival on the bonfire and burn her to a satisfying crisp. Vindictiveness was foul and self-defeating. Better far to work out a survival plan and stick to it religiously – not massages and manicures, or extravagant trips to Paris, but some activity or project that would allow her to lay claim to part of Daniel's vital essence, and to solemnize a past memory that couldn't be erased, or shared with the new upstart.

As she stood pondering the matter, the silhouettes of trees began to take blurry shape against the sombre, starless sky and, all at once, an idea sprang to mind. It wouldn't cost much in terms of cash or effort, nor would it involve Avril, Pat, or any of her other friends, who might insist that she be positive and impossibly upbeat. Instead, it would be solitary, peaceful and allow her to grieve rather than to celebrate, yet still, she hoped, be ultimately consoling.

Two thousand years old, he'd told her, ninety-foot tall, and with a trunk-girth thirteen feet in diameter. She had halved all the figures, allowing for his habitual exaggeration, but now, looking at the tree again, it did seem exceptionally large for a yew and, with its thin, peeling bark and distorted, sagging branches, awesomely old and venerable. All those years ago, he had called their visit here a 'pilgrimage', in which they would make a mystical connection to ages long past, and honour the yew's endurance and resilience. They had been married then a mere eleven months, yet she had already grown used to his all-consuming passions – whether for chess, cheeses, Damien Hirst, performance poetry, Wittgenstein or, in this particular case, spiritual transformation. Whatever the rapidity with which one craze succeeded another, she never mocked his whims or wearied of his interests. Why should she, when, as his zealous pupil and eager disciple, she was continually learning and growing under his tutelage?

And the yew-tree pilgrimage had remained in her mind as a magical turning-point, because only then had she stopped mourning her miscarriage two months earlier. Daniel had devised a touching ceremony in honour of the lost and much-lamented baby and, as they'd stood within the sheltering tent of branches, he had declaimed an ancient Celtic prayer, in which death was regarded not as final, but more as a kind of transformation. Each end could be a new beginning, the prayer insisted, and she had, in fact, felt renewed and healed, standing in the empty churchyard with no witness but the circling rooks and the sacred yew itself. And, as if to prove Daniel right, she had conceived again, that very weekend and, nine months later, given birth to Chloe.

Remembering both the death and the birth, she gazed up at the dark reaches of the tree, its branches a-flurry with greedy birds gorging on the glistening berries. She hadn't known until he told her that only the female yews had berries, nor how the birds discarded the highly poisonous seeds, before feeding on the harmless scarlet flesh. Poisonous females recalled her to Gabriella, even at this moment walking down the aisle, with innocently traitorous Chloe and Clare holding up her magnificent white train. And, yes, having checked the forecast for Siena, she knew the sun would be shining; the temperature a smug twenty-five degrees. Indeed, even here in England, the weather had surpassed itself, despite it being mid-October. The sun was not just shining, it was veritably gloating, enamelling all the autumn colours, glinting on the cotton-wool clouds in the postcard-perfect blue sky, as if to taunt her with a snapshot of the splendiferously radiant wedding day in Gabriella's home town. Yet, if nature had any pity, Siena, far from basking in sultry heat, should be ravaged by a storm: thunderclaps drowning out the wedding march, vindictive hail-showers stinging and slashing the bride's young, flawless face.

She turned on her heel, stalked away from the yew and began stomping round the churchyard, kicking out at the disrespectful weeds choking many of the gravestones. All too easy to deny death, when corpses clogged the ground here – mouldering flesh, whitening bones, loving couples separated: one deceased, one flourishing. It seemed bitterly appropriate that male and female yews were separate; only the male trees producing pollen, only the females bearing berries. Weren't males and females always separate, whatever the sentimental tosh about twin souls, or lifelong unions, or flesh of one flesh? Daniel had taught her the word 'dioecious' – one she'd never heard and couldn't spell, but which came from the Greek and meant, literally, 'two households'. Neither of them had dreamed that, one day, there *would* be two households, separate and apart; their daughters forced to switch between them, with two homes in two different countries, even two mothers.

No, she thought, with a new lightning-flash of fury, Gabriella would never be a mother to the girls – except how could anyone prevent them, young and impressionable as they were, being tempted and seduced by presents, treats and frequent plane trips to Siena? That huge extended Italian family – a whole tribe of clucking aunties, grannies, cousins – were bound to indulge the pair in extravagant, unusual ways she had no chance of rivalling.

Her anger and the sunshine were making her uncomfortably hot, so she followed the path back to the church, pushed the heavy oak door and slipped inside, to be immediately enveloped by the cool breath of ancient stone. As she inhaled the faint, curdled smells of lilies, must and candlewax, a sense of peace and timelessness began gradually to calm her vituperative mood. Colours from the stained-glass windows were reflected on the flagstone floor like stone embroidery, and the highly polished brass altar-rails gleamed against the dull wood of the pews. Instinctively, she closed her eyes, longing, all at once, to have the comfort of a deity, some kindly Father-God who could kiss her better and make everything all right. She remembered visiting a church in Rome, on honeymoon with Daniel, and seeing hundreds of petitions left by trusting pilgrims beside a statue of the Virgin Mary, begging for babies, cures, interventions, miracles. Even then, she had envied those with faith, the resources they could call on, the supernatural powers to reverse sterility or terminal disease or the break-up of a marriage.

People even left petitions tied to yew trees, so Daniel had informed her, when, just the following year, they made their pilgrimage to this very spot. She had dismissed the notion as empty superstition, appropriate for credulous Celts, or ardent early Christians, but not for twenty-first century agnostics with a rigorous cast of mind. Now, however, some irrational, intuitive part of her yearned to believe in Somebody or Something that could offer help from some mysterious realm – help that would far surpass the Positive Thinking pep-talks supplied by her crass friends.

On a sudden impulse, she rummaged in her bag, withdrew her Filofax and tore out a clean white page. Then, frowning in concentration, she tried to compose an appropriate petition. No use begging for Daniel's return, or for her broken marriage to be magically repaired. Whatever the yew tree's powers, it could hardly work outright miracles, so wouldn't it be better to beg simply for the courage to endure? She owed it to Chloe and Clare not to be bitter and resentful, even to welcome a new addition to the family, should Gabriella produce her own child. Such an outcome would call for strength and resilience way beyond her normal reserves, yet the yew, as the most resilient of trees, surely provided the perfect exemplar. It had stood firm throughout the ages, even if completely hollow inside – as *she* was, too, since the divorce had hollowed out her vital inner sap – yet still able to survive centuries of storms.

Leaning back against the pew, she continued her attempt to find some apposite words, whilst also struggling to silence the doubting, derisory voices in her head. If Daniel were here, he would urge her to respect the wisdom of past peoples and religions, rather than mock them for their naïveté. So, when she finally decided on her petition – one for fortitude, forbearance, perseverance, patience – she wrote it out in her neatest and most careful script, as if to signify the importance of the exercise.

Then, page in hand, she ventured out into the still swanking sunshine, dazzled for a moment by the contrast with the cool gloom of the church. Relieved to see the churchyard totally deserted, she made her way back to the yew, moving close in to the trunk this time and allowing the thick foliage to serve as a protection against the glare of the noon daylight and the gimlet-sharpness of her grief. The bark felt scaly and rough-edged beneath her hand, yet, according to Daniel, yew-wood was prized for its toughness and durability, and had been since primitive times. Admittedly, the tree was not a beauty, with its unkempt foliage, asymmetrical shape and air of being worn down by the years, but it was that very weight of years that gave it majesty and nobility, as one of the longest-living plants in the whole world. Her own brief life had impinged on it for a mere fraction of its span. Established here long before her, it would continue aeons afterwards; witnessing in its time great swathes of human history. Didn't all that make it worthy of respect?

Deliberately, she leaned against the trunk, in an effort to absorb some of the tree's own tenacity and stoicism, then folded her frail piece of paper and pushed it deep into a hole in one of the lower branches, trying to mark this important moment with some prayer or invocation.

Embarrassed all at once, she peered behind her, as if Pat and Avril might have somehow tracked her down and, contemptuous of her 'mystic' ritual, were now endeavouring to drag her off to some spa, or spree, or trip on Eurostar. But no one was there at all, no human sound or footstep, only the flutter of birds in the branches, the hoarse squawk of a crow, and a melancholy salvo as the church clock chimed the quarter. She was only imagining the derision and could, if she desired, commit herself, heart and soul, to this otherworldly experience. Indeed, she was already beginning to feel more deeply rooted, less impervious to gales and storms, as if the yew tree's ineffable powers were slowly working a transformation.

She remembered Daniel saying that the earliest yews had survived the great climatic changes of the planet, even thriving in the Ice Age, somehow finding ways to adapt, whatever the adversities. So wasn't that a lesson for her? Her husband had left, their once deathless marriage expired, but those were irreversible facts, so it was time she stopped indulging in vain and futile regret. Of *course* it was a searing loss, and no way could she shrug it off or – God forbid – celebrate it, as her more superficial friends advised. But, having mourned the loss so long, she did now have the option of simply picking up the pieces and quietly moving on.

A squirrel suddenly darted up to the tree but, sensing her presence, sped instantly away with a frantic scurrying of feet. Only then did she notice that the ground beneath the yew was completely bare of vegetation. Clearly, nothing could grow in the shade of this dense tree: no blade of grass, no smallest, slightest plant. As she continued to gaze at the empty, barren patch of brown, she was struck by an analogy with Daniel. He had always been so dominant, no one and nothing could flourish in his shadow. Throughout the years of their marriage, she had been dimmed by his brilliance and dwarfed by his achievements. Forced into the pupil role – even the parasite role on occasion –– she had lived only through his nourishment and obedient to his whim. Yet extraordinary as it seemed, she had never really realized till this moment, let alone resented it. It was as if the yew itself was showing her a revelatory truth: that, if she freed herself

127

from her ex-husband's stifling shade, she might find light and space to be herself.

The notion was a shock, requiring a fundamental rewrite of eleven years of marriage. Perhaps Pat was actually right in criticizing Daniel as highhanded and overbearing. Certainly, she, as wife, hadn't had much chance to develop her own talents or follow her own interests; *his* had always taken precedence, just as *his* decisions had invariably been sacrosanct.

Disoriented by such a shift of viewpoint, she needed time to speculate on who she might become if she removed herself from Daniel's custody and compass and struck out on her own. Would she develop as a person, begin to grow in her own right? As if daring to test the theory, she emerged cautiously from the dark sanctuary of the tree, taking her first hesitant steps from engulfing shadow into air and sunlight. And, as she stood in the full light of day, between the tree and the church-porch, the sun no longer seemed gloating or spiteful, but just a simple fact of nature. She could even see it as a blessing that she had come to this peaceful village on such a benignly mellow day. And, because this was Sussex, not Siena, she had to make a conscious effort to shift her mind from the wedding reception – due to start at any moment – and, instead of feeling excluded and rejected, try to move on, as she'd vowed.

Slowly, she began walking back towards the churchyard gate, suddenly recalling the pub she'd passed when driving through the village an hour or so ago – an attractive-looking, ivy-covered structure, its window-boxes glowing with gold and red chrysanthemums. After a scanty breakfast of tea and toast, her stomach was growling with hunger, so a pub lunch would be welcome before setting out on the long drive home. The prospect made her nervous, though. She never went to pubs on her own, let alone in an unknown place and when feeling so lonely and fragile. Yet couldn't the very fact of her aloneness provide a chance for change; transform the lunch from an ordeal into a small but solid achievement: her first tiny success in learning she was sufficient in herself? And surely it was significant that the pub was called The Rising Sun, because, if the yew had any lesson to impart, it was that, after night, the sun would always rise, and that cold and darkness must simply be endured, because, like all else, they would pass.

What might take longer to accept was that every end, however hard and heart-breaking, could be a new beginning, and that even death might – sometimes and just possibly – herald a rebirth. But, however tough the challenge, she had to make a start on crawling free from the crushing weight of her former Daniel-centric universe. The task would call for wisdom, and what better source of wisdom than adopting the perspective of the dispassionate, judicious, far-seeing, grounded yew.

Determinedly, she turned to face her future and began running down the path towards the car and – she was probably just imagining it – but already there was a strange sensation that she was actually putting out new shoots.

'TA-RA!'

My God! She was actually *there* – at last, in the flesh, just five or six yards from his work-station, miraculously alone at the water-cooler. He had been watching that cooler since Rosie first joined the company, yet never caught a glimpse of her, so far. Not only did they work in different departments, but the firm was so large and anonymous it was easy for a new employee simply to be swallowed up. So why was he sitting paralysed, instead of seizing this one perfect chance to get to know her better?

He smoothed his hair, straightened his tie and got up from his desk – only to sit down again, not daring to cross the tantalizingly short space between them. Yet, only a month ago, he had actually had the audacity to follow her almost home. By a stroke of luck, he had seen her leave the building – although not alone, alas, but arm-in-arm with Harriet from Accounts, which made it impossible to speak to her. He'd shadowed the pair to the tube, keeping a safe distance behind them, then continued down the escalator to the Piccadilly Line and boarded the same train, watching surreptitiously from behind his newspaper as they talked and laughed together. Sadly, Rosie was oblivious of his adoring scrutiny, but, when, eventually, she alighted at Arnos Grove, he remained in close pursuit. However, although Harriet was no longer with her, he hadn't liked to approach her in the street, for fear she might realize he'd been stalking her.

But now there was no need for stalking, because, if he could only pluck up courage, all he had to do was stroll across and join her. Indeed, if he didn't act immediately, there might never be another opportunity, and he'd spend the rest of his life single, loveless, frustrated and alone. So, despite his semolina legs and steam-pistoning heart, he tried to assume a casual, spur-of-the-moment manner, as if he merely needed a cup of water, rather than being absolutely desperate to initiate a relationship with the woman he'd fallen in love with at first glance.

'Hi! You're Rosie, aren't you?' He cleared his throat. A damned great boulder was obstructing it, making his voice ludicrously high and squeaky – hardly a turn-on for any female. 'We were introduced your first day here, but I expect you've forgotten.'

'Not at all. You're Stephen. I remember your red hair.'

Bugger his hair – the subject of countless jibes. No redheaded man was ever taken seriously. And, now, to humiliate him further, he was blushing like a teenager; his crimson face clashing, no doubt, with his curly, carroty mop. That brash and bumptious hair, with its defiant corkscrew curls, continually resisted his attempts to dampen it down. If only *he*, its owner, had as much sheer chutzpah, he would have stormed into Rosie's department weeks and weeks ago and simply carried her off to some island paradise, where they would now be living blissfully as man and wife.

'I was just wondering if' – the boulder in his throat had assumed the dimensions of the Himalayas, making it hard to speak at all – 'if you'd, er, have time for a coffee one day, or maybe lunch or…. There's a nice little place in Earlham Street – inexpensive and simple and….' God! That made him sound mean, as if were trying to ration her. He'd gladly take her to the Ritz, if only she'd say yes; spend the rest of his life paying off the debt.

'I'd love to, Stephen, but I'm afraid things are pretty hectic at the moment. You see, I'm about to move to America.'

'*America?*' he gasped. And he'd considered Arnos Grove to be achingly far.

'Yes, it's terribly exciting! My dad works for Adobe in London, but a fabulous new job came up for him in their Seattle offices, so he and Mum have decided to settle out there permanently. And they're so thrilled with all things American, they suggested that I join them and, if it grabs me, too, start a whole new life there.'

His mouth tried to say, 'Great!' or 'Good luck!' or something appropriately congratulatory. Instead, it was screaming 'Horror', 'Disaster', 'Tragedy', 'Don't *do* this or you'll kill me, Rosie.'

A lame 'Oh', was all he finally managed, although he began

desperately seeking reasons why the plan was fundamentally flawed. 'But how will you find a job?' he demanded. 'I mean, it's tremendously difficult getting a Green Card, or being allowed in to the country at all.' There must be some reason she would be barred from ever setting foot there: she was a terrorist, a drug addict, a Communist, a spy – or, to be absolutely certain, all four at once.

'Oh, Dad's already pulled strings, found me a temporary niche at Adobe. It's very low-key, of course, but I prefer that anyway. I've never been an ambitious type, so it suits me fine doing something small but useful.'

They were gratifyingly alike in that respect. Indeed, the very reason he was attracted to Rosie was her simplicity and naturalness, her soft voice and self-effacing manner, which tallied with her looks. Her face, as rosy as her name, was free of all the gloop and glitz most other females wore; her long, flowing hair not stiff with lacquer, or coloured an unlikely shade. He would be terrified to touch such women, for fear of disarranging their coiffures, or kissing off their lip-gloss or whatever it was they wore. Nor did Rosie go in for the sharp, threatening talons that Harriet seemed to favour, painted shiny blue or bilious green, or even studded with fake rhinestones, and looking nothing like real nails at all. He'd bet his bottom dollar that Rosie had never visited a nail-bar in her life – except he mustn't even *think* of dollars, because they reminded him of her imminent move to America.

'Er, when exactly are you going?'

'Three weeks' time. I've given in my notice and I stop work on the tenth. Then I have a week free before my actual flight. My boss is pissed off, of course, because I've only been here a couple of months, but I just have to take this chance, Stephen. My parents have already found an apartment – a fabulous one, they say, with plenty of room for me!'

Three weeks still offered hope – time enough to make her change her plans, although, first, there was the little matter of getting to know her better. A hundred schemes began flashing through his mind. He must move to Arnos Grove, so he could catch the same train home, bump into her at the local shops, join her at the weekend in some trendy North London café. And, once they were seeing more of each other, he would find the courage to declare his undying love

– the only problem being that he couldn't afford to rent a flat in *any* part of London. Yet, on second thoughts, who needed a flat at all, if Rosie were at hand? He would happily sleep on cardboard, or spend the nights on a park bench, so long as he could see her, touch her, smell her scent, hear her lilting voice.

He noticed, with alarm, that she'd finished her water, put the cup down and was obviously about to leave. He must be bolder, for heaven's sake, stop wobbling like a jelly and arrange some sort of meeting before it was too late. 'Look, I … I totally understand how busy you must be, with all that going on. But how about a quick drink after work?'

Before she could say no, he resorted to a little creative improvisation. 'You see, strangely enough, I'm hoping to move to the States myself. It's always been a dream of mine to work on the West Coast, so if you could spare the time for a brief chat, just to fill me in on job opportunities and immigration procedures and—'

'I'm afraid I know very little about them. My dad's taken care of all that.'

'Just half an hour,' he begged, not caring if he sounded desperate. He *was* desperate. 'There's a Café Nero in Long Acre, very close to your tube station, so at least it wouldn't take you out of your way.' Shit, he thought, he wasn't meant to know where she lived. He blundered on, however, determined to persuade her. 'Is there the slightest chance you could meet me there today – say, at five-forty-five, after work?'

By nature bashful and accommodating, he was acting totally out of character, maybe actually alienating her by coming across as insensitive, even overbearing. But this was a crisis situation and he dared not risk losing the woman who made all other females seem crass, false, lumpen, plain and pushy.

The pause that followed his audacious invitation lasted so long he felt himself grow old. His hair was turning white, his back was sprouting a hump, and he now walked with a stick and wore a hearing-aid.

'OK, Stephen, I guess half an hour won't hurt. And, anyway, it would be great to get to know you better.'

The walking-stick and hearing-aid fell magically away. He was not only young again, he was tall, dark, handsome, courageous and utterly irresistible. 'Fine,' he said, trying to sound as if all he had in mind was just a casual coffee, and not, to use her own phrase, the start of a whole new life.

'I must get back to work, but see you at Café Nero, quarter to six. Ta-ra for now, Stephen.'

'Ta-ra for now' – he savoured her farewell like a sweet, pink puff-ball of candy-floss. But it was those other unforgettable words that were replaying over and over in his head: 'It would be great to get to know you better.' Not only would she get to know him; she would realize they belonged together. Indeed, work was out of the question for the rest of the afternoon, since every shred of his concentration was focused on the challenge of how best to effect that miracle in so worryingly short a time.

'Stephen! What the hell are you doing? Your supper's getting cold.'

He groaned aloud at his mother's wrathful summons. How could cold chips or a congealing lamb chop be of the slightest importance compared to trying to sort out the intricacies of obtaining a visa to America and, more difficult still, a Green Card? He had long ago given up on the official sites – too complex and too technical – and had now resorted to Yahoo, where there were yards and yards of detailed answers to the basic question: 'How hard would it be for a Brit to move to the States?'

Extremely hard, apparently. He could apply to study at an American university – so long as he could lay his hands on $60,000 for the fees. Or he could become a nurse, a special-needs teacher, an Olympic athlete, or a famous actor or rock star, none of which seemed exactly feasible. If he owned a business worth $200,000 or more, America would welcome him with open arms – as it also would if he held at least $1 million in assets and planned to invest the lot in the States. Alternatively, he could discover Jesus, train as a minister of religion and follow his calling in an American church – tricky for an atheist. The final route open to a would-be immigrant was to make a claim for political asylum; one likely to be supported by a private bill from Congress – not a hope in hell.

He had, in fact, given every option due consideration; even toyed with the idea of taking up the guitar and adopting a Mick Jagger look (not easy with his pallid skin, impossible hair and non-existent musical talent), but apart from robbing a couple of banks, the only possible means of entry was marriage to an American citizen. And the more he thought about it, the more satisfyingly simple that solution seemed to be. If Rosie applied for citizenship, then all he would need to do was book a holiday to Seattle and, after a couple of weeks with her, go down on his knees and whip out the engagement ring.

However, he had to face the depressing truth that they were nowhere near the ring stage yet. After a scant half-hour in Café Nero, she had rushed off home, claiming an evening engagement, which had left him devastated; forced to consider the possibility that she already had a boyfriend, or, worse, a live-in partner. Desperately, he had asked around the office, even quizzed the forbidding Harriet, but no one seemed to know, or, if they did, had no intention of telling him. So his number-one priority was to arrange another meeting and somehow bring up the subject. *How* he hadn't yet decided.

What he did know, after those thirty enchanted minutes – and the Café Nero was now analogous to Heaven – was that Rosie was utterly his type: sweet-natured, unaffected, in a word, angelic. They both loved cats and country walks and both supported Spurs. Indeed, he'd been so thrilled to learn more about her, it had proved extremely difficult to keep up the pretence that he merely wanted information about moving to the States, when it was all he could do not to strip off her clothes and make love to her right there. In his mind, he did exactly that, ignoring the disapproval of the waiter to lay her tenderly on the counter and trust that the throbbing gurgle of the espresso machine would muffle their ecstatic cries, as they embarked on the most passionate encounter in the whole history of the world.

'I'm not calling you again, Stephen. If you don't come down this minute, that's the last meal I ever cook for you!'

His mother was now yelling from the bottom of the stairs, drowning out his fantasies. Once he married Rosie, his bewitchingly beautiful wife would never need to summon him to any meal or activity. He would be cemented to her side morning, noon and night – especially night. He had taken her to bed so many times, he now knew every nook and cranny of her body; had sucked her nipples, tongued her breasts, let his mouth move slowly lower, lower, until it penetrated the glorious thicket of her bush....

Another bellow from below. Hastily, he banished Rosie, leaping naked from their dishevelled double bed. 'Sorry, Mum. Just coming!'

But, once at the door, he couldn't resist doubling back for one last look at the screen. *Millions of Americans are being made redundant, so you haven't got a dog's chance of employment, unless you can offer something really, really special.*

Did they have to be so damned depressing? His lowly job as an assistant credit controller in an obscure hire-purchase firm was hardly likely to cut much ice with the American Embassy. And, of course, it was also pretty pathetic to be still living with his parents in a dreary part of suburbia, but he couldn't afford the rent on even a tiny bedsit, let alone the deposit on a house. However, Rosie would inspire him – that he knew as a fact. Once they were together, his earning power would magically increase; he'd be promoted to CEO, manage a vast portfolio of investments, own a string of racehorses, even the odd Picasso or two.

'Stephen, your mother's going bananas!'

His father suddenly erupted into the room. Quick as a flash, Stephen closed down his laptop. The last thing he wanted was his parents getting wind of his immigration plans. His dad, however, glanced from his guilty face to the now-blank screen, looking increasingly suspicious.

'Look here, Stephen,' he said, sounding both accusing and embarrassed, 'your mother and I are beginning to suspect you're watching porn up here. I mean, the hours you've been spending closeted alone of late, and the fact you've just turned off your computer shows you're up to no good. I'm well aware how easy it is to log on to these so-called adult sites, but I need to warn you, son, you could end up as a sex-addict, unable to have any normal relationships.'

'It's *not* porn, Dad, I swear.'

'Well, what is it, then, that's so damned secret, and means you never join us downstairs these days, for your favourite telly programmes?'

'I'm er ... just studying facts and figures – all that sort of stuff.' Those figures were hardly encouraging: a miniscule number of Green Cards issued every year, as against millions of applications.

'Well, all I can say, Stephen, is that you're not the son we used to know and love. You've changed in these last two weeks – and changed for the worse, I'm sorry to say.'

Yes, he thought, dead right. The once mild-mannered, obliging Stephen was now contemplating robbery and perjury – not to mention matricide. But desperate situations required desperate solutions and, one way or another, he intended to live with Rosie in Seattle, whatever extremity it might require.

'If it's any help, Rosie, I could drive you to the airport.' Forget the fact he didn't own a car and that his mother was unlikely to lend him hers – not that a ten-year-old Ford Fiesta was worthy of Rosie anyway. No, he planned to hire a limousine and had already been online to suss out the various options: Mercedes, Bentley, BMW, or, if she fancied something more way-out, a pink stretch limo, or vintage Chrysler in wedding-white. OK, it would cost, but he was cutting down savagely on all other expenses and, in fact, felt secretly relieved that Rosie had opted for coffee over lunch for this, their second meeting.

She hadn't yet responded to his offer and seemed to be playing for time, spooning the chocolate-sprinkled froth from the top of her cappuccino in such a provocative way he longed to *be* that froth, licked by her, consumed by her, gently drifting down to her intimate regions and taking up residence in her delectable stomach. But he was on tenterhooks until she spoke, since his offer of a limousine was really a ruse to discover whether she already had a boyfriend. If that should prove to be the case, then the loathsome fellow would presumably be the one who would take her to the airport, whereas if she accepted his Merc, or Chrysler, or sky-blue-pink Rolls Royce, he could more or less assume he had no serious rival.

'No, I'm sorry, Stephen. It's sweet of you to suggest it, but my parents warned me not to go by car. You see, they hired a cab themselves, but it got bogged down in the most horrendous traffic and they were almost late for their flight. So Dad said I'd be better off catching the Heathrow Express, which takes only fifteen minutes.'

He was still in with a chance. No mention of a boyfriend – yet. 'Well, why don't I come with you anyway, just to help you with your luggage – save you humping heavy cases around?'

'To be honest, I haven't finalized my plans. Admittedly, the Heathrow Express is quick, but it's also jolly expensive, and I've been spending a bomb as it is, on new clothes and stuff for the States.'

I'll pay, he longed to say, but she might think that rather peculiar when they were still only casual acquaintances – well, in her mind, anyway. He was obviously a pathetically slow worker; should have bought the ring by now, or at least dared to hold her hand.

'It also means schlepping out to Paddington and changing tubes and everything. Whereas if I go the whole way by underground, I can simply stay on the Piccadilly Line, *and* save money, too. OK, it's a hell of a trek, but it's actually less hassle.'

'Well, I could still come with you, whichever way you go, and help you with your cases on the tube, or train, or whatever you decide.' A 'hell of a trek' sounded much more promising than a meagre fifteen minutes, and he certainly needed time to move from casual acquaintanceship to throbbing intimacy.

'But why should you bother, Stephen? I mean, it's a drag for you and you hardly know me, anyway.'

Yes, he thought, that was exactly the problem. In four days' time, she'd be 5,000 miles away, so it was imperative to move faster.

Daringly, he reached out for her hand, at precisely the same moment as she picked up her Danish pastry. His fingers closed on sticky icing, resulting in a furious blush. She'd think he was trying to nab her food – all the more humiliating when he had declined a pastry himself, not only on the grounds of cost, but because he'd embarked on a new fitness regime, to get in shape for the wedding. What an incompetent fool he was, if he couldn't even hold her hand without an embarrassing cock-up. Indeed, it hardly boded well for any prospect of a speedy marriage proposal. He was even beginning to hope she'd refuse his offer of accompanying her to Heathrow, since he was bound to disgrace himself, maybe trip on the escalator and drop her cases from top to bottom, or lose her in the crush of people, or—

'Here, have a bite. It's yummy!'

Lord! She was actually moving the Danish pastry towards his mouth, holding it close to his lips, as he bit into the tempting, yielding dough; her beguiling fingers brushing against his chin. This was truly intimacy and, in his mind, he was whooping with such full-throated jubilation they could hear him in John O'Groats.

'And, if you really don't mind coming with me to the airport, it would be a great help. You see, originally, Harriet promised to see me off, but she's broken her ankle, poor thing, and can't travel anywhere, let alone lug cases around. So a nice strong guy like you, Stephen, would be extremely welcome.'

He had eaten a mere morsel of the pastry, yet his whole body was suffused with sweetness because, miracle of miracles, she needed him. And the phrase, 'a nice strong guy' had instantly added a good ten inches to his height and endowed him with the physique of a champion body-builder.

'But, must fly, Stephen! Work's piling up, as usual. Ta-ra for now.'

'Ta-ra for now' had become her signature farewell. the same lilt to her voice, every time she said it, the same radiant, sun-burst smile. And, as he sat on in the café, he, too, was smiling – with exhilaration, excitement, triumph – since he knew in his bones that their journey to Heathrow would prove thrillingly significant.

He stood by the tube-doors, guarding Rosie's adorable fondant-pink cases, but unable to see her for the mass of heads and bodies in the way. Some guy had offered her a seat – little wonder when she looked so fanciable – but his plan to declare his love as he sat beside her, arm around her shoulders, had been, once again, frustrated. He hadn't reckoned with the crowds – a sweaty scrum of people, most lumbered with bulky luggage – nor with the roar of the train, which made it more or less impossible to speak, even had he been sitting close. If only she hadn't chosen August to depart, at the height of the tourist season when every other person in the UK seemed to be fighting their way to Heathrow. And it was such a sweltering day that, although he had larded himself with deodorant and cologne, he feared he might smell of sweat, rather than of alluring musk. Certainly, by the time they reached Terminal 5, he would have disgusting damp patches under his arms and his insolent hair would have long since rebelled against its restraining morning gel.

But all that was nothing compared with the fact that he had got nowhere with a Green Card and was beginning to think it highly unlikely he would ever find employment in the States – unless he offered to do the housework and gardening for Rosie's parents, or worked as their general factotum. He would even beg in the streets, for pity's sake. Whatever the humiliation, he would willingly accept it, so long as it meant he could be near her. OK, in the absence of a ticket or passport, it was hardly practical for him to fly out with her today. Besides, his mother would shit herself with worry if he simply disappeared, rather than joining her and his dad for their usual Friday evening fish pie. And if he absconded from work without giving in his notice, they would never give him a reference, which he might desperately need, if some fairy godmother should suddenly materialize and offer him an opening in a prestigious American firm. He allowed himself the fantasy of becoming the next Bill Gates – not that he craved wealth or power in themselves, only so that he could purchase a huge villa for Rosie in the swankiest part of Seattle, complete with swimming pool, jacuzzi, private gym and menagerie. (She liked guinea pigs, she had told him, as well as cats.)

For God's sake, he muttered, get real. Banish the wildlife and fix your mind on what you're going to say to her, the minute there's a chance. He had less than four hours left before she'd be summoned to the departure lounge and forced to leave him this side of the Atlantic, while she went winging across it to a far-distant alien shore. But before that dreaded moment, he must have made his position absolutely clear: he couldn't live without her and intended to join her in the States in just a matter of weeks. He was, in fact, due for some leave and, although he had originally planned a week's holiday exploring the Yorkshire Dales, there was no reason why he couldn't change it to a fortnight in Seattle, laying siege to Rosie. Well, no reason except the cost: £500 odd against a flagrant £2,000. There were always loan-sharks, of course, or he could even beg his father for help, although it might be rather tricky trying to explain why he was contemplating the hassle of a long-distance flight to a big, anonymous city, when his natural preference was for quiet, rural UK breaks.

He was rambling again, going off the point. Nothing mattered at this juncture save working out the most persuasive formula to win the woman of his dreams. And, however brief the time left to him, he was determined to succeed.

Pinned against the wall by some moronic heavyweight who also happened to be treading on his foot, he couldn't help recalling those lust-inducing movies where couples actually copulated in lifts. Hardly a possibility in this jam-packed Heathrow lift, where the space was so confining he could barely breathe, let alone make glorious love to Rosie. A backpacker's rucksack was digging into his chest – a distraction, at least, from the pain in his foot – and the anguished infant wailing in its space-consuming buggy was setting his already frazzled nerves on edge. Rosie, for her part, seemed unaccountably cheerful, considering they were about to be parted for what seemed like an eternity, but that only heightened his resolve to make his feelings clear as soon as they reached the terminal.

And Terminal 5 proved to be a pleasant surprise: spacious, ultramodern, spankingly clean and also unexpectedly quiet, given the crowds of passengers. He blessed the clever acoustics and the absence of canned muzak, which should make his task just slightly easier. His role at this moment, however, was to take charge of the proceedings, find the check-in desk with the shortest queue and carry the cases over in a capable, confident manner – act, in short, like the authorative husband he hoped soon to become. There would certainly be no problem recalling her flight-number. BA 0049 was steel-etched into his mind; the two zeros symbolizing the void that would open up in his heart once he'd taken his leave of her, however brief their separation proved to be. And the BA stood for the Blistering Agony, Burdensome Affliction and Buttock-clenching Anguish he would endure this evening, as he sat chatting with his parents about his 'hard day at the office', while Rosie sped further away from him with every passing second.

'It's so kind of you, Stephen, to take all this trouble. I'd never have managed without you.'

Not only did she need him, he was now indispensable: a definite advance. In fact, he must focus on the joy of being the person actually seeing her off, instead of on the pain of their temporary parting. He yearned to take her hand as they stood waiting in the queue but, if he let go of the cases, they might be nicked, or fall on her foot, so he contented himself with telling her how much he liked her outfit.

'It cost nine pounds ninety-nine at Primark. Are you sure it doesn't *look* cheap?'

'Absolutely not. I'd have guessed Harrods or Harvey Nicks.' How lucky he was that she didn't mind economizing. If he couldn't afford the Seattle villa, she'd probably be content with a modest one-bedroomed apartment – if they had such things in America. Wasn't everything and everyone supersized out there – another worry on his mind? At five-foot-seven, he couldn't compete with those strapping, broad-shouldered Yanks. Suppose Rosie sat next to one on the plane – a sophisticated fast worker who would nab her there and then, while he was sitting with his mum and dad in Norbiton, shovelling down stewed prunes and custard.

The thought was so appalling, he failed to notice that they had reached the head of the queue, until Rosie tapped him on the arm. 'Stephen, the man's waiting.'

Hastily, he lugged the cases up to the desk, relieved when they were placed on the scales. Her luggage was so damned heavy, he'd been in danger of a hernia.

'Are you travelling, too, sir?' the British Airways clerk enquired.

He was tempted to shout an exuberant 'Yes!', but Rosie got in first. 'No, just me,' she said. But shouldn't she be weeping at the fact, rather than sounding so heartlessly jaunty?

As the cases disappeared along the conveyor-belt, he longed to squeeze inside them and be carried into the baggage-hold, to be reunited with Rosie in Seattle for the start of their new life. Indeed, everyone but him appeared to have a route-map and a destination; only he was adrift and spare. But this was no time for self-pity; he had to move his marriage plan a little closer to reality.

'Right,' he said, authoritatively, once the check-in procedures were complete. 'I think we need a coffee.' There was a Café Nero at one end of the terminal, which was surely both propitious and appropriate, since all their meetings so far had been in some branch or other of the chain.

'Sorry, Stephen, but I'm dying for a pee. Could you hang on a moment?'

'No problem.' He ushered her over to the toilets, glad that he'd mugged up the layout of the terminal last night, and so knew his way around – impressive in her eyes, he hoped. 'See you here in five minutes, OK?'

He had better pop to the gents himself, for a hasty wash-and-brush-up, and to spray himself with Lynx again, which, according to the ads, made women flock in droves – not that he'd noticed in his adult life so far.

Five minutes was barely long enough for any major transforma-tion, but it would be crazy to waste his all-too-brief time with Rosie, so, after exactly four-and-three-quarter, he was outside the toilets waiting for her.

The minutes crept on – and on. What on earth could she be doing? Not reapplying make-up, or varnishing her nails – that simply wasn't Rosie. Maybe, God forbid, she'd been taken ill, or was even now being brainwashed by some female terrorist seeking her help in blowing up a plane.

'Sorry, Stephen. I noticed this dirty great ladder in my tights. I must have caught it on the case or something. Anyway, it meant I had to change them. Fortunately, I had a spare pair in my bag.'

A provocative image of her peeling off her tights and revealing sexy knickers – perhaps with wisps of pubic hair poking out entic-ingly – engulfed him in such extremes of lust, he could barely resist running his bare hands up her thighs. 'Now for our coffee,' he gasped, breathless with the imagined thrill of fingering her luscious flesh.

'Would you mind awfully if we went to Boots and Smiths first? I need to buy some baby-wipes, to freshen up on the plane, and a book to read, and....'

Couldn't she have bought them in advance, or given him a list, so *he* could do her shopping? Boots and Smiths were hardly suit-able locations for a declaration of love, and the shops were at the opposite end of the concourse from the Café Nero, thus thwarting his action-plan.

'Yes, fine,' he said, trying to suppress his annoyance and walking as fast as he dared, since every minute counted. As they continued their quick-march, he glanced up at the departure-boards: flights to every city in Europe, even domestic flights to Edinburgh and Manchester. Why did she have to travel so *far*? He wouldn't need a Green Card to work in Manchester, and it was under five hours by coach, with a fare costing less than a tenner. But he had to face the fact that Rosie had expanded his formerly cramped horizons, so he was duty-bound to follow her to the very ends of the earth, even to the most distant of the planets.

Actually, he couldn't help reflecting that she spent so much time in the shops, they could easily have gone to Uranus and back, while she stood in Boots, dithering over every smallest purchase, and then browsing the books in Smiths.

'These all seem a bit stodgy. Maybe I'll try the "Beach Reads" section.'

He plunged from Uranus into another delicious fantasy: Rosie on the beach in the skimpiest of bikinis, inviting him to unfasten her top and rub sun-cream into her ravishing back. Soon, they were having it off, right there on the golden sands; the gulls competing with her love-cries, and the tempestuous pounding of the breakers matching his own rhythm, as he threshed insistently against her yielding shore.

Only a maddeningly long wait at the till brought him crashing back to reality; the magically secluded cove giving place to a raggle-taggle queue of clod-hopping shoppers, all of whom appeared to be losing their purses or fumbling for their credit cards – with Rosie still stuck in its midst.

Once the 'Beach Read' was finally bagged, after what seemed like half a century, he steered her back across the concourse, determined to be masterful, for once. 'I decided we should revisit our old haunt, the Café Nero.' 'Our old haunt' made them sound an item; a couple who'd had time and opportunity to establish comforting routines.

'I don't really want a coffee, Stephen. I'm a bit hyper as it is, with all the excitement and everything. And, anyway, I don't have that much time.'

No wonder, he all but expostulated, when you've squandered it all on baby-wipes and trashy books. And, as she consulted her watch yet again, a tidal wave of jealousy reared up in his breast. She had never studied his face with as much focus and attention as she lavished on the watch-face – an inimical object maliciously counting down the seconds until they parted.

'In fact, there's no real need for you to hang around. You've been absolutely brilliant and I just can't thank you enough, but now....'

This was rejection pure and simple; ingratitude on a massive scale. 'But it's only ten past one,' he objected, 'and your flight doesn't leave till three.'

'I know, but I'd prefer to go straight through to the departure lounge, so I can look round all the shops.'

This was worse than rejection; this was downright cruelty. How could any shop – Dior, Tiffany's, Cartier, or all three rolled into one – come before his five-star, solid-gold love? 'Surely you can spare ten minutes?' he said, with undisguised pique. 'I mean, I could do with a drink, even if you don't want one. And, anyway, there's, er, something I want to ask you.'

'Can't you ask me now?'

'It's impossible to talk here,' he retorted, although struggling to regain his composure and remain, in her estimation, Mr Calm-and-Kind, 'with all these people milling around.'

They were, indeed, causing an obstruction, having come to a halt in the middle of the concourse, surrounded by passengers with loaded trolleys or oversized pushchairs, and whole clans of Asians complete with grannies, aunties, parents, kids and babes in arms. Thank God, he thought, his own relatives weren't here; his mother dispensing unsolicited advice about diarrhoea or jet-lag; his Granny Walker dribbling and demented, and his embarrassing Aunt Ellen with her peroxided hair and brazen mini-skirts. At least he had Rosie to himself – bar a few hundred strangers, that is. The only problem was she didn't appear to want even another minute of his company.

As a stewardess teetered past in her smart blue uniform and unsuitably high heels, an outrageous plan flashed into his mind. If he kidnapped that woman and all other airline staff, no plane would be able to fly, Rosie would be grounded and he could whisk her off to some sequestered spot, with no danger of temptation in the form of retail therapy. *He* was her therapy, her *raison d'etre*, her only destination, so somehow he must persuade her to fall in with his plan of a romantic *tête-à-tête* in the auspicious Café Nero, leading to a definite commitment on her part.

'If you don't want coffee, why not have a camomile tea or something nice and calming? You won't be late, I promise. I'll keep a very careful eye on the time.' Hardly any need when, once again, she was peering at that hateful watch.

'Oh, all right, Stephen, I'll let you twist my arm.'

Twisting her arm wasn't what he had in mind; her sucking his cock might come a little closer but, at this rate, he'd be lucky if he managed to touch so much as her fingernail.

There was yet another queue at the Café Nero counter and, much to his chagrin, she refused all food, which would have given them much longer for their crucial conversation. Rosie always ate in a slow, unhurried fashion; even a single cake or sandwich taking her ages to consume. To extend their time together, he would have ordered her hundreds of cakes, fifty-dozen sandwiches, twenty tray-fuls of Danish pastries. But she settled for nothing but a miniscule bottle of water, which made his own hot chocolate seem blatant in comparison, topped as it was with an avalanche of frothy, foaming whipped cream. As he took his first sip, he imagined coating every inch of her body with that same sensuous cream, then slowly licking it off, from her neck to her nipples, from her belly to her bush, down the insides of both thighs to her captivating—

'Oh, shit! I've forgotten to ring Harriet and I promised to call her from the airport. She's due any minute now to see the doctor – you know, about her broken ankle, so I'd better phone her right away. You don't mind, do you, Stephen?'

Yes, I do mind, he all but bellowed. They had actually found a table to themselves – a chance to speak, at last – yet, instead of saying an impassioned yes to his marriage proposal, she was already jabbering to her unspeakable friend. And, to make matters worse, the couple at the adjoining table were kissing with such fervour, their mouths seemed literally glued to each other; the man's tongue thrust in so deep, it was probably halfway down his girlfriend's gullet. He *loathed* the couple, not only for showing up his own pusillanimity, but for being such expert kissers. If he tried the same with Rosie, he'd probably bang his teeth against hers, or ignominiously choke, or bite her lip, by mistake, and draw shaming rivers of blood.

Should he simply give up, resign himself to lifelong celibacy and bachelorhood, while she rabbited on to Harriet? It seemed unut-terably humiliating that she clearly had much more to say to some stupid cretin in Accounts than to her future husband and the father of her children. In his mind, those children were already born – four entrancing replicas of Rosie; his own red-haired genes savagely repressed.

'Harriet sends her regards,' Rosie said as, finally, she finished the call, adding with a laugh, 'and she says she's sorry she lumbered you with the chore of seeing me off!'

Wasn't this his chance? He must make it absolutely clear that, far from being a chore, it was the deepest honour and privilege. However, once he had made that declaration in a supremely heart-felt and poetic tone, she simply gave another giggle and said, 'Oh, Stephen, you are quaint!'

'Quaint', for Christ's sake, when there were countless other adjectives he would have given his right arm to hear: sensational, irresistible, hunky, manly, drop-dead-gorgeous.

'Anyway, I really must make a move.' Watch-checking time again. It was all he could do not to wrench that damn watch off her wrist and graft their arms together, so they could live hereafter as mutually worshipping Siamese twins.

'Dad told me to go through Security as soon as possible, not just to buy duty-free and stuff, but to make sure I have plenty of time to find the right gate for my flight.'

He wouldn't know, having never flown in his life – another humiliation, to add to all the rest.

'But I don't want to rush you, Stephen, so why not stay here and finish your drink in peace? Security's not far, so I can easily make my own way now.'

He gulped his drink so fast it burned his mouth, but what was a scalded tongue compared to the horror of being finally defeated? He refused to give up – could still declare his love, even if forced to do so at the very entrance to Security. Rosie, however, seemed so keen to be off, she was already bounding up to a uniformed official who was checking passengers' boarding-cards.

'Rosie!' he yelled, not caring who heard. This was a crisis-point in his life: it was now or never, win or lose, the ecstatic bliss of heaven as against the endless torment of hell.

As she turned to face him, he lowered his voice to a passionate whisper, knowing he had to match his tone to the sheer drama of the moment. 'Darling,' he breathed, throwing caution to the winds and breaking with a lifetime of restraint and inhibition, 'I love you, I adore you, and I know beyond all doubt that you and I belong together. Just say you'll be mine and, whatever it takes, I'll find a way to join you.'

Waving a jaunty hand, she wheeled back again and proceeded along the passage that led to Security – a passage totally out of bounds to him. He stared, open-mouthed, at her retreating back. Obviously, she couldn't have heard. She would never dream of snubbing him so cruelly, or wave a callous goodbye in the middle of his ardent declaration, however great her haste. It was his own stupid fault, of course – he had spoken far too softly, in his usual timorous mumble, so it was imperative to repeat his spiel, or risk eternal separation.

But just as he was drawing breath for a passionate reprise, she suddenly turned back once more. The situation was saved! Clearly, all she had required was a moment or two to formulate her response – something equally fervent and committed.

'Ta-ra!' she carolled, with the usual radiant smile, but he registered, with a stomach churning pang, that, instead of saying Ta-ra for *now*' – her usual phrase for any leave-taking – she had said 'ta-ra', full-stop. Did that mean Ta-ra for ever: *adieu*, not *au revoir*?

No, impossible. She must simply be feeling thunderstruck to realize the depth of his devotion and just needed time to adjust. Any minute now, she would come running back, to tell him she'd been thrown off-guard, but was profoundly thrilled and flattered by his love.

She was, indeed, just breaking into an eager little jog, but – could it be? – yes, it was: *away* from him, not towards. And she was moving so fast he could barely gather his thoughts, as the space between them was swiftly swallowed up. He, though, was blunderingly slow to grasp that, far from re-joining him, she wasn't even looking back – no, not the merest glance – and was now disappearing round the corner, out of sight, lost to him irretrievably.

'Ta-ra,' he repeated, in a hollow, anguished whimper, as the full implications of the phrase gradually sank into his mind: it was ta-ra to his whole future, ta-ra to his hope, his happiness, ta-ra to the whole point and meaning of existence.

With devastating despair – indeed a sense of being truncated – he slunk back to the café, as if to gather up Rosie's traces. Their table was still uncleared, her empty Evian bottle lying on its side. Her hands had touched that bottle, her lips had been clamped around it, so, cradling it with the deepest reverence, he tipped the last few drops of water down his throat, then, leadenly, began retracing his steps towards the underground, pushing the bottle into his trouser pocket.

But, as he stroked its awkward bulge, he suddenly realized, with a jolt, that, having consumed the last of her water, some tiny essence of Rosie was now inside his body. And, with that sustaining thought, the bottle itself seemed no longer a redundant plastic shell, but had become a sacred vessel, his glittering battle-honours for having loved – and lost.

A CUPPA AND A BISCUIT

'Ah, Cecilia, come in, child.'

Cecilia pushed the door a little further open and slunk across the expanse of polished wood, not daring to look up. Her heart was beating so violently, it must have jumped out of her body and be clearly visible on the outside of her chest, like the picture of the Sacred Heart that hung in the antechapel. That scary heart was red and gory, and had a crown of thorns around it and a gash in its side that oozed drops of lurid blood. She could feel the spiky thorns pressing into her own heart; hear the drip of her own blood splattering onto the floor. No girl was summoned to Reverend Mother's presence unless she had committed some serious offence and, although she couldn't recall any crime, she had learned, in her three years at St Botolph's, that you could sin without actually knowing.

'Sit down,' Reverend Mother commanded, and Cecilia perched obediently on the edge of the hard-backed chair. Reverend Mother's chair had a high carved back and padded arms and seemed more like a throne.

'And look at me when I speak to you, child.'

With an effort, Cecilia raised her eyes and met the ice-blue gaze. The nun's face was whitish-grey; her lips greyish-pink and thin. You never saw nuns' hair or legs or bodies. They were just gliding black robes that crept up on you unawares if you had pulled another girl's hair, or picked a leaf from the flowerbed or – worse – an actual flower. Although she hadn't picked anything, or pulled anybody's hair, she suddenly remembered that she *had* wished Mother Jude would drop down dead. It was only for a second and only after Mother Jude had rapped her hard on the knuckles with a cruelly stinging metal ruler. Nonetheless, it was still a terrible sin. And, because the nuns could see into your mind, Reverend Mother was probably going to tell her that, if she didn't go to Confession this minute, she would burn in Hell for ever. A year ago, she'd scorched her arm and the nuns had said that, however bad the pain, it was nothing compared with the flames of Hell, and had explained, in frightening detail, exactly what Eternal Damnation meant. Later, she'd wondered why *people* couldn't be eternal, then her mother wouldn't have died.

'The reason I want to see you, Cecilia, is to discuss the problem of you fainting during Holy Mass. You seem to be doing it more and more often, which causes huge disruption. This week, for example, you've fainted almost every day, so you have to make an effort to put a stop to it.'

Cecilia suppressed a gasp. No one could stop themselves fainting. It just happened automatically. One minute, you were kneeling at the altar-rails, and the next, everything went black and there was a sickening sort of thump and you found yourself flat-out on the floor. And then there was the blank bit, where you couldn't remember anything until you woke up in the infirmary, and that was the most unsettling part of all.

Reverend Mother clasped her hands together. The fingers were long and bony – a bit like claws. 'It means one of the nuns has to miss part of Holy Mass, in order to look after you. And, on top of everything else, Father Mark is finding it extremely embarrassing. Imagine what he must feel like when he's about to place the Host on your tongue, and then you suddenly keel over and cause an obstruction to the other girls trying to come up for Communion.'

'I'm sorry, Reverend Mother, but I don't think I can help it. I don't mean to faint. It just sort of … takes me over.'

'It's a matter of willpower, Cecilia. I suspect you allow your attention to wander and then, of course, it's all too easy to drift into a dreamy state where you're no longer in control. But if you banish all distractions and fix your thoughts on the wonder of the Eucharist – that you're about to receive our Blessed Lord's own precious Body and Blood – I'm sure you'll master what's become a most pernicious habit.'

Cecilia wondered what 'pernicious' meant. It rhymed with 'vicious', so it must be something awful. Actually, she knew that fainting was connected with her mother's death, since she had never fainted in her life until she'd gone to boarding-school, and *that* had only happened because her father couldn't cope on his own with bringing up a daughter. The nuns kept saying her mother was safe with our Blessed Lord in Heaven, which secretly she thought unfair, when our Blessed Lord already had His own mother sitting right beside Him in the sky.

'You need to work on the problem, Cecilia. I can't have the priest incommoded, morning after morning. He's doing us a favour, you know, saying daily Mass for us here in the convent, on top of all his parish work.'

'Yes, Reverend Mother.'

'It's no good just saying, "Yes, Reverend Mother". What I want to hear is that you intend to try your best to change the situation.'

'Yes, I will, Reverend Mother.'

'Right, run along now, child. And I shall be praying for you, of course; asking the Lord to give you the necessary help and strength.'

'Thank you, Reverend Mother.'

Reverend Mother's prayers were more powerful than the other nuns'. Even so, she felt frightfully worried as she walked back along the corridor, since she knew it was impossible to stop that floaty, slipping-away sensation that seemed to come from her body, not her mind. According to the Catechism, bodies were sinful by their very nature, because they felt hungry during Lent when you were meant to be fasting and not even *thinking* of food, or they got fidgety in chapel, where you were supposed to kneel really quiet and still, or they kept making you cry about your mother, instead of being submissive to God's Will.

In fact, she could feel tears pricking even now – not just about her mother, but about the mortifying prospect of what might happen if she fainted again tomorrow. Reverend Mother would say she had no willpower and that she hadn't even tried, and might send her to the Penance Room all day.

All at once, she spotted a black-robed figure at the far end of the corridor and immediately doubled back the way she'd come, keeping close against the wall. She was sobbing really hard now, so if any nun should see her, there'd be more lectures on self-control. She dashed around the corner, then made a hasty escape by slipping through the small green door that led into the garden. The garden was mostly out of bounds, but you were allowed to walk in the rose garden, as long as you said the rosary there. The rosary was Our Lady's special prayer, just as roses were her special flower, so the rose garden was dedicated to her – and the garden as a whole was dedicated to St Phocas, who was the Patron Saint of gardeners.

Cecilia fished her rosary-beads from the pocket of her summer frock and began reciting the Sorrowful Mysteries. Although it was wrong to cry for mothers, it was a sign of true devotion to cry for Christ's Passion and Death. In fact, some of the saints were so affected by Our Blessed Saviour's sufferings, they cried for weeks at a stretch, or even months, non-stop. So, if anyone should see her tears while she was actually saying the rosary, they'd just assume she was really holy. And she might even get a miracle, because scores of miracles were connected with Our Lady of the Rosary, who had appeared to three children in Fatima, one exactly her own age. Our Lady had given the children three secrets, the first of which was a terrifying vision of hell and described thousands of sinners plunged into a pit of fire, shrieking and groaning in agony. And repulsive black demons, misshapen and deformed like hideous beasts from a nightmare, tortured them, for ever, amidst raging flames and choking clouds of smoke.

'Hello, Tuppence! How are you?'

She jumped. The gardener had come up behind her and put his hand on her shoulder. But she wasn't meant to talk to him, because men were dangerous. They were also more special than women, since only men could be popes or bishops or priests, and only boys could serve at the altar, not girls. And men did all the important jobs, like being doctors and dentists and judges, whereas hardly any women worked at all. There were only two things God intended women to do: become a nun and be the Bride of Christ, or marry an ordinary man and have loads of children, to create more souls for Him. She didn't want to do either, because nuns had to shave off all their hair, and giving birth to children was the worst pain imaginable, except for the torments of Hell.

Actually, she hardly saw any men at school, as the only ones around were Father Mark (who wore a dress and didn't count) and this nice, old, smiley gardener, Mr Johnstone. And, even in the holidays, her father was mainly at work, or out, and the auntie who

looked after her – who wasn't really an aunt – didn't have a husband
or a son.

'Why are you crying, Tuppence? What's happened?'

She gave a quick glance round the garden to make sure they were
alone. Surely a few words couldn't hurt? She always felt better when
she talked to Mr Johnstone, partly because he called her Tuppence,
which she much preferred to her real name. Cecilia was a Virgin
Martyr and the Patron Saint of Music, so it was completely the
wrong name for her, since she was useless at music and not brave
enough to be a martyr. St Cecilia had been beheaded by a Roman
soldier and then staggered around for several days, bleeding and
half-dead, because the axe had been too blunt to kill her outright.

'Is it your mum again, poor love?'

'Not just Mummy, but....' Suddenly, the words were pouring out:
the whole complicated story about fainting, and embarrassing the
priest, and making a nun miss part of Holy Mass, and her shameful
lack of self-control.

Mr Johnstone shook his head so hard, the weird floppy hat he
wore fell off, revealing long, untidy hair. 'Tuppence, it's nothing to
do with self-control. It's a very simple problem and all you need to
solve it is a cuppa and a biscuit.'

'How do you mean?'

'Well, you're fainting because your blood sugar's low – which
is hardly any wonder when you young girls don't eat a thing from
early-evening supper to breakfast the next morning, a whole hour
after church. But if you had a cup of nice sweet tea *before* you went
to church, and a few digestive biscuits, there'd be something in your
stomach to give you energy, and then you wouldn't faint.'

She stared at him, profoundly shocked. 'But we're not allowed to
eat or drink before Communion. It's a very serious sin. And, if I did
have a biscuit or something and then received Communion, the Host
could actually choke me or even kill me.'

'That's nonsense, my love. You don't want to believe everything
the Sisters say.'

'My love' was even better than 'Tuppence' and 'poor love' best
of all, because it meant he cared about her. And she really liked his
crinkly blue eyes and soft grey hair, the colour of bonfire-ash, and
the fact he smiled so much (which nuns never did), although, when

he smiled, you could see he'd lost two teeth. And his voice was sort of rough but comforting, like the rough red blanket the ambulance men had wrapped around her mother before they took her to the hospital. Of course, it was wrong of him to tell her that she shouldn't believe what the nuns said but, she had to admit, it gave her rather a thrill.

'Look at it this way, Tuppence – Reverend Mother said you were embarrassing the priest, so you'd be doing Father Mark a favour if you stopped yourself from fainting by having a little snack. And you'd be obeying Reverend Mother, and not causing any fuss, or making another Sister miss the service. And that seems better all round.'

'But suppose I go to Hell?'

'Of course you won't! God is merciful and He loves little children especially.'

How could that be true? A merciful God wouldn't kill people's mothers and, as for Him loving little children, the five-year-olds in the kindergarten here often cried themselves to sleep, so why didn't He make them happier?

Suddenly, the booming, growly courtyard clock chimed five. 'Oh, no!' she cried. 'I'm late for Benediction.'

'Off you dash, then. But remember what I said.'

'OK,' she called, already running at full pelt. Remembering it was easy, but doing it was a different matter entirely, since it involved her immortal soul.

'Pssst!' a deep male voice hissed, as she came down the stairs from the dormitory, teeth well-brushed, white veil secured with hair-grips. 'Tuppence, over here!'

She swung round at her name – or rather not her name. If anyone should hear it, or know she'd been talking to Mr Johnstone, she was bound to be reported. But the gardener didn't seem to care; just repeated her name, louder, and beckoned her over, despite the disapproving looks cast in her direction by some of the other girls on their way downstairs. Darting over to where he stood at the bottom of the staircase, she put her finger on her lips, to indicate the need for silence. You weren't allowed to say a single word during the twelve hours of the Great Silence, which stretched from 8 p.m. to 8 a.m. Even if you asked to close the window, or said you were feeling ill, you'd still broken the rule and could be sent to the Penance Table in the morning, to eat your breakfast there alone – again in silence. Mr Johnstone wasn't a proper Catholic, so he wouldn't understand.

She felt sick with nerves, as she stood beside him; the focus of curious glances from the long line of girls proceeding to the chapel. One of them was bound to sneak, so, whether she talked to the gardener or not, the damage was already done. However, she kept her finger on her lips and tried to make her face look as stern as Reverend Mother's, until the last of the girls had moved on along the corridor and were safely out of earshot.

Apparently unaware of the risks he posed, Mr Johnstone was smiling broadly as he handed over a well-worn canvas bag. 'I've made you a flask of hot, sweet tea and wrapped four or five biscuits in greaseproof. You get that little lot down, Tuppence, and I'll bet my life you won't faint!'

She couldn't reply because of breaking the Great Silence, but it seemed horribly rude not to thank him. It was only 5.45, so he must have got up especially early to make the tea and find the Thermos and greaseproof. Yet no way could she eat or drink before Communion. So she just smiled and nodded, instead, hoping he'd know she was grateful, then tapped her watch to show she had to go.

The minute he'd disappeared, waving over his shoulder, she headed straight for the Flower Room, knowing it would be empty at this hour, since all the girls and all the nuns were already in the chapel. She could hide the bag in one of the extra big plant-pots that were kept in the largest cupboard, stuff it into the bottom and cover it with chicken-wire and artificial moss. And, as she still had fifteen minutes before Holy Mass began, she could take her time making sure it was totally concealed. Mother Frances came here in the morning, to do the altar flowers, but not till nearly noon.

As she stole in and closed the door, she was engulfed in a strange, stale smell of mustiness and heat and rotting flowers. Then, all at once, her attention was caught by a picture on the wall, showing Christ as a gardener, and a doctrine lesson she'd totally forgotten suddenly jolted into her mind. Mother Ignatius had told them that Mary Magdalen was the very first person to see the resurrected Christ, but had failed to recognize Him, because He'd been disguised as a gardener.

Cecilia moved closer to the picture. She had never seen a painting of the incident, but as she studied the details, she realized to her astonishment that Christ did actually look like a younger, fitter version of Mr Johnstone. Both had twinkly blue eyes, strong, muscly hands, and long, untidy hair. Christ wasn't missing any teeth, of course, and his hair was brown, not grey, but he was carrying a spade and wearing a weird floppy hat, not that different from Mr Johnstone's spade and hat.

Could it be, she thought, in an agony of fear and wonder, that Christ Himself had actually appeared to her at the bottom of the stairs just now, disguised as Mr Johnstone? Which would mean it had been Christ Himself who had advised her to eat and drink, in order not to faint. Certainly, in the Gospels, He had seemed surprisingly keen on food and wine – far more so than the nuns themselves. And if He was genuinely merciful, as Mr Johnstone said, then He wouldn't want her to have that frightening, floaty, sicky feeling and then hit her head on the floor (not to mention all the shame of causing obstructions and disturbance).

She glanced from the picture to the canvas bag which looked very old and shabby, as if it did indeed date back to the disciples. Of course Christ wouldn't have had a Thermos or McVitie's digestive biscuits, but since there was no Time with God, details like that probably didn't matter. Surely the important things were to trust in His mercy and accept the gifts He'd brought. She must also remember that Mary Magdalen had sinned much worse than *she* had. The nuns never specified what actual sins they were, but they must have been quite monstrous, since she had needed to be exorcized to rid her of seven devils. Nonetheless, Christ still loved Mary Magdalen; in fact, He loved her more than anyone, except for His mother and St John.

She continued staring at the picture, daring to believe, for the very first time ever, that Christ loved *her*, as well. And He must have sent the tea and biscuits to show she was forgiven for talking to the gardener, and even for wishing Mother Jude would die. So she would have to treat this humble snack like another form of Communion, and eat and drink with the utmost reverence and devotion. She made the Sign of the Cross, then poured some of the tea into a small glass posy-vase and laid the biscuits on an earthenware saucer she'd found underneath a flowerpot. And, doing her best not to make any vulgar gulping or chewing noises, she began solemnly to sip the tea and nibble the crumbly biscuits.

It felt strange to eat in her veil, but no way could she remove it, because there wasn't a mirror in the Flower Room and, if she tried to do it blind, she might put it back on askew. Actually, she hated wearing a veil, but the nuns said it was a sign of respect, so never, ever, must she enter the chapel without it firmly in place. Veils were another reason she didn't want to get married. Brides had to wear a really long one, and wear it right over their eyes, so they couldn't see out properly. Boys were lucky, because they could be respectful even without a veil. Boys were lucky anyway.

Aware she was already badly distracted, when she'd just vowed to keep her mind on God, she decided to say a prayer between each mouthful, to help her concentrate. 'Thank you, dear Lord, for your blessings,' she repeated, fervently, until she had swallowed the last biscuit-crumb and drained the last drop of tea. She then stowed the flask and greaseproof paper back into the bag and hid it in the largest of the plant-pots, as she'd planned to do originally.

Keeping one eye on her watch, she made another Sign of the Cross, then opened the door a crack, emerging only cautiously once she'd checked that no one was in sight. And, by three minutes to six, she was safely back in the chapel, eyes closed, hands clasped, ready to rise to her feet when Father Mark made his solemn entrance.

'*In nomine Patris, et Filii, et Spiritus Sancti,*' he intoned, bowing before the altar. '*Introibo ad altare Dei.*'

'*Ad Deum qui laetificat juventutem meam,*' she responded dutifully, along with all the other girls. Normally, at the start of Mass, she would be feeling weak and empty, with a great, grumbling hole in her tummy, so it was something of a miracle that, on this particular morning, she could focus fully on the prayers without sinful thoughts of breakfast intruding, or fears she might faint and let everybody down again. And never before had the service passed so quickly – *Confiteor, Introit, Kyrie* and *Gloria*, all went by in a flash. Even the Gospel, which often seemed worryingly long, because you had to stand for it and she sometimes felt quite shaky on her feet, caused no problems at all. And those parts of the Creed she never understood, even in English, let alone in Latin – 'begotten, not made; consubstantial with the Father', or 'incarnate by the Holy Ghost' – just wafted past her ears today, as if Christ were saying, 'Don't worry, my child. In the fullness of time, all things will be made clear.'

Christ seemed kinder altogether, now that He had given her new energy and strength, and suppressed her usual hunger-pangs and dizziness and that frightening feeling of being not quite 'there'. And, when it was time for Holy Communion and she processed out of her pew and walked slowly up the aisle, towards the altar, she felt wholly confident she could remain upright, as instructed, and not embarrass the priest, or inconvenience the girls on either side of her.

'*Corpus Domini nostri Jesu Christi custodiat animam tuam in vitam aeternam, Amen. Corpus Domini nostri Jesu Christi custodiat animam tuam….*'

She could hear Father Mark's repeated murmur, as he placed the Host on each girl's tongue – first, the older girls, then the middle forms and – in just a few minutes – *her* class. Despite the wait, she didn't feel the slightest bit unsteady, but seemed to be rooted firmly, like the cedar tree that grew tall and strong and powerful, just beyond the chapel.

And, yes, now it was her turn to take her place at the altar-rails, so she knelt devoutly, watching out of the corner of her eye as Father Mark came slowly along the row of girls, carrying the ciborium. Never before had Communion seemed so special, because she was about to receive the Body and Blood of a new, kinder, merciful God, who had actually intervened in her personal life to save her from humiliation and from Reverend Mother's fury.

As the priest drew nearer, she opened her mouth and extended her tongue, in readiness for that important moment when he would stand directly over her.

'*Corpus Domini nostri Jesu Christi custodiat animam tuam in vitam aeternam, Amen,*' he whispered, lowering the tiny white wafer towards her, but, suddenly, appallingly, a saggy, swimmy feeling seemed to turn her bones to junket and her blood to lemonade. *Fight* the feeling, she willed herself, as Reverend Mother had urged and, desperately, she strained every muscle to stop herself from fainting.

In vain. She was becoming limp and droopy, like a blurred pencil mark on a fuzzy page, about to be rubbed out. Yet, still she struggled, determined to use every ounce of willpower, so that she could somehow find the strength to grope up from her knees and return to her pew, without actually keeling over. But, all at once, her will-power failed, along with her lollopy body, which, of its own accord, collapsed on to the floor like a lumpish sack of flour. And, as she hit the hard wood with a sickening thud, she realized to her abject terror that she wasn't simply fainting, she was plunging into Hell. She had sinned beyond redemption, not only by eating and drinking before receiving Holy Communion, but by her unpardonable pride in imagining that the gardener's snack had been a gift from Christ, instead of a devilish temptation. Perhaps it had even been the Devil himself who had given her the bag, deliberately disguised as Mr Johnstone, to test her strength of mind. And, since she had failed that test horrendously, the only fitting punishment was Eternal Damnation in the all-consuming flames of Hell, tortured by all the monsters and demons described by Our Lady of Fatima.

Even worse – in fact, too terrible to contemplate – she would be eternally banished from her adored and much-missed mother, who would spend her own eternity a million miles away, in Heaven.

And it was all happening *now*, this minute, the pain, the torture, the darkness, and the unbearable, horrible loneliness of being cut off from the person she loved best in the whole world – cut off not just in this life but in the Next, separated from those safe and sheltering arms for ever and ever and ever and....

MARSHMALLOWS

Typical, Helen thought, as she made her way, with difficulty, along the aisle of the train – too many people and too few seats. The 9.06 to Exeter was invariably noisy and crowded, but today of all days she had been relying on a stress-free journey. Dipping and ducking to avoid the jutting elbows of those already seated, she stepped over bags and rucksacks obstructing half the space, forced to squeeze past querulous people coming in the opposite direction, presumably in search of an empty seat. She gave silent thanks for her reservation – a table seat in the Quiet Carriage, which should, at least, be mercifully free of phones and afford her room to work.

Having finally located it, she was surprised to see the whole table unoccupied, despite the fact it was only a couple of minutes before departure time. Each seat bore a reservation slip, so, with any luck, the other three passengers might join the train at Reading, which meant half an hour free not just of mobiles, but of distracting chatter or boisterous kids.

She settled herself by the window, plugged in her laptop, and did her best to ignore the announcements about safety procedures and buffet opening-times, as the train made ready to leave. There wasn't a minute to waste: her presentation needed serious rethinking before the all-important meeting in just over three hours' time.

But barely had she brought up the file and begun reassessing the notes she'd made last night, when an inordinately overweight couple came lumbering down the aisle and stopped at her table to check the seat-numbers.

'Yeah, this is it, Barry!'

Despite the fact that 'Barry' was following close behind, the woman's voice was megaphone-loud. She then attempted to squeeze her bulk into the opposite window-seat, puffing and wheezing as she negotiated the cramped and narrow space.

'I know I'm built on the big side,' she laughed, compressing her podgy stomach, in order to slide further in, 'but, even so, you'd think they'd give us a bit more room!'

Helen merely nodded, although the comment had been addressed to her. She was not normally unfriendly but, with this presentation weighing on her mind, she had no desire to encourage idle chit-chat. Not that she could do much work while Barry was struggling to settle himself, hampered as he was by a couple of capacious holdalls, a bulky wicker picnic basket and several plastic carriers.

'Mind if I put these here?' he asked Helen, indicating the free seat next to her.

'Wouldn't they be better up on the luggage-rack?'

'No, we need this stuff for the journey, and I can't be fagged keep getting up and down. I'm Barry, by the way.'

Helen refrained from saying that everyone in the carriage was probably aware of that fact, given the volume of the woman's voice. Instead, she resorted to silence again, in the hope that this chummy pair would take the hint.

'And this here is Tracey, my other half.'

Another brief nod on Helen's part, which didn't deter Tracey from proffering her podgy hand, like a party-guest expecting formal introductions. 'What did you say your name was?'

I didn't, Helen bit back, instead giving her name grudgingly, whilst extricating her fingers from the sticky, sweaty handshake.

'And are you going all the way to Newquay?

'No, just to Exeter.'

'Oh, that's a coincidence! We're getting off there, too. But then we have to take a taxi to a village about three miles out, where my parents have just bought a house. It's a dear little place, but unfortunately it isn't on a bus route.'

'It was a real bargain, though,' Barry chipped in, 'much cheaper than a house in the town centre. Admittedly, it needs a fair bit of work, but they're not too bothered, to tell the truth. What's important for Tracey's mum is the fact it's a bungalow, because she can't manage stairs too well now. Anyway, they've laid on this house-warming picnic in the garden and invited all their friends and neighbours, so it should be quite a knees-up!'

'I'm sorry,' Helen said, tersely, deciding she had better take a stand before she was regaled with the picnic-menu and guest-list, not to mention further details of Tracey's mother's ailments. 'I'm trying to finish an important piece of work, so I'm afraid I can't talk, OK?'

'Yeah, 'course,' said Tracey. 'I completely understand. Barry knows all about deadlines, don't you, sweetheart? The doctor put him on tablets for his blood pressure and, after that, he had to quit his job. The stress was almost killing him.'

His weight seemed more likely to kill him, Helen reflected. Built on the same generous scale as Tracey, his paunch was clearly outlined beneath his tight white singlet, along with prominent man-boobs. The pair of them couldn't be more than thirty, yet both looked in danger of imminent heart attacks. She knew her mind should be on her work, not on these strangers' health or longevity, yet somehow her eyes kept stealing back to them. Both were distracting presences, Tracey because of her jangling bracelets, wheezy breath and continual fidgeting (the seat clearly inadequate for her sizeable dimensions), and Barry on account of his tattoos. There was hardly a centimetre of skin on his bare arms not covered with a writhing tangle of multicoloured snakes and hearts and flowers, and what intrigued her in particular were the repetitions of 'TRACEY' in elaborate Gothic-script, enclosed by several of the hearts.

With a conscious effort, she returned to her work and began typing with deliberate emphasis, to stress the point that she was under pressure and wanted no more interruptions.

Fortunately, the couple were soon preoccupied with their iPads and, since each had a set of headphones, there was no further noise – apart from a few tuttings, groanings and triumphant exclamations, presumably marking the progress (or otherwise) of the computer games they were playing.

The respite was short-lived, though, and, after a scant ten minutes, Barry struggled to his feet and reached over for the picnic-basket. 'I'm starving!' he announced, bringing out a Thermos flask and a large green Tupperware carton. 'Fancy a scone, Trace?'

Did they have to talk so loudly, Helen wondered? They were sitting so close to each other, their respective folds of surplus flesh overlapped, so surely a low murmur would suffice. And now Barry

was making an annoying rustling noise, as he unwrapped the scones
from their greaseproof swaddlings. She couldn't help glancing in his
direction as he set out four apiece, each oozing a calorie-laden spume
of butter, jam and cream. He then unpacked two plastic beakers,
filled them with coffee and dipped into the basket again for a jar of
Coffee-Mate and one of sugar. Indeed, he'd laid claim to so much of
the table, there was little room for *her* stuff.

'Do you prefer these to the Sainsbury's?' Tracey asked her
husband, as she began munching the first scone.

'I can't tell any difference, love,' Barry mumbled through a mouthful. 'I like this raspberry jam, though.'

'So you should! It's what they call "pure fruit preserve" and twice
the price of the common-and-garden strawberry I used in the Tesco
scones. Here, give me a bite, so I can see how the two compare.'

Far from just a bite, Tracey demolished it all, then they both
started on their second scones, discussing the relative merits of the
plebeian jam as against the posh preserve. Helen moved her folder
from the table to her lap. It was already dotted with crumbs and
flecked with swirls of cream, and there was also danger of a coffee-
spill if the train should lurch round a bend. Yet that was the least of
her problems. More serious was her fatal lack of focus, as she found
herself riveted by the progress of the scone-athon – all eight devoured
in less time than a normal person would take to consume just one.
And scones must be aphrodisiac, since, the minute their mouths
were empty, the couple began passionately smooching – kissing and
canoodling with the same undisguised relish as they had brought to
eating their food.

She dragged her attention back to her laptop, suppressing a pang
of envy. Barry obviously adored this mountain of a woman, with
her tree-trunk thighs, flabby bosom and general air of undisciplined
neglect, whereas *she*, a fit size twelve, had no man on the scene – and
little time to attract one, given the demands of her job. She tried to
imagine a partner so totally besotted, he had her name tattooed right
across his body – ridiculous, as well as totally unlikely, and further
proof of her deplorable grasshopper mind.

She had barely typed two more sentences when she was interrupted by snuffling and snoring noises, and realized the pair had
dozed off, Barry's head pillowed against his wife's capacious breasts,

while Tracey dribbled serenely, dead to the world. Well, at least that should put paid to more ear-splitting conversation, so she used the lull to run through her list of marketing ideas, already fairly comprehensive by now: features in the nationals and the regionals, advertisements in the travel press, a stand at the International Travel Show at Olympia, inclusion in the top Wedding Fairs, celebrity endorsement....

Pitching to a five-star hotel was, in fact, less challenging than some of her previous jobs; nonetheless, she knew she wasn't working with any of her usual application. She could no longer blame her two immediate neighbours, now both fast asleep, but the four people at the adjacent table had been prattling and giggling since the train left Paddington, and there were also endless, unnecessary announcements from a logorrhoeic guard. Normally, she could block out such distractions, but today she felt strangely restless, due doubtless to the anxiety engendered by the project. If the Garden Court Hotel were to reject her pitch in favour of a rival PR firm – as had happened only last month with the Elegance Boutique – her boss would hardly overlook two failures in succession. Forget a lover tattooed with her name; the more likely prospect was to be stuck at home, alone, poring over the Situations Vacant, or, worse, having to swallow her pride and register at the Job Centre.

'*Stop* it!' she reproved herself, aware that such negativity was totally counterproductive. It was essential that she radiated confidence at the meeting and impressed the Garden Court contingent by her upbeat spirit and strong sense of conviction. In an attempt to change her outlook, she ran through some of the mantras gleaned from a book on positive self-talk: 'I am successful in all I do. I meet every challenge with assurance and zeal.' Then, drawing on that zeal, she began thinking up ways to make more of the hotel spa. Obviously, a few well-placed features in luxury magazines would attract the right type of client, but perhaps she should go further and suggest a total rebranding – new name, new image, new beauty treatments. And maybe persuade a famous actor to eulogize the fabulous break he or she had just enjoyed at the revamped Garden Court: the amount of weight they'd lost, the attentive staff, the sense of total peace....

Her own peace was shattered by a couple of kids who came racing down the aisle, shouting taunts and insults at each other. Fortunately, they dashed on to the adjoining carriage, but not before they had woken Barry and Tracey.

Barry yawned hugely, shook his head and stretched his arms, to rouse himself from his stupor. 'I must have gone out like a light,' he exclaimed.

'Me, too,' said Tracey, her equally extravagant yawn accompanied by a long-drawn out, groaning sigh.

'Hungry?' he asked her, again reaching for the picnic-basket.

'I wouldn't say no to a sausage roll.'

Would she say no to anything, Helen wondered? Barry was already levering the top off a second Tupperware carton, packed tightly with sausage rolls. The enticing smell of warm pastry was a distraction in itself and she couldn't help but watch as Barry doled out four apiece again. If four helpings were the norm for this couple, was it any wonder they were obese? That picnic-basket, she'd originally assumed, was their contribution to Tracey's parents' housewarming but, at this rate, it would be seriously depleted long before they reached the bungalow.

'Fancy one of these?' Barry offered, passing her the carton.

'Er, no, I won't, thanks.' She was touched, despite herself, but disliked the idea of grease and crumbs messing up her work and, anyway, if she started fraternizing, it might simply open the flood-gates. 'I need all my concentration for this job.'

'What are you working on?' Tracey enquired, displaying a mouth-ful of half-masticated pastry.

Helen had no wish to explain her role as PR consultant, since it would only prompt further questions. 'It's, er, confidential,' she fudged.

Tracey gave a guffaw. 'MI5, you mean!'

'Something like that.' Helen broke off as the train suddenly jerked to a halt and, after a brief glance at her watch, she realized to her dismay that they were already delayed, without this additional hitch. They should have stopped at Reading a good ten minutes ago and this certainly wasn't Reading, or any recognizable station – more a sort of no-man's-land. Yet there had been no announcement explain-ing the delay.

The longer the train continued to stand idle, the more her worry increased. If she was late for the meeting, she would be seen as unreliable, however fool-proof her excuse. A few pernickety people were bound to ask why she hadn't caught an earlier train, to guard against any such mishap. Indeed, she had every cause to reproach herself for just such a lack of pre-planning. Nonetheless, she tried her best to return to work by considering a new idea: a special range of luxurious Garden Court toiletries, to be sold nation-wide, as another way of marketing the spa. However, when Barry started rooting in one of the bags again, it interrupted her train of thought, especially when he banged down a giant-sized bottle of Coke. In contrast to her own agitation, he and Tracey seemed totally unfazed and, having finished the last of their sausage rolls, now began gulping the Coke from a couple of plastic tumblers in a violent shade of puce-pink. Barry touched his tumbler to Tracey's and drank a toast to his 'wonderful wife'; his final words swamped, as the guard's booming voice echoed through the carriage.

'Ladies and gentlemen, I am sorry to announce that the train in front of us has broken down, and a large number of passengers are stranded. So we shall have to make an unscheduled stop at Slough, in order to pick them up. I'm afraid this will delay our service, so, on behalf of First Great Western, I apologize for any inconvenience caused.'

Inconvenience! Helen all but wept. Even with a perfect presentation, this could cost her job, and the most frustrating aspect was her total lack of control. There was nothing she could do to speed up the train, and no way of knowing just how long the delay might be; she was simply at the mercy of indifferent Fate.

Having refilled his tumbler, Barry pushed the Coke bottle in Helen's direction. 'Help yourself. There's enough for a tribe!'

'No, honestly, I'm fine.' She needed not Coke, but a double vodka, just to calm herself. When in God's name were they likely to reach Exeter, when they hadn't yet made it to Reading?

'Last year, we went to the Lake District,' he informed her, chattily, 'and the journey took fifteen hours!'

'Yes, it was fearfully hot, you see' – Tracey took up the story – 'rather like today, and there was this sudden thunderstorm, and the lightning brought the power-lines down. We all had to get out at Crewe and wait an age for another train, and that was delayed, as well.'

'And the year before,' Barry added, with obvious relish, 'we were coming back from Cambridge and a man threw himself in front of the train, which brought the whole damned network to a halt. We were all turfed out halfway and just stranded in the middle of nowhere, with no trains running in either direction.'

'It was boiling hot on that day, too,' Tracey chimed in, holding her tumbler out to Barry for a refill. 'And people were fighting for the few available taxis – not that we could have afforded one, even if we'd been lucky. The railway staff handed out free bottles of water, but we were still sweating like pigs, weren't we, Barry? In fact, several people fainted, and one man actually had a stroke, or so we read in the paper later.'

'Yeah, poor sod – although he was quite an old geezer, they said. But the bloke who topped himself was only twenty-three. Apparently, more and more people are throwing themselves under trains, some of them only youngsters. But it's the train-drivers I feel sorry for. Often, they never recover from the shock – you know, burdened with awful guilt the rest of their lives.'

Increasingly discomfited by this talk of death and delays, Helen was severely tempted to try to find a seat in another carriage. But it would seem extremely rude to unplug her laptop and simply decamp, when this couple were only trying to be friendly. So, after struggling with her conscience, she eventually resorted to a lie. 'I've, er, decided to get out at Slough and not hang about any longer, but I'm desperate to use the toilet first, so if you'll please excuse me....'

'But how will you get to Exeter?' Tracey asked, with maddening logic. 'Surely no other trains will be running, if passengers are stranded there.'

'I have, er, contingency plans.'

'A helicopter, courtesy of MI5?' Tracey suggested, with a giggle.

'Sorry, must dash to the loo!'

Blithely disregarding Helen's bladder problems, feigned or otherwise, Tracey began explaining her own camel-like capacity to go all day without a pee, however much she drank. 'I suppose I'm lucky that way. And Barry's the same, aren't you, love?'

Helen merely gathered up her possessions, replaced her laptop in its case and struggled out of her seat.

'Good luck!' Barry gave her a thumb's-up sign.

'Yeah, great to have met you and don't forget to....' Tracey was still babbling, as Helen made her way along the aisle, the siren-shrill voice echoing in her wake with further calls of farewell.

Good riddance, Helen murmured to herself, as she continued through to the adjoining carriage, which seemed to have more than its fair share of children, all with voices louder than Tracey's, if that could be believed. The only free seat was next to a harassed looking mother with a grizzling baby and an obstreperous toddler – hardly ideal company – so she walked further on, this time to the buffet car. Since it wasn't particularly crowded, she decided to buy herself an espresso, then move forward up the train and hope to drink it in peace.

However, once she had paid for her coffee and stumbled along to the next coach, she found it was standing room only. A gaggle of young lads was blocking the aisle, all armed with beer-cans and already belligerently loud, which made it impossible to squeeze her way through – at least not without harassment and catcalls. So she returned, defeated, to the buffet car, although it offered no solution, since there was no way she could work without a proper seat.

She stood pondering her options. She could walk down the opposite way, in the hope of finding an empty seat, but that would mean passing Barry and Tracey. Anyway, was she really likely to find a peaceful carriage, free of intrusive conversations, squabbling children, or people endlessly yakking on their mobiles? All things considered, Barry and Tracey might actually prove the best bet. At least they were kindly disposed and neither drunk nor aggressive.

As she retraced her steps to the previous carriage, she could hear the baby screaming hysterically. Its poor mother also had her toddler to contend with – a mini-Mafioso, furiously kicking his seat, whilst also bashing the table with a lethal-looking toy gun. It was almost a relief to return to her original seat, and even to Tracey's effusive welcome.

'Great to see you back, Helen! Barry was just saying what a lovely person you seemed. But why the change of plan?'

'Well, I, er, made a couple of phone-calls and it seems they'd ... prefer me to sit tight.'

'The problem is,' Barry declared, 'we don't know what the devil's going on. I mean, the guard told us we'd be making an unscheduled stop, but the train hasn't budged an inch since then, and there's been no more information.'

'Well, I'd better get back to work,' Helen said, refusing to indulge in useless speculation, so, having set up her laptop once more, she prised the lid off her paper cup.

'Oh, you drink your coffee black,' Tracey observed, with interest. 'Barry and I like it really milky, with loads of froth on top. In fact, Barry's all-time favourite is frothy hot chocolate with marshmallows and whipped cream. Which reminds me – we brought some marsh-mallows, didn't we love, as an extra little snack?'

Needing no further encouragement, Barry rummaged in one of the bags, produced a giant-sized pack and ripped it open.

'Want some for your coffee?' Tracey asked, with another of her irrepressible giggles.

'No, thanks.'

'Well, why not a few just to eat? You haven't had a thing, so far.'

Helen forbore to point out that it was still only ten o'clock and thus not yet time for elevenses, let alone for lunch.

'Are you on a diet or something?'

'No. I just prefer not to eat between meals.' Even as she said it, she was aware how priggish it sounded, if not downright judgemental, since Barry and Tracey had been eating more or less continuously. Besides, refusing all their offers of food was hardly likely to stop them talking, so she allowed herself to weaken. 'OK, give me just a couple.'

Tracey shook a good dozen from the bag, placed them on the carton-lid and pushed them over to Helen, who gazed, intrigued at the small, spongy, cylindrical discs, half of them white, half the palest pink. She hadn't had marshmallows since childhood – in fact, not since her father died. It was he who had taken her camping and taught her how to toast marshmallows over a camp-fire; the pair of them sitting side by side beneath the stars, relishing the taste and texture: the soft, liquefying sweetness inside contrasting with the caramelized, semi-charred outer layer.

They had always wolfed down a huge number, unconcerned about rotting their teeth or ruining their appetites. Those were her *mother's* concerns and her mother never joined them on the trips. She particularly hated camping and considered holidays in general to be indulgent and unnecessary, having been taught as a girl that work must come before play. And, after she was widowed, there was, in fact, a pressing need for her to slave away all hours, just to pay the bills. And she herself, the dutiful daughter, soon learned to follow suit; adopting her mother's view of life as precarious and perilous. If a husband and father could die so young, then it was essential to avoid all risks and try to secure a stable future by continually striving and saving.

'See, you *were* hungry!' Tracey crowed, and Helen realized to her shame that she had devoured all twelve marshmallows, with truly gluttonous speed. She tried to stop the woman from giving her yet more, but the Tupperware lid was already piled high. And they were hard to resist when they prompted such happy memories: her father's warm, protective bulk pressed against her side, as he sat with his arm around her, outside the tent in Wales; him stealing into her room on Christmas morning, before her mother was awake, to share the packet of marshmallows he had slipped into her Christmas stocking; he eating all the white ones, she the pink. She could still recall the sweet, scented taste in her mouth that lingered joyously till breakfast-time. There were no Christmas stockings after he died; no treats of any kind.

'Of course, the best way to eat marshmallows,' Tracey pronounced, 'is to dip them in melted chocolate. Barry gave me this fabulous chocolate-fountain for my twenty-fifth birthday, last year. We tried out various mixtures and our favourite, we decided, is equal parts milk chocolate and double cream. It's really yummy, isn't it, love?' She paused to scoff a few marshmallows, as if needing further reserves of fuel to power her conversation. 'And, if there's any left, we spread it on toast for breakfast the following morning. It's a pity we didn't bring chocolate today, but it tends to go all gooey in hot weather. Still, we have loads of other food, Helen. I mean, you can't exist simply on marshmallows. Barry, be a love and get out the ham-and-cheese sandwiches.'

'No, really, I—'

Despite her protests, Barry handed her yet another plastic carton and was just urging her to help herself, when his voice was suddenly drowned by an announcement.

'Ladies and gentlemen, I apologize again for the delay, but we are now ready to depart and we should arrive at Slough in approximately eleven minutes.'

As the train lurched into motion, Helen dared entertain a scintilla of hope. She might just make the meeting in time, if the stop at Slough wasn't too protracted and the train picked up speed *en route*. She must try to take a positive stance, view this initial hassle as just a mere minor inconvenience and assume that things would ultimately work out. Which meant all further distractions were strictly banned, whether sandwiches, marshmallows or pointless chatter. Her number-one priority was to keep working on her presentation until it was polished to perfection.

Decisively, she pushed the carton back to Barry's end of the table. 'It's really kind of you, Barry, but I'm not hungry, honestly, and I need my full attention for my work.'

Both he and Tracey seemed to accept her statement with gratifying (if uncharacteristic) compliance, and began tucking into the sandwiches themselves. And, despite their chewing and slurping noises, she did actually manage to concentrate until the train pulled into Slough.

However, Slough was a scene of commotion, as a whole influx of visibly harassed people came pouring into the already crowded train, some complaining vociferously about the heat, the endless wait and the deficiencies of the train service in general. The carriage was soon packed with sweaty bodies and resounding with querulous voices. The only free seat – the one next to her – was immediately claimed by an officious-looking woman who wanted it for her daughter, a plump, spotty girl about thirteen. First, Barry had to shift those bags he hadn't yet moved to the table, although he merely piled them inelegantly on his and Tracey's laps. The mother watched the manoeuvre with displeasure, then deposited the child in the seat and told her to sit still and shut up.

Barry made no move to transfer his gear to the overhead rack, in order to give up his seat to one of the people standing, who included several elderly folk. And, although Helen felt obliged to offer her own, she allowed her pressing need to work to overrule her conscience. Now that her normal concentration had, at last, returned, she simply couldn't afford to waste another second. And the train appeared to feel the same, as it pulled out of Slough with commendable rapidity, went zooming on to Reading and stopped there a scant twenty minutes later.

However, further chaos was evident at Reading, where yet more passengers shoved their way into the carriage, despite the fact that the train itself made no attempt to continue on its journey. She eventually realized, to her horror, that three other trains on adjoining platforms were also stationary, and she was compelled to face the daunting possibility that the entire network had ground to a halt.

Barry and Tracey remained their cheerful selves, of course, but then being late for a picnic hardly compared with her own highly stressful predicament. She found herself reflecting on how the couple paid the bills. Being basically young and strong, they were unlikely to be on benefits, so, presumably, they had some sort of job, but perhaps they'd deliberately settled for easy, undemanding work, as being infinitely preferable to health destroying pressures.

'Ladies and gentlemen, I'm sorry to inform you that there will be another delay to our service. The broken-down train is causing problems further down the line, so we are unable to proceed. On behalf of First Great Western, I apologize for ...'

What use were mere apologies, she fumed? Things were now looking so serious, she would have to contact the Garden Court and warn them she'd be late. Yet the very idea appalled her, smacking as it did of failure and defeat – both crimes in her mother's book.

But as the minutes ticked on – and on – and all four stranded trains appeared totally immobilized, she realized she *was* defeated. They were already fifty-eight minutes late and no train could make up that amount of time, unless, miraculously, it changed into a spaceship. So there was no option but to inform the hotel, however apprehensive she might feel. Although calls were technically forbidden in the Quiet Carriage, many people were already on their mobiles, explaining their missed connections, or simply deploring the delay.

She reached for her own phone, wondering how she would make herself heard in such a noisy atmosphere. But, since it would be more or less impossible to squeeze her way to the vestibule, with a mass of bodies clogging up the aisle, again she had no choice. On the other hand, the thought of a personal confrontation with her main contact, Desmond Stevens, made her distinctly uneasy. An irascible man at the best of times, he was bound to explode in annoyance if she announced the slightest disruption to his plans. It would be less nerve-racking to text – except a text seemed worryingly casual to convey such a crucial message and might rile him even more. Yet, it was imperative to contact him in some way or another, otherwise he and his colleagues would eventually gather round the boardroom table, ready to start the proceedings, and become increasingly impatient as she failed to put in an appearance.

That prospect was so dire, she decided that, despite her misgivings, a text was still preferable to a one-to-one exchange, so she began trying to work out a message that sounded suitably apologetic, whilst exonerating herself from any blame. However, all her attempts sounded either servile or defensive. Another problem was her automatic tendency to lapse into text-speak, which seemed disrespectfully slapdash in the circumstances, and meant she had to keep changing her language to something more aptly formal. Typical, she thought, that even a few lines should cost her so much effort. It was the same with her presentations. However often she went over them and over them, they never seemed quite good enough and, on each and every occasion, her anxiety would mount about them being judged inadequate, or compared unfavourably with pitches from competing firms. She was already sweating with sheer nerves, imagining Desmond's reaction to her text – disappointment, disapproval, resentment, even anger – and all before she had even sent it.

She was so absorbed in her small, confining universe of dread and indecision, she failed to notice that Barry and Tracey were opening a box of doughnuts, and it wasn't until the deliciously greasy, sugary smell wafted in her nostrils that she was jolted back to their far less threatening world.

'Fancy one of these?' Barry asked the young girl sitting opposite him, who accepted with alacrity. But just as she was reaching out her hand, her mother intervened, watching hawk-like from the aisle.

'Myra, put that back immediately! You know you're not allowed to eat between meals.'

'But, Mum, we'll never have lunch at this rate and I'm jolly hungry already.'

'Well, you'll have to wait. And, anyway, you're meant to be getting on with your school-work. I've told you twenty times.'

'I can't do it here. It's too distracting.'

'Myra, I don't want any argument.' The mother's tone was so crushingly severe her daughter simply subsided, blushing furiously as she realized that the three people round the table had been listening to the exchange.

Helen gave her a sympathetic smile. She, too, had blushed at that age and, like Myra, had been cocooned in puppy-fat, deplored by her mother, of course, whereas her father had always approved of her, whatever her size or shape.

But, she wondered, suddenly, would he approve of the person she'd become: the skinny workaholic who spent long hours in a punishing job; was constantly worried about not quite making the grade, and tossed and turned at night about failed presentations, lost chances of promotion, or the risk of being sacked? Was that any sort of exist-ence, for pity's sake, let alone for someone whose natural inclination was, like his, for a simple life with few pressures and no deadlines? She didn't even *like* her job. Half the time, she was pushing prod-ucts and services she didn't actually believe in; forced to distort the truth, play down the disadvantages and enthuse about the positives. Whatever the self-help books might claim, being invariably positive could prove a strain in itself and, anyway, did she really want to be zealous and successful, rather than free of that persistent internal slave-driver who mercilessly oppressed her?

'*I*'ll have a doughnut,' she said, loudly – loud enough for her own mother to hear, way up in Peterborough.

'Great!' said Tracey, passing her a couple. 'To tell the truth, I was getting a bit concerned about you. I mean, you seem in such a state. And it can't be good for you to work so hard. You'll get blood pres-sure, like Barry.'

'Yes, it's already high,' she informed them; suddenly wanting to communicate; to tell the heedless world just how difficult it was always having to exert herself, justify her existence, slog, slave, achieve, succeed. She took a large bite of the doughnut, aware of Myra's envious glance. Her own mother had issued similar admo-nitions: 'Don't eat between meals', 'Get on with your homework', 'Do as I say', 'I've told you twenty times.' Her easy-going father had provided a buffer, of course, and would willingly relax the rules – at least when they were on their own. But the very morning of her eleventh birthday, he had suffered the fatal heart attack and, after that, what else could she do but join her mother's world – a more relentless and exacting world, in which even tiny derelictions of duty could be seen as major offences.

Barely had she finished the first doughnut when she started on the next, aware that she was breaking rules all round: being greedy, taking other people's food without offering some in return, leaving grease-marks on her papers, spilling grains of sugar on her clothes, and actually spewing tiny soggy morsels on to the table, because she was talking with her mouth full. Disgusting. Sluttish. Liberating. 'Fantastic doughnuts,' she mumbled, through another luscious bite.

'Yeah, aren't they great? They've just opened a branch of Donut Heaven right near where we live and I went out early this morning to buy a couple of boxes, so they'd be nice and fresh for the journey.'

Helen was startled to realize that this woman she had dismissed as greedy and idle must have lavished time and effort on preparing all the provisions for the train. Everything on show so far had been neatly wrapped and carefully packed; the sandwiches well-filled and freshly made; the scones bursting with jam and cream. You could 'exert yourself' and 'justify your existence' in ways completely different from those expected in a high-powered job. However unlikely it might sound, Tracey was a perfectionist, like her, striving to meet the highest standards by laying on a sensational spread. And both she and Barry were generous enough to offer their bounty to strangers and so brighten other people's lives by sharing their largesse. On the rare occasions her mother had prepared food for a journey, it had always been meagre fare. One mustn't 'pig oneself', or 'over-indulge', or 'rot one's teeth', or 'fill up on empty calories'.

Tracey's voice intruded into her thoughts. 'You haven't tried the iced ones,' she said, opening a second Donut Heaven box. 'Here, take one of those big squishy chocolate ones – they're my favourites by a long chalk.'

'No, really, I couldn't possibly.' Two was crime enough, let alone three in a row. Yet, as Tracey began elaborating on the scrumptious, velvety, intensely chocolaty icing, she found herself reaching out for one, almost against her will.

'And these are *my* favourites,' Barry put in, grabbing the box from Tracey and pointing out some custard-filled ones, sprinkled with chopped nuts. 'You just have to try one, Helen. The creamy filling and crunchy nuts are the perfect combination.'

'It's sweet of you, Barry, but absolutely not.'

'Look, love,' Tracey said, in a persuasive, almost maternal tone, 'we might be stuck here for hours, so, if you're doing all that work, you need something to sustain you. I can see you're making the same mistake as Barry – missing meals on account of the job-pressures – and all it did in his case was undermine his health. So, you really should think about your own health and try to build yourself up a bit.'

And, to her complete astonishment, she did indeed accept the proffered doughnut, although well aware that she wasn't hungry, didn't need it and that it was anything but healthy. It was as if Barry and Tracey were taking her over, subverting her normally rigid self-control.

'I'm *stuffed*!' she groaned, happily, once she had finished all four doughnuts. Weirdly, she was adopting Tracey's language and even the woman's sense of pleasure in sheer greed. Yet every bit as strong was the deep alarm she felt at this newly revealed gluttonous streak.

'No room for a blueberry muffin?' Tracey asked, with a laugh.

Vehemently, she shook her head, knowing it was time to call a halt. Yet she heard her traitorous voice saying – or was it Tracey's voice? – 'Actually, what I would like is another marshmallow or two.'

'Be our guest! Have as many as you like.'

Although she obeyed, guilt and gratification were still fighting in her mind, and she could only justify herself by swallowing each marshmallow as a tribute to her father. Marshmallows had been their secret transgression, bought only when their mother was absent, and eaten on their fun-filled expeditions: bowling, swimming, skating, or just taking the bus to the Odeon to watch a Disney movie. Always one for pleasure, he believed in enjoying life to the full, in contrast to his restricting, rationing wife.

She was suddenly aware that Myra must have witnessed her consumption of the doughnuts and was still watching her, with a deprived and hungry look. Indeed, she was clearly so distracted that her draconian mother was forced to intervene from the aisle.

'Myra, would you kindly get on with your work. How many times do I have to tell you?'

'I *am* working, Mum.'

'No, you're not. You're staring at other people, which is the height of rudeness. And, before that, you were gazing out of the window.'

'But only to see what was happening – or *wasn't* happening, more like.'

'Yes,' her mother snapped. 'This delay is quite intolerable. I intend to demand a refund on our tickets.'

The mother's ire was echoed throughout the carriage, as passengers continued to complain about the heat, the cramped conditions and their thwarted or aborted plans. Myra, for her part, was sitting hunched in her seat, still not working, just alternately biting her nails and jabbing her pen on the table. Barry and Tracey alone were immune from the general fury and frustration.

'If this train doesn't get a move on soon,' she wailed, 'we'll miss the whole festival.'

'Where are you going?' Helen asked her, kindly.

'Castle Cary,' she replied, blushing again at being the centre of attention. 'And it's a total nightmare turning up so late!'

Jolted back to her own nightmare, Helen's anxiety reached a record high. She had lost her concentration by gorging on Barry and Tracey's food, and still hadn't managed to compose a final text. Moreover, the tide of angry people now jabbering on their mobiles all around her seemed to reproach her own paralysis. Even Tracey had grabbed her phone – although far from sounding angry, she was happily bellowing to, presumably, her mother, explaining they'd be late for the picnic, but not to worry, they'd breeze in sooner or later.

Helen was struck by her tone: forceful yet relaxed, confident yet cheery. No apologies, no grovelling, just a ringing voice, a giggle or two, and an air of buoyant acceptance. Why agonize about things that couldn't be changed?

All at once, and prompted by the example, Helen seized her own phone and dialled Desmond's direct number, determined to ignore the flutterings in her stomach, the constriction in her throat.

'Desmond? Helen Bailey here. I'm sorry to report that the train ahead of us has broken down, and we're stuck at Reading, along with several other trains.... No, I'm afraid there doesn't seem much chance of—'

A more compassionate man might have expressed a smidgen of

concern for her predicament, or even managed a sympathetic word. But Desmond was impatiently tut-tutting and saying that, since time was of the essence for this project, could they please reschedule for tomorrow.

Yes, of course, her natural instinct inclined here to say – her mother's polite, compliant, ever-dutiful daughter. No trouble at all to make another reservation, spend an age on her make-up and her clothes, risk another hold-up, waste another day. Yet the acquiescent, deferential words failed to issue from her mouth. Instead, she broke off to eat a couple more marshmallows and, when she finally spoke, it was Tracey speaking through her, and speaking from a deliciously scented, sweet, pink, festive mouth.

'No, I'm afraid that's out of the question, Desmond. You see, as from now, I shall no longer be working at Taylor Thompson Matthews. ... No, of course they won't let you down. Someone else will take over from me. ... Yes, I know it sounds extraordinary. ... And, yes, as you say, most irregular. ... But no, I can't explain, not really. Let's just say that things have taken an unexpected turn.'

And, daringly, unpardonably, and in the midst of Desmond's expostulations, she simply clicked off the phone, scooped the last marshmallow from the bottom of the bag and murmured as she chewed it, 'Thank you, Barry and Tracey, for giving me back my life.'

VENUS

'So, ladies and gentlemen, please raise your glasses and let's drink a toast to Leon and to the success of his new book.'

'To Leon! To Leon!'

Her voice was scattily loud, Poppy realized to her embarrassment, in contrast to the others' muted tones, but this whole occasion had clearly gone to her head. Crazy, cocksure bubbles seemed to be coursing through her veins, as if the tepid, cheapo wine in her glass had turned into champagne. But was that any wonder when she was actually in the presence of the legendary philosopher she had admired since leaving school; seeing him in the flesh, at last, rather than on the dust-jackets of his seventeen prestigious books?

Peering towards him, as he stood beside his editor at the far end of the room, she marvelled that, at eighty-two, he looked still impressively youthful. His posture was upright, his white hair still profuse, his voice vigorous, compelling. He made Martin, at a mere fifty-eight, pale into a shadow – balding, pasty-faced Martin, who, despite his own eminence, spoke in a halting mumble, as if unsure of his opinions. Yet, today, she would gladly kneel at Martin's feet, because without his timely string-pulling, she would never have been invited to this launch party at all. Certainly, none of the other post-graduate students had managed to gain entrée, however influential their supervisors or well-connected their tutors. Indeed, she was nervously aware that she appeared to be the youngest person present.

The editor was now saying a few concluding words. In the general hubbub before the speeches began, Poppy had failed to catch her name, but she was certainly distinguished-looking, with her high cheekbones, aquiline nose and airy disregard for fashion.

'And, of course,' the woman continued, 'Leon will be signing copies of his book, so, Leon, if you'd like to sit here' – she gestured to the small table and chair prepared in readiness – 'I'm sure many people will be extremely keen to buy it.'

'Me for one,' Poppy murmured, about to squeeze her way to the front of the room, until Martin laid a restraining hand on her arm.

'The college has already purchased three copies for the library, so no need to buy one yourself.'

Couldn't he understand how vital it was for her to possess her own personal copy, inscribed with the great man's signature? No, he probably couldn't. Martin was always maddeningly blasé about the big names in his field and, since he himself had a superfluity of books overflowing the floor of his college room, he probably failed to realize that lesser mortals might only just be starting to build up book collections.

'I mean, it's fiendishly expensive, Poppy, and I know you're strapped for cash.'

'Yes, maybe, but I want a reason to speak to the author, don't you see?' Before Martin could detain her any longer, she hastily excused herself and joined the end of the queue. No chance of being bored while she waited, with so many academic celebrities to spot. Some of them looked as if the twenty-first century had completely passed them by, wearing trousers with turn-ups, or ancient Harris Tweed jackets, or even Fair Isle waistcoats – the sort featured in films from the forties.

Feeling a shade self-conscious at knowing none of the guests but Martin, she was gratified when the man queuing just in front of her turned round to introduce himself as Hubert Hodgkinson, a Professor of Philosophy. Bearded and bespectacled, he sported an alarmingly pink shirt and dapper blue bow-tie.

'Have you read the new book?' he asked, once they'd exchanged a few pleasantries

She would have hardly had a chance, since it was published only today. Hubert and his ilk would probably have been sent a proof-copy, or even a signed volume as a personal gift from the author. 'No, but I've read all the rest,' she said, in her own defence. And *From Hegel to Existentialism*, I've read four times.'

'Well, you're obviously a glutton for punishment!'

She bristled at his snide remark. Admittedly, Leon's books were written in a dense, convoluted style, but that was simply part of their challenge.

'And what's your own speciality?' Hubert enquired, raising his voice above the wine-fuelled babble throbbing all around them.

'Well, I'm still finishing my doctoral thesis, so I'm very much a novice.'

Another man ahead of them had now turned round to join the conversation – a more amenable type, judging by his tone. 'And what's the subject of the thesis?' he asked, genially.

'Gottlob Frege – mainly the distinction between concept and object.'

He seemed none the wiser – unsurprisingly, since he went on to explain that, unlike Hubert, he wasn't a philosopher, but worked in publishing and mainly on the fiction side.

While he expatiated on the current parlous state of the book business, she was distracted by the fact that the queue was moving fast and there were now only a couple of people in front of them. Since she was determined to make an impression on the great Professor Leon Kozlov, she needed a few minutes' silence, to work out what to say – some pithy but profound remark that would encapsulate her devotion and enthusiasm. It would be an appalling waste of this once-in-a-lifetime chance to stand tongue-tied in his presence.

Fortunately, Hubert had begun chatting to someone else, and the publisher had reached the head of the queue and was engaged in buying his book, so she used the time to prepare her opening words. But once he'd had his copy signed and melted into the crowd, she came face to face with her hero; his startlingly dark eyes looking directly into hers.

'What an incredibly beautiful woman!' he exclaimed.

The unexpected compliment, uttered in so dramatic a tone, threw her off-balance entirely. A furious blush began to envelop her from scalp to toe and the scintillating words she had so carefully prepared vanished in crimson confusion.

'Have we met before?' he asked, still gazing at her with a focus of attention that only intensified the flush.

'Er, no. I don't think....' She was behaving like an awkward adolescent, unable to formulate even one coherent sentence.

'What's your name?'

'Er, Poppy.'

'*Poppy*,' he repeated, spinning out the name in a long, exclamatory sigh. 'Yes, I recognize you as my Muse from long ago, so we must have met in another life.'

No way could he be serious. He knew absolutely nothing about her and, as for their meeting in a previous life, how could a philosopher of his standing ever entertain such a fanciful idea?

'Never would I forget such exquisite grey-green eyes. I'm drowning in their depths! And your hair deserves a poem in its praise. That fantastic shade of auburn rarely exists outside a Rossetti painting.'

Was he making fun of her? Or had he had too much to drink? The wine-glass on the table beside him was very nearly empty. But, pissed or not, it was surely inappropriate for a man of his age to take so intimate an approach. And his voice had changed completely. The magisterial tone he had adopted for his formal speech, as author, was now replaced by a velvet-and-Courvoisier purr, as if the two of them were alone together, rather than in a crowded room. And what embarrassed her particularly was that the gawky young man from Blackwells, in charge of selling the books, had overheard the whole extravagant spiel.

Disoriented, she thrust her credit card towards the lugubrious-looking fellow. 'I'd like to buy a copy, please.'

However, Leon reached out smartly for the card and pushed it back into her hand. 'I wouldn't hear of you buying it. As my miraculously resurrected Muse, you deserve a free copy – if not the entire pile!'

'No, really, Professor Kozlov, I couldn't possibly—'

'Call me Leon!' he interrupted, cutting off her objection, then, opening one of the books with a flourish, he grabbed his fountain-pen, scribbled something on the flyleaf and passed the tome across the table.

The ink was still wet and had splattered into tiny blue-black blotches, such was the force of his pen. His writing was exuberantly large and the inscription itself left her staring in disbelief.

You enchanting creature, I simply have to see you again. Phone me, please, on 07939 875593.

Beneath the squiggled signature, was one plunging, long-legged kiss, penned with such fervent emphasis, it had all but scored through the paper. This couldn't be happening, she thought. Instead of the polite but brief exchange she had expected, stranger to stranger, he seemed to be suggesting an assignation. Or did he intend them to meet simply to talk philosophy?

As if sensing her uncertainty, he seized a second copy of his book and began inscribing that one, too, the pen ejaculating another flurry of excitable blue-black spurts. Again, he passed it over; letting his cold, bony hand linger against her warm and fleshy one.

We just have to take this further, my enchantress. And make it soon, or I'll die of deprivation!

She stood stupidly dumb – elated by the inscription, yet also shocked and bewildered. How could she respond in the face of such excess, or respond at all in such a public place? The bookseller had slunk away, thank God, presumably aware that his presence was, to say the least, superfluous, but the editor was still hovering in the background. She had probably planned to take her author to meet various academic luminaries, yet Leon seemed oblivious of the fact he was holding up the proceedings.

'I'll be expecting your call,' he whispered, leaning across to grip her wrist, as if about to take her captive and spirit her away.

Suddenly decisive, she shook her hand free, thanked him for the books, then turned her back and made a beeline for Martin – safe, predictable, unextravagant Martin. Never once had Martin made a single comment on her appearance, let alone in such fulsome terms. And, anyway, her looks weren't particularly special – well, apart from her hair, which *was* her best feature, admittedly, being thick and wavy and naturally auburn, without recourse to chemicals. But her eyes were, frankly, boring, more slatey-grey than green, whatever Leon might say. Besides, if she were truly so exceptional, why didn't she have a current boyfriend? No one had shown the slightest interest in her since she had ended things with Edward, on the grounds he was too old. But, hell, Edward was thirty-five – a mere thirteen years her senior – so how could Leon possibly imagine that she would welcome a relationship with a man of eighty-two?

Well, she didn't and she wouldn't. His books she would treasure – undoubtedly learn a huge amount from this new volume on phenomenology – but the two inscriptions, however beguiling, must simply be ignored. Fuelled by too much Chardonnay, they were patently insincere.

'Come in, come in!' he enthused, as he tugged open the front door. 'I can hardly believe you're here, when you took so much persuasion.'

He seemed so disconcertingly different from the Leon of the launch, she instantly regretted having come. He also looked disorientingly older, as if the flesh had shrivelled on his face, allowing the skull and bones beneath to make their outlines felt. Yet how could that have happened in the mere six weeks since the launch party? On that occasion, he had worn a smart velvet jacket in an elegant shade of blue; now he was dressed in a crumpled off-white shirt and unflattering mud-brown trousers. Even his hair seemed different: straggly and overlong, so she suspected his dapper appearance at the party had been due to the ministrations of his editor, who must have taken him in hand, to make a good impression on the guests.

'Poppy, it's wonderful to see you!' he exclaimed, and the sheer fervour of his welcome made her feel ashamed of her initial negative reaction. What she had to remember was that a man of his towering intellect might well consider it frivolous and shallow to lavish time on his hair or dress. And, after all, his expression was just as lively, his voice as exuberant, his whole manner vivacious, as if the blood in his veins was frisky-young and super-charged, in contrast to his scraggy neck and arthritic, blue-veined hands. At least he had made no mention of enchantresses or Muses – a definite relief.

'Prepare for a climb to the heavens,' he said, with a smile, leading the way up a narrow flight of stairs. 'I warned you I live in a garret!'

Despite the warning, she was completely unprepared for the small, shabby bedsit they finally reached, five flights up, at the top. The address might be Bloomsbury, but the ambience was, frankly, slummy. How could a man of his distinction live in these cramped conditions and in such a total mess? The rug on the floor was threadbare and the cover on the small divan looked as it hadn't been washed in aeons. Books had overflowed the shelves and were piled ten-deep on every surface, making Martin's profusion of volumes pale into insignificance. A film of dust had settled on the battered mahogany desk, and the curtains at the window hung lopsided on their hooks.

'Forgive my modest home,' he said. 'But I bought this flat for a song when I was in my early twenties and have lived here ever since. And, because my needs are fairly basic, I see no reason to move.'

She marvelled that anyone should live so long in one place – most of her contemporaries were forever decamping from flat-share to flat-share, as their friends or prospects changed. And she couldn't help admiring his lack of materialism in having no ambition or desire to climb the property ladder, unlike most of the population. And, as for the general squalor, well, again, she tried to excuse him. Any true philosopher would have his mind not on tedious housework or interior decoration, but on logic, theory, rational analysis....

And, indeed, once he'd settled her in the one (well-worn) armchair and poured her a glass of claret, he turned the conversation to her thesis. 'So what made you choose Frege?' he enquired, perching on the edge of the divan and fixing her with the same intense, unsettling scrutiny she remembered from the party.

'Mere chance,' she replied, nervously, shifting in the lumpy chair. 'I happened to go to a Philosophy Society meeting, which was exploring his life and work. And I was immediately intrigued by the way he started as a mathematician and from there devised a logic he applied to other areas. You see, right from my late teens, I've been equally interested in philosophy and maths, and Frege seemed to bridge that gap.'

He nodded eagerly, genuinely interested, it seemed. "I, too, have always been struck by the way his thinking took him from mathematics to logic to semantics, then back to mathematics again. I reckon he was the first philosopher fully to understand the complexities involved in explaining what makes a statement true or false. Plato may have seen the problem of the unity of the proposition, but it took Frege to come up with a solution.'

She was profoundly relieved that they were now on safe intellectual ground and that she was managing to hold her own, despite the monumental gulf between his breadth and depth of knowledge and her own as yet shallow paddlings. And, as he embarked on a discussion of Frege's influence on Wittgenstein, she actually let herself relax. Of *course* she didn't regret having come. This would be something to relay to her children and grandchildren – an evening with a legend.

'Although one of the problems with Frege,' he added, leaning forward, as if to bridge the gap between them, 'is his anti-Semitism. It's always been a blot on his reputation and, personally, I find it hard to stomach.'

'Me, too,' she concurred, 'but, from what I've gathered, it wasn't too extreme until well into his old age. And, anyway, I try to regard it like musicians do with Wagner – you know, appreciating the work, while disapproving of the prejudice.'

'Talking of Wagner, shall we have a little music?' he suggested. 'And how about something to eat? I'm sure you must be hungry.'

'Well, yes, both would be lovely – so long as it's no trouble.' Inwardly, she was tingling with excitement. Dinner with the world's greatest living philosopher, in the sanctum of his home, and to the accompaniment of Tristan and Isolde.... She must be dreaming, surely.

With surprising agility, he sprang up from the bed and opened the lid of an ancient gramophone, positioned on one of the bookshelves. 'I'm afraid I don't have any Wagner,' he remarked, as he selected a record and placed it on the turntable, first blowing off the dust. 'But this is Eric Satie. Are you familiar with his music?'

'Er, no.'

'Well, he's a far cry from Wagner – in fact, he opposed the whole Wagnerian cult. He thought music should be pure and simple, not overloaded with weighty symbols or intertwining themes.'

Was there anything this man didn't know? Even his possessions were intriguing: the gramophone itself, with its pile of 78s, the black Bakelite telephone, complete with receiver and dial, the bottle of real ink on his desk – things she had never seen except online, or in old photographs. It was as if he existed in a time-warp; a piece of living history made flesh. Fascinated, she watched him set the gramophone needle carefully down on the vinyl and, after a few clicking, buzzing noises, a fragile stream of music stole into the room – spare and soulful music, although sounding rather scratchy and distorted.

'It's not exactly hi-fi,' he admitted, as if tuning in to her thoughts, 'but I'm too busy to be bothered with all this new technology. And, whatever its deficiencies, I'd like you to sit here and enjoy it, while I make us a little supper.'

'Can't I help?' she offered.

'No. My kitchen's barely bigger than a cupboard, so there isn't room for two. Anyway, I want you to relax. When you first arrived, you looked absolutely terrified. I don't know why, because I assure you I'm not an ogre!'

She flushed. Hardly surprising she'd been nervous, wondering what on earth to expect after his excesses at the party. She realized now, however, that, on such a glitzy occasion, all the wine and adulation must have gone to his head, so that he had acted out of character. This was the genuine Leon: the serious intellectual and erudite professor.

Once he'd refilled her glass and vanished into the kitchen, she took a long, appreciative swig of the wine. Being more accustomed to the cheapest offers at Oddbins, it was an unexpected luxury to savour a fine claret. Besides, a drink or two would help her to relax. She was still ridiculously anxious that she might reveal her ignorance by letting fall some naïve or artless remark.

While he was gone, she tried to focus on the music, so she could comment on it intelligently. However, the record lasted only minutes and then all she could hear was a scratchy noise from the needle as it continued to revolve. So she examined his expanse of books – there were shelves from floor to ceiling on three of the four walls – books not just on philosophy but on art, music, religion, history, politics…. If only she could imbibe that wealth of knowledge simply by looking at the volumes, so that, when he returned, she would be more worthy of his company.

In fact, he was back far sooner than she'd expected and not with anything resembling dinner.

'I've made you my speciality,' he announced, setting down a small plastic tray on the desk. 'A cheese-and-marmalade sandwich. They're the perfect partners, I find – the cheese smooth and bland and creamy, against the bitter, tangy, chunky marmalade.'

Her fantasies of lobster, quail or pheasant shrivelled into dust. But what stupidity, on her part, to imagine that such gourmet fare could emerge from a cupboard-sized kitchen, or from a bachelor who lived alone and had probably never learned to cook.

Having taken off the record and replaced it with another, he unloaded the tray and handed her a plate. 'I hope you don't mind eating on your lap. There just isn't room for a table and, anyway, I've never found one necessary. To be honest, Poppy, I'm usually too busy to bother eating at all.'

Being greedy by nature, she envied his asceticism, although, once she had studied the contents of her plate, it was all she could do not to grimace in distaste. The plate itself was a treasure – fine porcelain patterned with twining leaves and flowers – but the sandwich looked, frankly, inedible. He had toasted the bread and burnt it, and the two charred and blackened slices enclosed a slab of bright orange processed cheese, and were oozing a sticky amber gel she assumed must be the marmalade, although 'chunky' it certainly wasn't.

'*Bon appetit!*' he said, settling himself on the bed again and tucking in, with relish, to a similarly unappetizing sandwich. Indeed, he was eating with the avid concentration of a literally famished man, as if nothing had passed his lips since the dainty little canapés served at the launch party, six whole weeks ago.

She, too, was hungry, but not for this abortion of a snack. However, from courtesy alone, she took a reluctant bite. The cheese was hard and greasy but tasteless, while the peculiar runny marmalade began drooling down her chin and onto her best blouse. In the absence of serviettes, she couldn't mop it up and, in any case, her attention was engaged in the onerous task of trying to force the mouthful down. All she could taste was burnt bread, dry and acrid. Perhaps his eyesight was failing, along with his sense of smell, and he didn't even realize it was burnt.

Suddenly, embarrassingly, she actually started to choke and took refuge in her wine, gulping a good half of the glass, in an attempt to swallow the obstruction in her throat. Yet, the stubborn sludge of crumbs refused to dislodge and she was dismayingly aware that her rasping cough was obliterating the muted, mellifluous music.

Leon, all concern, quickly transferred his plate to the floor and rushed over to pat her gently on the back. Mortified, she continued to cough, which only made him more solicitous. 'Hold on! I'll fetch some water.'

Returning with a glass, he held it to her lips and encouraged her to sip. Although grateful for his ministrations, she knew she must look a sight, with her streaming eyes and smudged mascara. But, ever attentive, he put down the glass, whipped a hankie from his pocket and wiped her face with consummate tenderness. The handkerchief was mercifully clean, and cobweb-soft from repeated washings and, as it whispered against her face, she had a peculiar sense of being a tiny child, vulnerable and stricken but in safely nurturing hands.

'Better?' he asked, sounding genuinely concerned.

She nodded. The coughing had stopped; the obstruction disappeared – although her heart was beating ridiculously fast, from shame as much as discomfort. 'I...I'm terribly sorry, Leon,' she stammered, aware of her crassness in spoiling this magical evening.

His only answer was to take both her hands in his. 'You're a highly sensitive woman, Poppy. I realized that the minute we met. And you're *still* het up – which is wholly understandable. You see, I strongly suspect that my uncouth peasant food proved an affront to your delicate system. Forgive me, will you, please? To tell the truth, I've managed all these years without really needing to cook. Either, I dine out with my cronies, or get by on a bowl of cornflakes, or a spoonful or two of baked beans, so when it comes to entertaining a fastidious lady....'

'Look, the sandwich was fine.... Please don't think....' Was 'fastidious' polite-speak for 'fusspot'? Had she offended him, deep down? The second record had now come to an end and the irritable, scratchy noise, repeating and repeating, echoed the agitation in her mind. Leon, however, seemed oblivious of the noise and, far from looking offended, his eyes were fixed on her with something close to adoration. Without releasing her hands, he suddenly moved a little closer and kissed each of her eyelids in turn. Astonished, she was about to repel him, but the pressure of his lips was so innocently subtle, the gossamer caress seemed more nurturing and protective than intrusive and seductive. Or perhaps the wine had knocked her off-guard. She had to admit she did feel slightly woozy, having downed a morale-boosting vodka-and-Coke before setting out this evening, as well as Leon's claret. However, far from taking advantage of her, he led her gently to the window and drew aside the tattered curtain.

'I want to show you something, Poppy. See that bright star above the rooftops? That's the planet Venus and it's exceptionally bright at present.'

She gazed, enchanted at the small, glittering point of light – a star she would never have known or noticed had he not pointed it out.

'It's by far the brightest object in the sky, and that's probably why it got its name.'

'How d'you mean?'

'Well, Venus is the goddess of love and beauty, so she's also a dazzling presence.'

She experienced a frisson of excitement, as the pair of them continued to gaze out beyond the jumble of chimneys, spires and roofs, at the mysterious night sky.

'Amazing to think it's only slightly smaller than our earth, when it looks as small as a diamond solitaire' – he paused and turned towards her – 'a diamond I'd like to give you, Poppy, because *you're* a Venus, too: a goddess of love and beauty.'

However extravagant the compliment, she accepted it, this time, elated as she was by the whole tenor of the evening and by the sheer brilliance of the star itself. Why shouldn't she be Venus, if only for an hour, rather than an earth-bound poppy doomed to fade in some drab field of corn? She didn't even object when he slipped an arm around her waist. It felt natural, somehow, fitting, as if they were being drawn together by this shared experience. Rarely, in her ordinary life, did she spare a thought for the stars, or look beyond the narrow focus of the books in the library, or the papers on her desk.

Slowly but persuasively, he moved his lips towards hers. Instantly, she made to pull away – too late. Already, he was kissing her and the kiss was so wildly passionate, so sensuously erotic, she had no choice but to respond. This was a *young* man's kiss – ardent, fierce, emphatic – yet with subtleties she had never known before: his adventurous tongue exploring, seeking, flicking; forcing her own mouth to co-operate. All her misgivings melted in the wild fire of his embrace and, even when he coaxed her on to the bed and continued kissing her neck, her throat, her décolletage, she was powerless to resist. The sensations were exquisite, as if he were galvanizing new erogenous zones in her body, undiscovered till this moment. The kiss was going bone-deep, dissolving her previous rigidity into liquescent surrender.

He unbuttoned her blouse, skilfully and swiftly – no fumbling fingers or clumsy tuggings – then released her bra in a single adroit movement and began stroking her bare breasts. 'Poppy,' he breathed, 'your flesh is just exquisite – a miracle of loveliness. If only Titian could have met you, he would have banished all his other models and painted only *you* and you and you.'

His praise was pure hyperbole, but now she accepted it as of right. None of her previous boyfriends had ever been so totally bewitched by her body. Edward might grunt 'Nice boobs!' when about to 'shag' her – his word and one she loathed. With Leon, there would be no 'shagging'. He brought poetry to the art of love, and clearly cultivated passion as one of the highest arts. The bumbling men she'd met so far simply hadn't possessed the skill to peel off a woman's tights and pants in the easy and ingenious fashion he was now employing, as if the garments had simply dissolved beneath his hands.

'Darling Poppy!' he exclaimed, as he gazed at her naked belly and gently spread her thighs apart. 'I want every artist in the world to record your gorgeous body on their canvases, so it will go down to posterity.'

His adulatory words were set to the subtle music of his fingers, so how could she object? In truth, his touch was so lingeringly provocative, she seemed to move into a different realm where nothing else existed save her own voluptuous pleasure. Beneath his hands, she was indeed a Venus, experiencing extremes of sensation no mortal could ever know.

'I dared not hope,' he whispered, 'that your bush would be the same astounding auburn as your hair, but the two exactly match, I see.'

She shut her eyes to savour the electrifying feeling of his lips and tongue probing deep inside her: lapping, tingling, startling, in a whole symphony of impressions. This was a rite of passage, a vital initiation, as she morphed from girl to goddess.

But, all at once, he sat abruptly up and began tearing off his clothes. 'I must *have* you, Poppy – now!'

His voice was fierce, emphatic, but, as she stared at his thin, white, spindly legs – so suddenly and fatally revealed – and at the long, pale, dangly penis, only semi-stiff, her passion collapsed at a stroke. Seconds ago, she'd been revelling in the attentions of a vigorous young stud, so who was this old fossil, with his skeletally thin thighs and pathetically hairless body, and a face ravaged and creviced with wrinkles? Appalled, she pushed him off, deep revulsion replacing wild desire. 'I'm sorry, Leon. We have to stop.'

'Stop?' he repeated, astonished. 'But we've only just begun, my darling.'

She wasn't his darling – not now. The reality of his aged body, brought home to her so dramatically, had changed her mood entirely, and her overwhelming wish was simply to escape. Yet he was using every skill he had to overcome her resistance – fondling her buttocks, stroking her stomach, even exploring her anus – and actually holding her down with a physical force she could barely credit in someone of his age. How could the flame of lust burn so fiercely in a man of eighty-two, or his need to penetrate her be so all-consuming? Surely only a prostitute would be willing to couple with his pallid, stick-like body, or tolerate his drooping penis, as it struggled to maintain any sort of grip inside her.

Again she tried to heave him off, but he only redoubled his efforts to restrain her, apparently unconcerned whether he hurt or even bruised her in the process. But, with youth on her side, she managed to dislodge him, and then leapt off the bed and began struggling back into her clothes in a frenzy of impatience, determined to make her get-away.

But he, too, jumped up; his face contorted with rage. 'So now you're revealed in your true colours, Poppy, as just a selfish little prick-teaser – a taker, not a giver. You had no problem, did you, relishing every possible pleasure for yourself, but when it comes to *my* needs, that's a different matter, clearly.'

'Oh, you're accusing me, are you?' she retaliated, maddened by his bitter, vengeful tone. 'A minute ago, I was Venus – now I'm crap.'

'Yes,' he sneered, 'certainly you're Venus, but what I omitted to tell you, my dear little ignoramus, is that Venus is one of the least hospitable places for life in the whole of the solar system. In fact, it's the nearest thing we have to Hell – covered with lava flows and so blisteringly hot it could easily melt lead. Astronomers say that anyone who tried to visit would be roasted, crushed and corroded, all at once. And that's exactly what I feel you've done to *me*. I worshipped your body, lavished it with praises and caresses, and then you suddenly turn on me, insult and reject me in the most humiliating manner and—'

'Look, it wasn't like that. You don't understand.'

'No, I don't. And nor do I want to, you silly little bitch. I don't intend to waste my breath on someone so self-centred, so get out of my sight and don't ever dare come back!'

'I wouldn't if you paid me!' she yelled, forcing her feet back into her shoes, grabbing her coat and bag, and stampeding down the stairs, in a turmoil of emotion – humiliation, anger and, yes, guilt. She *had* been selfish. *And* rude. But....

She tugged open the front door and stumbled out into the night and, there above her, glittering and mocking, was her namesake, Venus, the brightest – and most hellish – of the stars.

'SORRY FOR INCONVENCE'

'Get a move on!' Anna muttered, willing the train to pick up speed – hardly likely when it was the slow, stopping-service to Chessington. Tom and Petra were just the latest of her contemporaries to move out to suburbia, once they'd started a family, claiming they needed a garden and more space. An abomination in her view to swap their trendy Camden flat for a hideous mock-Tudor semi in the sticks, and, of course, a hassle for their friends obliged to make the long trek out.

The train trundled into Clapham Junction, where a crush of people fought their way to the doors, pushing between the cluster of standing passengers. She collapsed gratefully into one of the now empty seats, her mind shifting to the meeting she'd just left and all its unsolved issues. It had dragged on, as always, way after half past five; her boss wilfully oblivious of people's plans for the evening, or their pressing need to get home.

Anxiously, she checked her watch, wishing she could transform this sluggish, backwoods train into a hurtling, high-speed express. It was pardonable to be late for a casual visit to friends, but not for a formal dinner party, least of all tonight, which was something of a landmark, being not just Petra's birthday, but her first foray into entertaining since she had given birth. It was as if she and Tom were announcing to the world, 'We've survived. We're back in harness. Normal service is resumed.'

Aware that her thoughts were all over the place, Anna opened her free *Standard* and tried to concentrate on the latest developments in Syria. The man beside her seemed to be overlapping his boundaries: his evening paper nudging hers, his elbows hogging the arm-rest, his aggressively spicy cologne assaulting the air-space. And opposite was a garrulous middle-aged couple, discussing last night's episode of *Celebrity Masterchef* – the final, so she gathered, and focusing on home-made ice-cream. She was so ravenous she could gobble down whole gallons of ice-cream. Lunch had long ago been squeezed from her daily schedule, and she was lucky if she managed to grab a sandwich at her desk. Today, it had been a tepid coffee and a tube of Polo mints.

At Earlsfield, more people alighted and, a few minutes later, once the train had lumbered on again, a tall, sultry-looking man came lurching along the aisle, stopping by each passenger and handing them a mini-pack of Kleenex and a tiny slip of paper. Curiously, she read the message typed in big black capitals, smudged, misspelled, unsigned:

SORRY FOR INCONVENCE. ME NO JOB AND NO HELP. CHILD OF 6 YEARS IS SICK. CHILD OF 4 IS HELTHY, THANK GOD, BUT BABY NOT DOING GOOD. I ASK FOR A MONEY TO PAY RENT AND EATING. THANK YOU. I PRAY GOD BLESS YOU.

She glanced up at the man, who was still distributing the Kleenex. He looked young, strong and fit, so why couldn't he find work? There was no shortage of jobs if one was willing to clean toilets or offices, or wash up in hotels – although, of course, many potential employees preferred to stay perversely idle rather than engage in such hard labour. Most of her fellow passengers seemed to share her own cynicism, since none had opened a purse or a wallet, and most had deposited the Kleenex on an adjoining empty seat, to signal that it was unwanted and unwelcome. Indeed, many looked uneasy or embarrassed at this blatant public begging.

Or was she being unfair? Perhaps it was downright callous to refuse to help a sick child and ailing baby. Admittedly, she'd been brought up to believe that having children without the means to support them was socially irresponsible, but for her the issue was more personal. Frankly, she'd had her bellyful of over-fecund mothers using their kids as a pretext for skiving off work. Neither of her so-called work-mates, Elizabeth and Ruth, ever stayed late, however great the pressures. Both had missed that last meeting today, one on the grounds of a parent-teacher function, the other because her toddler was unwell – apparently. Over the years, Anna had come to see that sick children were a wonderful excuse for not pulling one's weight in the office – and an excuse that could rarely be proved. Was Ruth really rushing home to relieve the nanny and take her child to the doctor, or just to put her feet up and watch a video? And who could say if Elizabeth was dutifully attending that parent-teacher meeting, or had simply dashed off early to fit in a hair-appointment? Whatever the facts of the matter, the result was invariably the same: the childless, harassed colleagues of these sanctimonious mothers ('doing the most important job in the world', so Elizabeth claimed) were left to hold the fort, regardless of the burden of staying on all hours.

The foreign man had moved on to the next carriage, so Anna screwed up his slip of paper and looked around for somewhere to offload the Kleenex – not easy, when the three adjacent seats were all still occupied. So she simply left it on her lap and applied herself to the *Standard* once more, although distracted again by the couple opposite, who had switched from TV to radio and were now debating the relative merits of *Moneybox* and *In Business*.

At Motspur Park, the train stopped for an unconscionable time, as if it had lost both heart and impetus and couldn't rouse the energy to drag its length through any more low-grade suburbs.

She sat drumming her fingers impatiently, before reaching for her mobile. She had already phoned Petra and told her not to wait dinner, but the thought of arriving when everyone else was already seated at the table made her both anxious and annoyed. However, as she was about to ring a second time, the train jerked into motion and continued in a halting fashion on to Malden Manor, where the tall, foreign man reappeared, now retracing his passage from the front of the train to the back, collecting up any unclaimed Kleenex, or cash from those with soft hearts.

Much to her surprise, the couple opposite handed him a five-pound note – enough to buy them two man-sized cartons of Kleenex, not this miniscule packet.

'Thank you, thank you,' he gushed, in heavily accented English. 'God bless you.'

She wondered who his God might be – Allah? Jehovah? Krishna? If he truly was down on his luck, then the deity in question was clearly failing in his duty to protect a devotee. The man beside her handed back his Kleenex with a grunt, patently unwilling to part with so much as a penny, perhaps fearing that the feckless bloke would only spend the proceeds on drink or drugs. She was about to return her own pack, when she noticed the fellow's large, ostentatious watch – clearly, an expensive one. In fact, his whole appearance gave no hint of penury or hardship – no ragged jeans, threadbare shirt, or shoes broken down at heel. As far as his clothes were concerned, he would pass muster at her office – except, of course, he wouldn't have the stomach for a hard day's work, let alone for long years of overtime and increasingly onerous deadlines.

Angrily, abruptly, she stuffed the Kleenex into her briefcase. She was damned if she'd return it. Admittedly, it was worth mere pence, but it was the principle that mattered – not to mention the fact she'd left work in such a tearing rush, she'd come out without several things she needed, including a handkerchief. A few tissues might prove handy this evening, if only for mopping up baby-slobber.

The guy was now standing over her, silently entreating either some money or his Kleenex back. But she continued studiously to ignore him until he eventually lost patience and shambled off to confront the next passenger; his English presumably too basic to engage in any argument.

And, five minutes later, when she finally reached Chessington South and found herself still reflecting on the encounter, she was surprised to realize she felt neither guilt nor shame – only a tiny stab of triumph for having made her stand in support of hard, honest work, as against skiving and scrounging.

'Fantastic ice-cream!' she enthused. 'Funnily enough, there was a couple on the train discussing an ice-cream recipe they'd seen on *Celebrity Masterchef*.'

'Yes, I watched a bit of that programme,' Petra told them, doling out second helpings. 'In fact, it gave me the idea of adding some Cointreau to my recipe. I was afraid it might curdle the cream, but it seemed to work OK.'

'It's delicious,' said Jonathan, the handsome, urbane barrister sitting on Anna's left. They had hit it off exceptionally well and, with any luck, he might suggest another meeting. She would certainly appreciate an intelligent, solvent man-friend, and one with a sense of humour and stylish taste in clothes. Her former testiness had vanished as if by magic – or perhaps magic was less the reason than the excellent wines Tom had selected from his father's Sussex vineyard. The meal, too, had been superb, and the other guests seemed a lively and articulate bunch. And as for the baby, there hadn't been a peep from it, nor any obligation to go upstairs and cluck and coo. Indeed, Petra had shown herself impressively proof against the usual need of most new mothers to discuss broken nights, or colic, or the advantages of breast-feeding but, instead, had steered the conversation into much more interesting channels.

Anna spooned in her ice-cream, relishing the kick of the liqueur and the jewel-like colours of cherries, raspberries and apricots studding the creamy-white mixture. 'In my opinion, Petra, you can tell Jamie Oliver, Hugh Fearnley-Whittingstall and all the pretentious rest of them they'd better hang up their chefs' caps, because now there's a serious rival on the scene!'

Everybody laughed, including Jonathan, who reached for her hand and gave it a flirtatious squeeze. Before the evening was out, she hoped to have his phone-number and a definite date in her diary.

Then, all at once, she was shaken by a sneeze, embarrassed by the hooting noise it made, although the others merely giggled or called out, 'Bless you!' The phrase reminded her of the man on the train, so she rummaged for his mini-pack of Kleenex and gratefully blew her nose. But, to her amazement and confusion, tears began streaming down her face – tears unconnected to the sneeze and with no cause or provocation. Indeed, the depths of pain and sadness she was experiencing seemed all the more unwarranted in light of her upbeat mood just seconds ago.

'Whatever's wrong?' asked Petra, leaning over in concern, to pat her on the arm.

'I ... I don't know,' she tried to say, although she was actually too choked to speak. She had been rejected for a string of jobs – not capable, apparently, of even cleaning offices or toilets, or washing up in seedy hotels. Not only were there four applicants for every one position, but her nationality and even education appeared to count against her – not that she could understand all the ins and outs. Her English was too elementary, and there was little time to improve it, with three children to look after.

The tears continued as she realized she would be forced to sell her grandpa's watch – the last remaining link with him, and thus precious as a keepsake and memorial. In the absence of her family, whom she knew she'd never see again, she'd been desperate to hang on to it, whatever else she was obliged to sell. But her children's empty bellies were of more importance than empty sentiment.

'Oh, Anna, please don't cry.' Now Caroline was trying to console her, then Petra got up and came round to her side of the table. She was profoundly embarrassed to have made such an exhibition of herself; wretchedly aware that she had disrupted a stylish dinner party, not to mention ruined her chances of making out with Jonathan. Yet, how could she *not* cry when she was being turned away from the Job Centre, forbidden even to register because her papers weren't in order?

'You're overworking, Anna,' Tom announced. 'I've been saying so for years, and now it's all come to a head – that's obvious.'

'No,' she tried to explain. 'I can't get any work at all. The system's horribly confusing and I don't know where to go for help.'

But no words were coming out. It was as if her voice-box had atrophied, or she had forgotten her own language. And those bitter, shaming tears were still sheeting down her face – tears no one here could understand and that were seemingly beyond control. Humiliated, she kicked back her chair, sprang up from the table and rushed upstairs to fetch her coat. It was imperative to go straight home before she disgraced herself entirely.

She groped out her hand for the alarm clock, peering at the illuminated figures. 3.04. Had she slept at *all*? She remembered tossing and turning, but then she'd had a terrifying dream, which meant she must have nodded off, at some point. Her nose felt blocked, so she reached for a tissue – the mini-pack of Kleenex she had left on the bedside table. But, the minute she blew her nose, another bout of weeping convulsed her body with gasping, choking sobs. Her father was out, as usual, desperately looking for work again, so she was all alone in their small, dark, smelly room. She could hear the baby screaming, but was too ill to get up and attend to it. Their neighbour had promised to babysit and look after *her*, as well, but, an hour ago, he had slipped out on some errand and not bothered to return. All she could do was cry – cry in pain and terror. The pillow was soaked with tears and her eyes were smarting and hurting. And her fever must be worse, because her head was throbbing terribly and her T-shirt drenched with sweat. But the most frightening thing of all was the fact her mother had vanished. She had no idea where she'd gone and, when she had asked the neighbour, he told her she was too young to understand.

'Mama, please come back,' she cried, over and over and over. But no one came; no one even seemed to hear. The only sound was the baby shrieking, louder.

The alarm shrilled through her sleep and, having turned it off, Anna eased herself out of bed. She vaguely recalled some disturbance in the night and some minor hitch at the dinner party, but she refused to clog her mind with trifling problems – it must be razor-sharp today for her meeting with the new client. And she had to look her best, of course. Once she had showered and dressed, she took pains applying her make-up: concealer first, to disguise the dark circles under her eyes, then blusher, to give her a healthy glow and, finally, a coat of her new, glossy, coral lipstick. She reached out for a Kleenex, to blot her lips and, instantly, as if a switch had been flicked, she began to cry hysterically. Her tiny belly was just a gaping hole of hunger; her nappy heavy and stinking, yet, however frantically she kicked and screamed, no one picked her up or fed her. Her lungs were breaking from the exertion of the sobs. She would *die* without her mother; die without a breast to suck.

Then, suddenly, she heard footsteps coming nearer and stopped crying for a second, in the fervent hope she would hear her mother's voice – be comforted and saved, at last, before it was too late. But all hope vanished when she realized it was just a child, a child she knew and recognized, peering through the bars, but a child too small and sick and weak to help.

Anna sat at her desk, delighted by her success with the new client, whom she had persuaded to sign up. Her boss had actually sent a congratulatory email – a rarity for him – but since she was bringing in new business and proving her worth to the company, he couldn't help but acknowledge that fact. With any luck, she would be in line for a pay-rise, and perhaps a bonus, too, come Christmas. But, right at this moment, she had the unaccustomed luxury of a little peace and quiet, to eat her lunchtime sandwich, undisturbed.

Determined to enjoy the break and not grab and gobble in her normal stressed-out fashion, she savoured the nutty wholemeal bread, the creamily ripe avocado and the generous filling of crab, swathed in lemon mayonnaise. Then, when the last morsel was finished, she sat back contentedly to sip her cappuccino, reaching for a tissue to wipe her messy fingers. But, once again, and without the slightest warning, she was engulfed in floods of tears, now lying in a narrow bed, with a mask across her face and connected to some frightening looking tubes. She had no idea where she was, except it was stark and white and claustrophobic, and she was all alone, apart from some white, starched, faceless nurses who didn't speak her language. She had seen her husband just the once and he, too, had seemed at breaking-point – haggard and exhausted – and had come only to explain why she couldn't see the baby. Apparently, the hospital thought she was too distressed to cope, since she was still bleeding very heavily after the traumatic birth, and also running a fever on account of her infected stitches, so they inisisted that she stay here, under observation. But that was wrong – totally and terribly – because her two other children needed her and, anyway, if she didn't feed the baby, he might not survive at all. So she *had* to get out, immediately, regardless of how ill she might be.

'Anna, what on earth's the matter?' Janet was looking at her anxiously from the adjoining work-station.

Anna glanced up, disoriented to see a colleague, rather than a foreign nurse. But, as Janet came over to her desk and she was jolted back to her work environment, she felt extremes of agitation and dismay. It was essential, as Janet's manager, to seem capable, efficient and completely in control, not someone prone to fits of wild emotion.

Unable to explain her state and, anyway, too mortified to speak, she headed for the door and stumbled on to the ladies' room, where she locked herself in a cubicle. And, sitting hunched on the toilet-seat, she tried to make sense of the last dislocated eighteen hours. Only slowly, and with a sense of sheer bewilderment, did she acknowledge the extraordinary fact that, every time she used a tissue from that foreign fellow's mini-pack, she experienced his own pain and suffering and that of his whole family. She had dismissed him as a scrounger and a skiver, without the haziest notion of how cruelly harsh his life was, how often he must fight despair, forcing himself to carry on only for the sake of his three children. Her shame was deepened by the knowledge that she had actually stolen from him, purloined the Kleenex and given him not so much as 10p in return. In the typed slip, he had apologized for any 'inconvence' caused, yet for *her* it would have been no inconvenience at all if she had handed over fifty pounds – just the price of a good dinner out, or half the cost of a pair of shoes.

Appalled by her failure to comprehend a life so wretchedly different from her own privileged and prosperous one, she knew she had to make some recompense. And, lacking any fool-proof way to find the man, she would have to trek to Chessington again, in the hope he plied the same route every day. And, if she didn't spot him on the first occasion, she'd be duty-bound to repeat the journey; perhaps ask the other passengers if anyone had seen him – at a different time, maybe – and whether he travelled that line regularly or switched to different routes. In truth, it seemed a crazy plan and might prove to be a total waste of time. And, since time was what she didn't have, it would add an extra burden to her already arduous day. Yet the alternative was to blank out the whole incident, which seemed an impossibility, when the experiences had been so searingly intense. She had lived the fellow's life, felt his pain, seen things through his eyes, so she was compelled to take some action that might improve his lot.

Again, she made her way to Waterloo; again, she bought a day-return to Chessington South; again, she boarded the crowded commuter train, forced to stand, as usual. She was becoming so fatigued by this tedious post-work journey, she had come to the decision that today would be her final trip. Several passengers had, indeed, assured her that the man *did* still board this line and *was* still distributing his Kleenex, yet she hadn't seen him on any of her trips, so far, and couldn't continue indefinitely in this exhausting and probably pointless way. She would simply have to send a cheque to some charity for the homeless or jobless, or for refugees or sick children, and allow that to suffice. Otherwise, she was in danger of losing her own job.

At Earlsfield she was offered a seat and smiled her thanks, glad to be no longer standing in tight, uncomfortable shoes and pressed against commuters' sweaty bodies. As always, she kept her eyes peeled, but not a sign of the man. In fact, she was beginning to doubt the testimony of those who claimed to have spotted him. They could well be unreliable, or confusing the recent past with the present, whereas, for all they knew, he might have returned to his country of origin, or moved out of London, to find cheaper accommodation, or even died from malnutrition or despair.

With far less cause, *she* felt close to despair, riled by these slow and futile journeys, by the apathetic train, the maddening music leaking from people's headphones, the litter of discarded *Metros* crumpled on the floor. But, however hungry, tired and frustrated she might feel, that was a triviality compared with the man's far more urgent hunger and fatigue. Up till now, she had more or less ignored such people and, if her friends condemned them as on-the-make immigrants, had never really bothered to present a more compassionate view. Yet, these last few nights, she had lain awake, haunted by graphic images of the man's grievous situation. Indeed, her sleep had been so seriously disturbed, she'd been feeling lethargic all week and, even now, was obliged to suppress a whole series of yawns; her eyes finally seeming to close of their own accord.

She had all but drifted off, when she was jerked awake by the woman on the adjoining seat trying to push past her, but hampered by her briefcase.

As Anna apologized and moved the case, she suddenly glimpsed the very person she had just abandoned hope of ever seeing. He was wearing the same clothes as before and progressing slowly along the carriage, his supply of mini-Kleenex at the ready. She was so overwhelmed with relief that her journeys hadn't been in vain, she did absolutely nothing except watch him for a moment. And she noticed, as she'd failed to do the first time, how gracious was his bearing; how dignified his stance. Far from approaching people sullenly, or thrusting the packets into their hands with ill-concealed aggression, all his movements were tentative and gentle, and he went about his task with a certain quiet humility, giving everyone a smile, however hostile or unresponsive their reaction.

Aware that he had almost reached her seat, she quickly withdrew the envelope she had ready in her bag. By now, it was a little crumpled, but its contents were the crucial thing and those were perfectly safe, since she checked them very carefully each time she set out. As he came to stand in front of her and handed her the pack of Kleenex, she passed him the envelope in return. Instantly, his expression changed, a look of terror on his face, as if he feared it was a letter of complaint, or an official warning that he was forbidden to tout for cash on public transport. He made no move to open it, so she tried to reassure him with a friendly nod and a smile, until, finally, he tore it open, still looking petrified. But the minute he saw the bank-notes, his expression changed again, from fear to astonishment and then to arrant disbelief.

She had failed to prepare for this moment, or work out how to convince him, without speaking his language, that so large amount of money was his, and his to keep. She tried to mime the action of putting something in her pocket, in the hope he would follow suit, but he only stared at her incredulously, then back at the wad of cash, as if this whole thing were a dream. No one in reality would ever give him a thousand pounds – a sum so prodigious it belonged in the realm of make-believe. Somehow, though, she had to show him that this was, in fact, reality; that he could use the money to improve his life in some practical fashion and buy food and clothes and medicines.

One or two passengers had witnessed the encounter and were still looking at her curiously, so she silently entreated the man simply to accept her gift and move on, if only to spare her further embarrassment. He seemed paralysed, however; gazing at the bank-notes once more, as if scared he was hallucinating. Realizing she would have to take the initiative, she rose to her feet and pushed the envelope firmly into his jacket pocket, stuffing it deep down, and reiterating, 'For *you*, for *you*!'

Still, he didn't move or speak, despite the fact that more people were now staring, making her feel uncomfortably conspicuous. If only one of them could speak his language, or use some other means of persuasion, so that she would feel less impotent. Then, suddenly, as if in answer to her plea, his stupefied silence gave way to a torrent of impassioned, ardent thanks.

'Thank you,' he repeated, over and over and over, in so delighted and effusive a tone, she couldn't help but be touched. 'God bless you, kind lady. God bless you.'

His face was totally transfigured, his radiant relief apparent in his very posture and, as he finally moved away, she did indeed feel blessed. Her tiredness, hunger and frustration – along with the shame and sadness that had oppressed her since she had filched the Kleenex – were magically lifting from her mind and body. It was as if she were being resurrected from what she realized, only at this moment, had been a sort of living death, where she had allowed herself to be constantly oppressed by the stresses of her job, resenting all the deadlines and demands, and angered by the extra burden placed on her by Elizabeth and Ruth. But now, in a sweet epiphany, she was struck by just how lucky she was to have a job at *all*, as well as the wherewithal to pay the rent on her luxurious central-London flat. And blessed, too, in that she had no children to support, since children only increased the pressures and forced their hapless mothers to engage in endless juggling-acts. Ruth's toddler was ill again, so she was forever phoning the nanny, to check on his condition – even dashing back home during office hours – then desperately trying to catch up on her workload.

She, in contrast, was mercifully free – no dependants, no sick kids or school-runs, not even any meals to cook. In fact, she decided, on an impulse, to take herself out this evening for a celebratory dinner and toast her own good fortune in having the means and independence to eat out when she wanted, with no family demanding her return. So, as the train pulled into Malden Manor, she alighted there and crossed to the other side of the station, to catch the next train back to Waterloo. There were several decent restaurants near the station, so she wouldn't even bother going home first, but simply revel in her freedom.

And there was something else she needed to celebrate – something more important than a sense of her own privilege. Just for once – rarely and surprisingly – she had proved herself a 'kind lady'. Kindness had always seemed a wishy-washy virtue, almost akin to weakness, in that it could lead to exploitation. But only now did she see how wrong that was – how wrong she'd been about a lot of things. So could this be a turning point, a whole new change of direction in her life?

'UNBELIEVABLY WONDERFUL!'

'Keep the change,' she told the cab-driver, her buoyant mood unaffected by his crabbiness. He had kept up a peevish monologue most of the way, irritated, apparently, by the traffic, London in general and Boris Johnson in particular.

As she approached the heavy plate-glass doors of the restaurant, she could see Duncan through the lighted window, seated at a table at the front, engrossed in a sheaf of papers – an overflow of work, no doubt, since his job in corporate finance was even more pressured than hers in advertising. He dressed the part, of course – impeccable clothes, well-cut silver hair, general air of stylishness – a strong contrast to some of the oddballs she had dated in the last few years.

Suddenly nervous about her own appearance, she peered at her reflection in the doors. Was the new swept-up hairstyle ageing; the figure-sculpting scarlet dress too blatant, compared with his understated suit?

Too late now to worry. The *maître d'* was already gliding forward to greet her and, as he led her to their table, Duncan sprang to his feet and held her in a close embrace; his touch sensuous, suggestive. As always, she gave silent thanks that, at six-foot-four, he was in perfect proportion to her own sometimes embarrassing height. Short men made her awkward, as if being a female of five-foot-eleven was a personal affliction, even a social catastrophe, whereas Duncan had told her from the start that, with her gracious bearing and statuesque proportions, she resembled a top fashion model. Having been labelled by her parents as 'clumsy' and 'unfeminine', she had stowed his compliment in her mind like treasure in a bank-vault. Even after all these years, it was hard to dislodge the image that had haunted her since childhood of a gawky, clumping giraffe.

Once settled at the table, Duncan ordered their drinks, then touched his glass to hers. 'To us,' he murmured, gazing directly into her eyes.

'To us,' she echoed, the phrase as much daunting as thrilling, since it was too early in their relationship for them to be an item. Yet, from the moment they'd first met at Fiona's 'February Blues' party, she'd had a strong gut-instinct that this might well be more than just a run-of-the-mill entanglement.

'How was work?' he asked, his eyes gazing directly into hers. Such scrutiny made her self-conscious: was her mascara smudged, her make-up less than flawless?

'Oh, the usual problems with the Taylor-Hodgson client. Between you and me, he's a bit of a shit, but the account's worth mega-bucks, so we're all forced to humour him. How about you?'

'Not the easiest of days, to be honest. But let's not spoil our evening. I suggest we leave work behind, order our food and relax.'

'Suits me!'

As they opened their leather-bound menus, another waiter sauntered over and began reeling off the 'specials': basil-and-gruyere tortellini, hand-dived scallops, swathed in a coriander crust; salmon and crayfish paté, with lime and saffron dressing....

As a working-class child, she still felt slightly diffident in face of gastronomic pretensions, despite her years of high living. Words like 'aged balsamic', 'jus', 'rouille', 'en croute' would have been double-Dutch to her parents, who had been more at home with bangers, mash and tins of mushy peas.

Duncan looked up from the menu. 'I like the sound of the scallops.'

'Me, too.'

'And how about your main course?'

'I think I'll go for the quail galantine.'

'Exactly what I was going to suggest.'

It seemed an additional bonus that their tastes in food were similar – a strong contrast with her previous boyfriend, Geoffrey, whose predilection for pizzas had bordered on the tedious. If a man couldn't raise his sights from cheese-and-tomato-covered dough, meal after meal after meal, didn't it signal a certain rigidity, a mind closed to experiment? However, some lingering residual loyalty to her parents was forever clashing with her hard-won status as a successful account executive. She was well aware that her highly moral, Methodist father could have cited more heinous sins than guzzling pizzas.

She felt equally torn once their starters arrived. Her dad would have scorned their lavishly decorative presentation as a matter of style over substance. The chef had undoubtedly gone overboard, with a whole gardenful of tomato 'roses', lemon-peel 'flowers', and even butterfly wings made from slivers of cucumber; such a profusion of colourful garnish turning the over-large white plates into picture-frames for exhibits in an art gallery. Nonetheless, she murmured her appreciation. Fernando's had just received its second Michelin star, so who was she to demur? 'I'm glad you introduced me to this place. They do everything so beautifully.'

Nodding in agreement, Duncan reached across to clasp her hand. 'Frances, I happen to know it's your birthday next weekend.'

How did he know? Just because he was canny and had a flair for digging out facts, or had Fiona told him, maybe? 'Yes, a rather unwelcome birthday, I have to admit.'

'But fifty's the new forty, everybody says, so I really shouldn't worry. Wait till you hit sixty, like me!'

She wondered sometimes if he resorted to a little secret Botox. Certainly, he looked years younger than his age, and kept himself in shape with daily 6 a.m. gym sessions.

'Anyway, remember a month or so ago, we talked about going away for a couple of days? Oh, I know we've both been too busy to arrange it yet, but I'd like to put that right. What I propose is a special birthday-surprise weekend. Would you allow me to set that up – somewhere nice in the country, perhaps? I'll make sure it's to your taste.'

'Sounds wonderful!' Surprises were rare – and welcome, when so much else in her life had to be rigidly structured and pre-prepared. 'Left to myself, I was planning on going into purdah!' Fifty was different for women, signalled the menopause and thinning bones – not that she had missed a single period, so far. But the prospect was always looming, with its attendant threat of old age and decline, and the continual sting of sadness about never having given birth.

'All you'll need to do is bring your lovely self, a frock or two for the evenings, and some gear for country walks.'

And a sexy nightie for you to remove, she added, silently, feeling a slight frisson of unease. The fact they hadn't yet been to bed was entirely her decision. With Geoffrey, it had all been too precipitate, if not undignified; the drunken shag on just their second date, and waking in his grungy bed, with a stinkhorn of a mouth: the foul and fetid fumes of hangover-fuelled regret. She knew instinctively that Duncan was too special for such casual sex, and was determined to save herself, like a virtuous Catholic or bashful ingénue, in order to make their first time an 'occasion'. Hence, the idea of a romantic weekend in some idyllic spot, to provide a fitting ambience. Fiona, of course, had snorted in derision at the very notion of chastity for someone with her extensive sexual history, but Duncan himself was sensitive enough to understand. However, now faced with the reality of finally making love, she couldn't help but worry that, if the chemistry proved wrong, not only would the idyll fall apart, the whole relationship might crumble. Yet *why* should it go wrong, when his passion was obvious in just his kisses and caresses? Their titillating sessions on the sofa in her flat had given her a foretaste of how satisfying things could be, once she stopped playing vestal virgin.

Duncan had not yet touched his food, clearly more concerned with arranging the weekend. 'I'm afraid the rest of my week's going to be pretty hectic. I'll be working late most nights, so there's not much chance of seeing you until the Friday evening. But I'll be sure to get off promptly then, so if there's any hope you could also leave early, then I could pick you up at home and we could set off before the rush-hour.'

'I'll do my utmost, darling, but would you mind if we waited till nearer the day to fix a specific time?'

'No, that's eminently sensible, especially with your current pressures.'

His easy-going, adaptable nature was more important in a relationship, she was only now beginning to realize, than many other qualities – particularly for someone of her anxious temperament. And, as she felt his hand make contact with her thigh, feathering and stroking with erotic expertise, she dared to build her hopes for next weekend.

It was past 8.30 when they finally hit the road. The Taylor/Hodgson client had surpassed himself, rubbishing the campaign he'd approved only the previous day, and insisting that she and the whole creative team stay on late and brainstorm for new ideas. And yet, when she'd tried to—

All at once, a fox darted across the road, jolting her thoughts from the office. The reckless creature was clearly bent on self-destruction, although, by some miracle, it escaped scot-free. 'Fancy a fox on the motorway!' she said, admiring Duncan's sangfroid. If an elephant had come charging out in front of them, he would have probably kept his cool.

'Oh, they're everywhere. A chap I know who lives in Dolphin Square found a mangy little vixen last week, careering around the basement, as if she owned the place!'

She laughed, determined to distance herself from the problems at work. She owed that to Duncan, who had accepted the delay with graciousness and patience and was now doing his best to make up time. It helped that his car was built for speed – a new red Jaguar F-Type, bought, she suspected, to foster his 'youthful' image. And at least they had missed the usual Friday-evening congestion and the M4 was now relatively clear. In any case, there was no real rush and it was actually something of a luxury to have nothing else to do but sit back like a duchess and let herself be chauffeured to some as yet undivulged destination. She knew they were heading west, of course, and that seemed agreeably apt: striking out for uncharted lands, discovering new horizons – including, she hoped, sexual ones. Relaxing back, she surrendered to the pleasurable sensation of speeding through the night, with an almost-full moon dappling the rushing-past trees and the shadowy darkness beyond, while the whine of the wind and the whoosh of the engine provided a steady soundtrack.

Even the forecast was benign, with a promise of balmy spring weather, once daylight broke tomorrow. The countryside would be burgeoning and budding; new young leaves unfurling in the warmth; daffodils prancing and boasting; birds heralding the longer days with crazy carillons of song. And perhaps she, too, would experience some sort of rejuvenation. It had been achingly long since she had permitted herself to feel even the slightest sense of girlish abandon.

'Tired?' he asked, allowing his hand to linger on her knee a moment.

'No, energized! Which reminds me,' she added, aware she'd been lost in reverie, when she ought to be conversing, 'did you see that programme on sleep last night? Apparently, even the smallest light-source, from, say, a laptop or a mobile, can suppress your melatonin levels and play havoc with the quality of your sleep.'

'Lord,' he groaned, 'not another thing to worry about! On top of the depleted soil, the polluted London air, our rubbish diet and imminent climate change. They're all Jeremiahs, those doom-mongers, ignoring the fact we're richer, healthier and live far longer than any society before.'

Not my parents, she couldn't help but think. Her mother had died at fifty-four and, although her father was still alive, his health problems took up most letters of the alphabet, from 'a' for angina to 'v' for vertigo. As for being richer, the only largesse in his life came courtesy of *her*. Left to himself, it would be little more than subsistence. But she must banish her parents as fiercely as work, or she would plunge into her usual guilt about the clothes or shoes she bought that cost almost as much apiece as her dad had once earned in a week. This was a time for celebration, not for guilt, remorse, resentment.

And, as if on cue, Duncan broached the subject of her birthday. 'Do you want to keep it on the "official" day – the Sunday – or would you prefer to celebrate tomorrow? I have a few surprises planned, so you'd better let me know!'

'It all sounds very exciting – although I think I'll stick to the Sunday, if that's OK with you? I'm in no great rush to be fifty, even a day in advance.'

'Well, since most of us alive now have a sporting chance of making it to a hundred, you can console yourself with the thought that you may only be halfway through your allotted span.'

Speculating privately about the next fifty years, consolation seemed a little thin on the ground. Apart from the threat of job-loss, there would be no escaping the purposeless vacuity of retirement, not to mention the fearsome prospect of cancer or dementia.

Duncan urged her to shut her eyes and doze, presumably interpreting her silence as fatigue. 'You say you're not tired, darling, but you've had a pretty gruelling day and, once we reach the hotel, I want us both to be supercharged. And, anyway, I'd rather you didn't see exactly where we're going, otherwise it won't be a surprise.'

Although she did her best to obey, it proved impossible to doze, especially once they swung off the motorway and then turned on to a narrower road, where the oncoming headlights assaulted her eyes. Besides, a new surge of apprehension had begun snaking through her stomach at his mention of being 'supercharged'. Wasn't that setting the bar too high, with an attendant risk of disappointment? Yet she cursed her habitual pessimism – probably unjustified, as usual. After all, when he'd arrived at the flat this evening, she had responded without the slightest hesitation to his lingering, explosive kiss, despite her highly stressful session at the office. Indeed, she had been strongly tempted to peel off her clothes there and then, rather than wait tepidly till tonight. And, in any case, her gut-instinct had kicked in again, assuring her that the weekend would go well; might even prove the start of a whole new supercharged existence.

'Wake up!' he said, gently nudging her shoulder. 'We're here.'

She opened her eyes, amazed that she had managed to nod off in a car, when she often found it hard to sleep in her quiet and comfortable bedroom. Maybe things were truly changing and Duncan's calm, optimistic nature would temper her own tendency to jittery disquiet.

But, as she peered from the car-window at the brightly lit, impressive grey-stone mansion, her mood plunged in mini-seconds from hopeful to startled, even horrified. A tide of fierce but long-suppressed and painful memories suddenly besieged her, throwing her off-balance, inducing her to turn tail and flee. The Lone Oak House Hotel, she spelled out, blinking several times to ensure she wasn't still asleep and dreaming. There couldn't be *two* Lone Oak House Hotels, least of all in the same part of the country – it was too distinctive a name. Besides, there was the same ancient oak she remembered from her previous visit, standing tall and gnarled, some twenty yards from the house.

'What's wrong?' he asked, aware of the expression on her face.

'N ... Nothing.'

'You're not disappointed, I hope.'

'No way!' Still floundering, she could manage only halting monosyllables.

'It was highly recommended as one of the best hotels in....'

Yes, that was the huge difference. Its present air of luxurious grandiosity was in total contrast to the shabbiness and decrepitude she remembered from thirty years ago. The house itself had been the same, of course, in its basic size and structure, but its hapless owners had left it to moulder and crumble, lacking the cash for repairs or even maintenance.

'And it's just been extensively renovated,' Duncan continued, as if in answer to the puzzle. 'A four-million-pound job, so I'm told. They restored all the stonework, repainted and refurbished it throughout, upgraded the plumbing and electrics and transformed the garden from a jungle to a miniature Versailles! So I do hope you'll like it, darling.'

'I know I will. It's … wonderful.' How could she stay here with Duncan when the place was sacred to Josh? Even in its decrepit state, the cost of just a single night had been far beyond his means and he'd been obliged to save up for months. But that had made it still more special – a night she had vowed never to forget. Yet she *had* forgotten it – deliberately – buried it deep in her subconscious and labelled the memory as dangerous, self-defeating and strictly out-of-bounds.

'Well, shall we go in?'

She let Duncan help her out of the car, screwing her face into the semblance of a smile. It was imperative to make an effort when he had gone to so much trouble.

A tall, personable man in elegant gold-and-green livery ushered them in, summoned a porter for their luggage, and led them to the reception desk, where they were greeted by a smart, young receptionist.

'Ah, Mr and Mrs Pritchard,' she said, warmly, passing Duncan the register.

So he had booked them in as a couple and under his name – exactly as Josh had done. Yet, whereas she had experienced the heights of elation at posing as Josh's wife, she felt seriously conflicted at suddenly being Duncan's. This whole parallel situation was deeply disquieting, and she was forced to rely on her acting skills, just to maintain her composure.

While Duncan signed the register, she glanced around the majestic hall, recognizing only its general shape and proportions; certainly not the expensive period wallpaper, ruched velvet curtains and

215

elegant Regency chairs. On her first visit, a lifetime ago, the paint had been peeling, the curtains faded and shrunk, and the furniture only noticeable by its absence.

'Well, they've obviously done a fantastic restoration job,' she remarked, again making a conscious attempt to sound appreciative. They were now following the porter to the lift. She and Josh had trudged up four flights of stairs, stopping to kiss on each landing, until they finally reached their attic room at the top.

'Yes, apparently they called in experts in several different fields – to match the period wallpaper exactly, and restore the crumbling cornices and try to return the house to its former glory.'

'And they've succeeded brilliantly.' Despite her valiant efforts, the words sounded hollow and false.

The porter led them along a lushly carpeted corridor, hung with gold-framed portraits. She glanced at each bewhiskered face, as if seeking help from these unknown dignitaries, but no kindly eyes or friendly smiles offered reassurance.

They stopped outside the Grosvenor Suite and, as the porter unlocked the door, she was confronted by a room of such stylish opulence, the small attic room seemed to slink away in shame. This high-ceilinged, spacious sitting-room was decorated throughout in subtle shades of ivory and cream; the twin sofas upholstered in oyster-coloured watered silk, which exactly matched the exquisite floor-length curtains. The room was lit by a glittering chandelier and two ornamental table-lamps, and boasted a Regency desk, two walnut-inlaid chairs, and a vast glass-topped coffee-table – strangely out of keeping with the rest.

Next, the porter showed them into the bedroom and placed their luggage on the rack. 'Sir, madam, if you would like someone to unpack for you, there is a maid still on duty.'

Frances could only shake her head. She and Josh hadn't bothered to unpack, but simply fallen on the bed in a tangle of limbs and swiftly shed clothes. Nor had they needed foreplay. The long and draughty train-journey, with two changes and multiple delays, had been anticipation enough and, by the time they arrived, they could barely keep their hands off each other. She could almost see the lumpy mattress and not-quite-clean, limp nylon sheets; a jolting contrast to this present bed, with its elaborate padded headboard, huge expanse of ivory-satin quilt, and more pillows than any couple would ever need or use.

'Is there anything else I can do for you, sir and madam?' the porter enquired.

Yes, she begged, get me out of here. Take me somewhere else – any hotel, any place at all, so long as it's not the Lone Oak House.

'I ordered dinner in our room,' Duncan said, delving in his pocket for a tip. 'But we're much later than we planned, so I hope there won't be any problem.'

'No, sir. It's all taken care of and should be here any minute.'

Any hotel that could lay on food at so unsociable an hour must be pretty exceptional, yet despite the fact that, in an attempt to make up time, they hadn't stopped *en route* for even a snack, she had lost all appetite.

'And your champagne's already cooling in the other room.'

She and Josh had made do with a bottle of plonk and a brown paper bagful of cherries. He had looped the cherries over her nipples and, later, they'd played cherrystones, and he had blown up the bag and burst it with a boyish, exuberant BANG. But she simply must remove her mind from that could-have-been-life-changing romance. That she *hadn't* let it change her life was the deepest of all her regrets, and no way must she revisit so disastrous an error of judgement, either now or ever.

At last, the porter left, gratified by his lavish tip, and Duncan immediately took her in his arms. But, instead of his tall, broad-shouldered body, she was pressing close to Josh's short, skinny one. How could she have permitted something as trivial as height to scupper the relationship with the only man she had ever truly loved? Admittedly, she had towered above him and some of her (ruder) friends had called them Lofty and Shorty to their faces. That had mattered deeply at the time, but only now, after a whole dispiriting series of subsequent relationships – too many for comfort and most of them abortive – did it seem ludicrously petty as the reason for dumping her soulmate.

'Darling, is everything all right?' Duncan had released her and was looking at her anxiously. 'You seem a little ... distant.'

'No, I'm absolutely fine.'

'Starving, though, I'm sure. I could certainly do with—'

He was interrupted by a polite tapping on the door. 'Ah, that'll be our food,' he said, calling out a loud 'Come in!'

A waiter entered with a silver trolley and began unloading its contents on to the coffee-table, along with knives and forks, starched linen napkins and two fluted crystal glasses.

Again, she forced a smile, adopted an upbeat tone. 'It all looks quite delicious.'

The waiter nodded to her respectfully, before addressing Duncan. 'Sir, would you like the champagne opened now?'

The celebratory pop of the cork seemed like a rebuke. She was still struggling in the quagmire of the past, despite Duncan's generosity and thoughtfulness.

'Sir, madam, if there's anything else you require, don't hesitate to ring down to reception.'

'Thank you,' she and Duncan said in unison. If only unison was easier in all the other spheres. Josh was making her feel an adulteress, daring to defile their personal love-nest by coming here with another man.

Duncan gestured her to a chair, unfolded her napkin and spread it on her lap. 'I ordered all your favourite things – I just hope I got it right!'

'I'm sure you did.' It would be the height of ingratitude – not to say bad manners – to fail to respond, when he had gone to such lengths to please her. And there would be more largesse on Sunday – birthday gifts and surprises, putting her still further in his debt. Yet, although she was physically present with him, she was still with Josh in heart and mind and spirit; recalling how, on that enchanted night, they hadn't wasted a single minute on sleep, but giggled and chatted in bed between each urgent bout of lovemaking. It seemed aeons since she had giggled, decades since she had shared a flat, as she and Josh had done, once. How could she have forgotten that precious sense of coupledom, the joy of cuddling up in bed to another warm, receptive body, not just for casual affairs, but night after night after night?

Post-Josh, it had been mainly three-month flings, or even one-night stands – all profoundly unsatisfying, compared with someone who knew you through and through, and who didn't care whether you looked a mess, or earned a pittance, or weren't *au fait* with the latest fashionable trend or celebrity sensation. Josh had been blessed with a basic integrity, so that, instead of judging people by their façades, he pierced right through to their real, essential core. And she had been foolish enough to ditch him, let her superficial lust for wealth and status suppress her deeper longing for permanence, security, a family and children.

'The paté's superb,' she said, all but cracking from the strain of trying to drag her attention back to the present.

'Yes, venison and duck liver. And the toasted brioche's rather good, don't you think? – much nicer than plain toast.'

Still on automatic pilot, she did her best to enthuse, although it was *Josh*'s culinary skills she was actually remembering: nothing highfalutin, just simple, unpretentious meals. He'd possessed many different talents, yet, as a struggling artist, had little chance of making anything but a basically unpredictable living. Her own childhood had been precarious enough, so it was only natural to seek out a high earner.

Or was it? Hadn't she known, even at the time, that abandoning Josh had been the most self-destructive decision of her life? And wasn't that the very reason she had buried the affair, refusing even to contemplate the full extent of her short-sightedness? His devotion had been obvious, and he had proved his commitment by begging her to marry him, even going down on his knees and whipping out a cheap but pretty ring. Yet, to her lasting shame, she had found herself worrying about the wedding photos, of all things, fearing that with her so tall and him so short, they would look a peculiar couple. Indeed, were the giraffe and the pygmy to stand side by side at the altar, some guests might be forced to suppress a few secret sniggers. In light of her greater experience, how petty that seemed in retrospect; proof of her fixation on image and appearance, even in her youth. If only she had been wise enough to go ahead with the marriage, she could be a mother now, a grandmother, part of a large, extended family in the shape of his five siblings and numerous cousins, instead of a lonely singleton, with her widowed father as her sole living relative.

Duncan would, of course, grace *any* type of photograph, with his handsome profile and gratifying height, yet, for all his merits, he could never fill the void inside her. For one thing, she couldn't confide in him, as she had with Josh from the start, or let him see her shaky, damaged real self. Besides, except for superficialities, they were just too unalike. For Duncan, the 'right' car, the 'right' restaurants, the 'right' friends, the 'right' career-plan, were all absolutely crucial; indeed, as natural as the air he breathed. Admittedly, those things were equally important in her own job – and no one could deny that she was cocooned – indeed ensnared – in that whole beguiling scene, yet she was uncomfortably aware that her motivation had been venality and vanity; further proof, were it needed, of her irredeemable shallowness.

'You're very quiet,' he said, leaning forward to touch her face.

'Just enjoying the paté. I can taste a hint of brandy in it and something like juniper berries. It's utterly delicious!' This person she had become, the urbane, sophisticated gourmet, with primped demeanour and purring voice, was it really *her*, or had she created a false self to win approval and esteem? Before Josh had burst back on to the scene, Duncan had seemed the perfect match, not just tall and good-looking, but a director in his firm, with a salary to match, and an entrée into places that gave her lustre and distinction simply by dint of being seen there.

'He's the one,' Fiona had said, approvingly. 'You've been waiting all your life for a Duncan, so for God's sake go for it this time!'

But Fiona herself – a wealthy socialite with a Chelsea penthouse and a Daddy in High Places – was just another aspect of the whole meretricious world she now inhabited: a world where expense was of no consequence, where the cut of your suit and your choice of vintage wines was proof of your inherent worth, and where you learned a patronizing condescension towards porters, waiters, lackeys. To her eternal discredit, she had totally forgotten that her own dad had been a 'lackey', although he would have bristled at the term. Her nicer, younger self – the self her father had influenced – would have told her she'd sold out, compromised her values for the sake of power and prestige.

'Don't let your champagne go flat.' Duncan passed her the glass and, for the first time this evening – indeed, the first time ever – she heard a note of rebuke in his voice. And who could blame him? Neglecting her champagne was a trivial offence; neglecting *him* unpardonable.

Desperate to make amends, she savoured the bubbly with exaggerated moues of pleasure, then, once they started on the sea-bass, pretended to relish every mouthful, pressing close to him as they ate, stroking his hand when he paused between mouthfuls – relying once more on her acting skills, as she'd done most of her adult life; the gawky giraffe determined to transmogrify into a graceful, high-born gazelle.

Fortunately, the charade convinced him and his normal unruffled demeanour returned, as she continued to play the role of attentive, appreciative mistress – so much so that he was now the one neglecting his food.

'I'm getting more and more hungry for *you*, darling! Let's leave our dessert till later.' His fingers stroked slowly down her throat, lingered teasingly just above the plunge-neck of her dress.

She couldn't help but tense. He had taken so long to make any outright sexual move (in total contrast to Josh), she had dared to hope that perhaps they could postpone things till the morning. By then, she would have had more time to eject Josh from their suite, lock, stock and barrel, and could concentrate solely on Duncan. But he was clearly in no mood to wait, so what excuse could she possibly fabricate for so unjustified a delay? She could hardly claim to be tired, when he was the one who'd done all the driving, while she had enjoyed an extended nap. Besides, he would be seriously insulted if she repulsed him on what was, after all, a sort of honeymoon weekend.

Already, he was slipping the dress off her shoulders, cupping her breasts in his hands – yet she was still standing ramrod-stiff. It was deplorably self-defeating to allow the past to ruin the present, when that past was irretrievable, erased from the slate entirely.

However, when he pulled her urgently towards him in a kiss, it was *Josh's* kiss she was actually recalling – her first kiss ever, as a virginal lass of eighteen – a tentative and fumbling kiss from an equally inexperienced Josh. But, with remarkable alacrity, he had gained confidence, even chutzpah; kissing her on every possible occasion and some impossible, as when they canoodled in church – her parents still struggling to coax their disappointment of a daughter back to the Methodist fold.

Duncan, blithely unaware of her traitorous thoughts, unhooked her bra with practised expertise and began gently flicking his tongue against her nipples.

'Let's go into the bedroom,' he urged, seizing her hand and steering her into that ostentatious sanctum, where he flung off the satin quilt with an exuberance worthy of Josh. And, all at once, Josh was *there*, and she was young and virginal again, without the slightest idea as to what to do, or what he might expect. For his part, he was so excited, he began ripping off her clothes with feverish haste and, although worried about being called a slag, she seemed powerless to resist. And, as his mouth inched down her belly towards her private parts, shockwaves of astoundment lasered through her body, especially when his tongue did things she hadn't known tongues *could* do.

'You're so beautiful,' he gasped, coming up for air a moment. 'I've been imagining this ever since we met.'

But, when he guided her hand towards his zip, she hesitated a second. Wasn't it terribly forward and blatant to unzip a man's jeans, and, in any case, she kept fearing instant punishment from her father's avenging God. But no punishment was forthcoming – only a swollen, frantic, self-important thing, springing up and surprising her – a thing she had no name for, which filled her with dread and longing both at once, a thing determined to get inside her, however much she might hear her parents' warnings about sin and shame and appearing cheap.

'Oh, darling, that feels wonderful!' He was speaking in a fractured, panting sort of way, and was now lying right on top of her; his short, skinny, wiry body newly empowered, as it thrust and threshed and pounded, determined to take its chance before she changed her mind. But no change of mind occurred. In fact, her body seemed to be responding in some natural and instinctive way, as if, suddenly, amazingly, it had learned, of its own volition, how to match his frantic rhythm and thrust back fiercely against him, even copy his weird, half-strangled cries. At last, she had got out of her head, shut off all her worries about her parents discovering where she was, or her fear of falling pregnant, or him losing all respect for her. Instead, she had been transported to a new and freer world where nothing mattered except keeping time and pace with him, as they raced towards some destination she knew couldn't help but happen and that would make her someone different ever after.

How could he go faster? Yet he did. How could so small a body – five foot four, at most – possess such sheer ferocity, not flag or tire, despite his laboured breathing?

Then, all at once, he seemed to explode – she *with* him – except they were no longer him and her, but one joined and coupled creature rising up, then slumping back in a sort of glorious agony she could never, ever describe, even if she were Shakespeare, Shelley, Keats, or any of the other poets they had ever studied at school.

'Oh, darling....' His voice was a rag: harsh, breathless, indistinct.

She couldn't speak at all, needed time to adjust, to come to terms with the extraordinary fact that her devout and straitlaced parents must have done this – once, at least; come to terms with the equally amazing fact that it hadn't been difficult or painful or disgraceful, or all the things her mum had threatened. And her school-friends had been wrong, as well, with their giggly, petty accounts of two-minute wonders, soggy disappointments.

'Was it all right for you?' the voice said – a different voice, now – deeper, older, more refined.

'Oh, yes,' she breathed, still clinging to the other voice, to the younger, smaller, stupendous, awesome body. 'It was just—' She paused. There *were* no words, although she would have to find some, to let him know, formally and solemnly, that this had been a life changing experience and, because of it, she would love him for ever, never let him go. '... Just unbelievably wonderful.'